24

Love + Light

Shirley

The Midas Tree

By

Lesley Phillips

CONTENTS

DEDICATION

So often, we are touched by other souls, who appear from nowhere at just the right time to help us in our journey.

I dedicate this book with love and gratitude to all my helpers.

To Corry Kouwenberg, my loving partner who encouraged me in my journey to be a writer, and who after reading the completed novel exclaimed, "Wow, you can really write!"

To Karilee Orchard, my wonderful copy editor and friend, who really "got" my book and knew just the right amount of tinkering to make it read well, without altering the meaning.

To my parents Jean and Brian Phillips and my friend Helen Chadd, for providing quiet spaces and all the comforts of home for the traveling writer.

To Nadine Truter and her friend Siobhan Hunter, who were the first young adults to read and enjoy the book; and my friend Patricia Truter, Nadine's Mum for over-seeing the girl's summer project.

To my friends Vanessa Walsh, who runs a Kumon school in Seattle, for reading The Midas Tree and providing a perspective on reading age, even though spirituality is not her thing; as well as Virginia Dudley, also an English teacher and tutor of mindfulness and spirituality to young adults.

To all my teachers, most of all Mary Ellen Flora for her kind words of encouragement.

My thanks also go to all my readers and my spiritual helpers.

Thank you all for your enthusiasm and your light.

i

FOREWORD

Join Joshua on a magical adventure of self-discovery in The Midas Tree. Become enchanted by the characters, lessons, and experiences The Midas Tree offers Joshua. Lose yourself in the lyrical story of this spiritual awakening, and allow your own awakening to unfold.

Phillips has created a poetic world of life, color, and adventure. She blends spiritual mysteries and scientific information in an ingenuous manner that enlightens and entertains at the same time. Phillips' style is unique and refreshing, and also reminds us of the great classic "Alice In Wonderland".

You will be challenged to select a favorite character or adventure, because everyone is unique and fascinating. From the start of Joshua's journey to the new beginning, you will be inspired, enchanted, and informed of new ideas. Fun and excitement weave throughout the story, and every adventure brings a new realization and another adventure.

The Midas Tree is a wonderful book whether you are seeking adventure, education, spiritual awakening, or fun. It is a book to be enjoyed by all ages since everyone will see her/himself in Joshua and his experiences. Learn to do what Joshua did and take charge of your life. As in our lives, the ending is a new beginning, so follow Joshua through The Midas Tree to begin again in a new awakened way.

By *Mary Ellen Flora,*

Spiritual Teacher, Healer, Clairvoyant
Founder, CDM Spiritual Teaching Center
Author of Meditation: Key to Spiritual Awakening and other spiritual books

PREFACE

Once upon a place where there was no time, and once upon a time where there was no place, there lived a boy who wasn't quite yet a boy. He held within him the potential to be a great man or indeed a great woman, for the spark that creates a boy can, in the twinkle of an eye, also create a girl.

He lived in a garden of brilliant light, under the guidance of a mentor who helped him on his path to greatness. They agreed together that the boy would travel to a new world, where the light of home contrasted with darkness. The tension between these would stimulate new experiences, and allow new knowledge to spring forth.

The boy's chosen purpose was to become a teacher, who would help everyone who entered this world after him, so that they could choose peace between one another, and harmony with their world. Part of the agreement was that he would forget some things about who he was, and why he was there. He would have to search for his own answers first, before he could help others find theirs. In this journey of forgetting and remembering, his path would emerge, and he would be able to enact his full potential in the world.

Birth into this new world was painful. He arrived in a state of fear and panic, shocked by how different this place was, compared to the light from whence he emerged. Because he didn't know where he was, or how things worked, he became frustrated. The more he realized how little he knew, the more tormented he became. He suffered physical pain, emotional anguish, and mental turmoil. Then he blamed and became angry with his mentor for leading him to this place.

Nevertheless, his yearning to find his way home was so strong, that it compelled him onward. Initially through trial and error, and gradually through the application of what he learned, he grew in both stature and experience.

By observing the special ways of the creatures he met, he discovered how to heal his pain. He learned techniques that helped him overcome the agony and misery he was experiencing. He began to feel empowered to improve his new world.

Chapter 1

Journey to a New Realm

Joshua found a golden acorn. It was unlike any acorn he had ever seen. Not only was it gold colored, but it emanated light, and he felt inexplicably connected to it.

It was bobbing along in the stream. He was so curious, that he felt compelled to follow this intriguing object, and capture it, so he could examine it more closely.

He hurried along the riverbank as fast as he could, so as not to lose sight of it. He left his pile of sticks on the bridge, forgetting instantly about his game. However, he took one big stick that would be good for poking in the water, to retrieve his prize. Once ahead of the acorn, he waded out a little and coaxed it toward him.

Back on the bank, prize in hand, he breathlessly sat down on the grass and peered at his new treasure. Although it looked like metal, it was warm to the touch. It seemed to be vibrating in slow pulses. Apart from that, it looked exactly like any acorn does. After examining it closely, and finding nothing else unusual in the way it looked, apart from its gold color, he placed both hands around it and closed his eyes.

In a flash of light, his mind filled with visions the like of which he had never seen. There were strange creatures, inside a curious world of dark shadows. He smelled the dankness of the air, and he heard a faint humming sound.

When Joshua opened his eyes, he was back in the garden of color and light. This was curious indeed. He closed his eyes a second time and was instantly transported back to this strange new world. There were dark twisting tunnels, and eerie voices. Joshua felt he was being pulled toward them.

Joshua resisted the pull and snapped his eyes open again, and was back in the comfort and familiarity of his home in the garden of color and light. He had never known shadow or darkness before. He was a child of the light, and he spent his entire existence in the garden with his mentor Morfar.

"For sure, Morfar will know what this is, and what to do with it," he said out loud. He clutched his prize tightly and went in search of his mentor. Off he went, back across the bridge, where this had all started.

Moments before he spotted the acorn, he had been playing his favorite game of dropping sticks and leaves into the water, and watching them float away out of sight. Joshua enjoyed imagining where they might end up. Now he had more urgent matters on his mind.

As he crossed the bridge, Joshua paused to glance down into the water, to see if there were any more of these interesting objects floating by.

For a moment, the light sparkling and shining on the ripples of the stream mesmerized him. It was such a hypnotic kaleidoscope of colors that he almost forgot his quest. Whenever he played sticks, he felt he could stand there for an eternity, watching the lights in a trance-like state, and never grow tired. Indeed, each time he threw a stick in the water, it felt like the first time he had ever done so.

His brief trance was broken when he realized that the pulsing in the golden acorn was speeding up. This made Joshua feel an even greater sense of urgency. The faster pulses made him want to close his eyes again, but he was afraid of being taken away into that strange dark world. He mustered his strength. It was now even more important to him to find Morfar, as he was having trouble resisting this urge.

Morfar was around and about him somewhere in the garden, most probably laughing and chatting up by the source of the stream, which was a favorite place. Joshua headed off in that direction.

He left the bridge and drifted over to a patch of bright golden sunflowers. They looked the same today as they did yesterday; eternal yellow suns, shining at him with happy faces and open hearts full of joy. He usually spent his days like this, wandering around looking at all the beautiful things here in the garden. He distractedly stroked a few yellow petals, until the buzzing object in his hand brought him back into focus.

Further along, he spotted a patch of bright red poppies. Yesterday he had taken great delight plucking their petals, and watching them drift off on the breeze. Somehow, miraculously, today, there were still a myriad of red buttons, wafting ethereally in the fresh currents of air. They were so pretty, and their beauty was so distracting that it almost pulled him in, but the buzzing object became even more animated.

To Joshua these distractions in his attention were normal. In the garden, he never had to be anywhere apart from where he was. He never had to do anything, or go anywhere, and yet he was never bored. The garden was so beautiful that there was always something precious to look at.

From his childlike perspective, it was always sunny, it

always had been, and always would be. The flowers were always in full bloom, and the breeze was always fresh and light. All the days were long, and bled into one another as though time was a mere thought, that never really meant anything to anyone.

Today had felt exactly the same as any other day. Until, that is, he came upon the golden acorn. Now there was a sense of urgency that was pulling him out of his usual languid and dreamy state.

The golden acorn was now buzzing so fiercely, he was almost vibrating along with it. If he didn't find Morfar soon, he didn't know what he would do. The pull of the acorn was becoming so strong, much stronger than the pull of the garden.

"Morfar, please help me!" shouted Joshua.

"What is it, my son?" Joshua could not see Morfar, yet he knew his mentor was close.

"I found this golden acorn, drifting down the river. When I hold it and close my eyes, it gives me strange visions, and I feel as though it is pulling me into another world. Do you know what it is, and what I should do with it?"

"My son, I see you have found the seed of your beginning."

"What do you mean by the seed of my beginning?" Joshua asked.

"Long ago, when you were a mere twinkle in my eye, we made an agreement for you to be my companion here in the garden. You could play and experience its delights as much as you wished. However, from time to time, you may choose to leave the garden, and travel to other places. In this way, you can expand your experience beyond what is possible here. When you return, you will have new knowledge to share with me."

He looked at the golden acorn, which was now vibrating and squealing at a high pitch. "What does that have to do with this acorn?"

"Now it is time for you to go on a journey. Once you are gone, you may forget all about the garden for a while. This golden acorn contains the full potential of this journey. Follow it, and see where it takes you."

As soon as Morfar finished speaking, the acorn flew from Joshua's hand, across the garden.

"What are you waiting for?" Morfar's voice faded as the acorn moved further away.

Joshua followed the acorn, as fast as he could, but it moved so quickly it was soon out of sight again. He thought he heard the voice of Morfar calling him, so he headed in that direction, until he came upon an area of the garden he had not previously explored.

A passageway of purple wisteria and pink climbing roses surrounded him, as though beckoning him to follow a certain direction. As he ventured further the breeze seemed to blow stronger, until it became a tunnel of wind. In fact, there was a definite feeling of acceleration towards the far end of the flowery trellises.

As he popped out an entirely new vista greeted his senses. There was a green meadow with daisies, buttercups, and dandelions. It smelled fresh, like new mown grass, and at the same time sweet and ripe like cut hay. There was a feeling of anticipation; a feeling of a beginning and an ending; a feeling that this was a day unlike any other day in the garden of color and light.

Then as he looked up, right there in the center of the meadow he could see the most beautiful tree. Majestic, tall and yet well rounded; in fact perfectly balanced and in proportion. As he approached closer and closer, he could see that the tree had many branches and twigs. Some were bare, but others were replete with buds and blossoms, like a cherry tree in spring; covered with beautiful pink and white powdery flowers in full bloom.

As he reached the base of the tree, he peered upwards and could see that there were many branches with new green shoots and leaves. More curiously, other branches were heavily laden with dense, ripe sumptuous fruits; plums, cherries, and juicy red apples ready for the picking. As he circled the base of the tree, his eyes started to sink into the rich reds, gold, and russets of an autumnal feast. This was a curious tree indeed.

Joshua had never seen anything quite like this. It was a fiesta of colors, a smorgasbord of arboreal states of being. It was amazing. Morfar had never told him anything about this place. Anyway, where was Morfar? Joshua had ended up here because he thought he was being guided towards the golden acorn. He could sense Morfar was nearby, yet now there was near silence. Only the quiet rustle of the leaves in the breeze tickled his ears.

He sat down at the base of the tree under the cool shelter of its umbrella-like canopy. That was novel. He hadn't experienced shade before. Up until now, he was always playing in the bright sunlight. He let his back slide down the trunk of the tree, until he was lying on his back, gazing up curiously into its branches. Puffy clouds drifted across the pale blue sky. An autumn leaf gently drifted down and landed on his cheek. He plucked it off and examined it closely.

The leaf was a beautiful rich golden-brown, and it crackled in his hands as he played with it. He could see the veins, like an inter-woven network of orderly channels. He lifted it gently above his head and then let it go again, this time allowing it to fall to the ground beside him. He turned around on his side, and picked up a twig, so he could dig and poke around in the earth. Lying down facing the earth, he spiked the end of the twig into the ground. The soil was hard-baked and he barely managed to carve a small scar in it and stir up a mote or two of dust.

He pulled himself up so that he could tackle the job from a better angle, but the extra surge of energy caused him to snap the twig in two. He dropped it at his side and slowly glanced

6

upwards while still facing the tree. That was curious. There was a thin groove in the side of the tree. Unlike the grooves in the rest of the bark, this one seemed to go deeper. He traced it with his finger and found that it only went up so high, and then curved around in an arch and dropped right back down on the other side.

Joshua pressed on the arch shape outlined on the tree. Nothing happened. He leaned his weight against it, and still nothing happened. Finally, he dug his fingers into the far side and pulled with all his might. One big hefty tug was all it took, and the panel swung open.

Joshua had found a door, in a place where there were no doors. He cautiously leaned in. It was dark inside, but he started to make out the outline of a small hollow. "What a great hiding place!" he exclaimed. He knelt down, then bent into a crawling position, and slowly pulled himself inside.

There was just enough room for him to sit in there with his knees up to his chin. He could still see the bright light outside, as the door was still open. Then a particular thought overcame his curiosity. He had never known pitch-black dark before. He had always been in the light. "What will it be like if I close the door? What will it be like to be completely enfolded by a blanket of darkness?" He leaned forward and gently pulled the creaky door shut. Blackness enveloped him.

Moments later, he was clutching at the inside of the tree, screaming for the light.

"Let me out! Morfar, help me! Let me out of here!"

No matter how hard he pushed, the door would not open. Panic overcame him. He started to kick his legs and flail his arms, while he screamed for help at the top of his voice. He gasped great gulps of dank humid air into his little lungs. Then he realized... not one minute ago I was in a fetal position barely able to move. How is it that now I am able to freely move my arms and legs?

He sat once again motionless and quiet, and gradually his eyes began to adjust to the dimness. He found that he was in a large-sized circular chamber. It was not tall enough to stand up in, but he could sit comfortably, without his head touching the ceiling. As he explored this new space with his eyes, he could see that all around the perimeter of the chamber were entryways to what looked like tunnels. Some led down into the ground, and others reached up into the sky. The doorway through which he entered this world was nowhere to be seen. He continued to look around, trying to make sense of his new environment.

Joshua took in a few more deep breaths of the musty air. He was feeling disoriented in this new world. He crawled over to the wall of bark and ran his hand over its crumpled wetness. He pushed, to see if it would give way to the world of color and light. He knew it was close by, just the other side of this barky veil. No luck. He tried in a few more places, again with no luck, and then proceeded to explore the openings to the passageways. He could not leave through the door he came in by, but a myriad of choices of different directions that he could choose lay before him.

There were so many choices; however, it was completely overwhelming. Thoughts came to him quickly. How will I know which is the right path to choose? Which one will be the most direct route out of this place, to take me back to the garden of color and light? I don't want to be away from Morfar for long. Surely Morfar will notice my absence soon, and come searching for me?

As he crawled in circles, he squinted into the passageways one by one. He could not see too far ahead into any of them, and he was feeling very unsure of himself. At least he seemed to be fairly safe here in this chamber, but he wanted desperately to go home. He knew he must venture forth deeper into this new experience of being within the tree, if he wanted to find a way out.

Joshua was becoming more confused and frustrated with every new tunnel he investigated. Then he noticed that in the upper right corner of the passage he was currently peering into, was a sign made from bark. In the dimness, he had not seen it immediately, as it was done very subtly. When he looked closer, he could see that there were a series of strange symbols scrawled onto the surface.

He retraced his steps to the other tunnels. Each one had a similar sign, made of a piece of bark attached to the upper right corner with a wooden nail. The symbols written on each sign were clearly different. They obviously must give some clue as to what he would find if he ventured into that passageway. He struggled to understand them, because they were mostly unfamiliar.

He needed to come up with a system that would help him decode the symbols. He imagined it to be like a puzzle, where you had a few letters, and could work out the other words from there. "If only I could just figure out a few letters in the code, I am certain I could translate the signs and understand what they mean," he said softly out loud to himself. Picking up a twig, he quickly memorized the first few symbols on one of the signs and copied them in the dirt. Then he systematically started to copy all of the symbols on all of the signs, periodically stopping to see if he could figure it out yet.

This was exhausting work. His brain was in a cloud of numbers and letters and symbols, none of which he could relate to each other. Sometimes he would think he had something, only to find that he had taken himself down a blind alley. This is the hardest puzzle I have ever had to solve, he thought, as he began to become a little frustrated. He tried and tried again, scratching his head and puzzling over combinations and transmutations. He wished he had the key, so that he would know what it all meant, and make the right choice about which path to take.

It was all very frustrating. No matter how hard he tried, he didn't seem to make any progress at all. What was more, by this time he was feeling quite thirsty. He took to licking the drops of water from the inside of the bark to satisfy his thirst. Exhausted from his efforts, he lay down on the hard earth next to his scrawls and drifted off to sleep

*"Joshua's adventures within the tree are about to begin. For your chance to win a gift from the author go to **www.themidastree.com/readers** and download the scavenger hunt.*

Chapter 2

Meeting the Devas of the Tree

oshua stirred gently. He was in a deep state of relaxation. His dreams had taken him back to the garden of color and light, into the loving arms of Morfar. His lips spread in a broad smile, and he was happy in his blissful ignorance. Gentle, mellifluous music drifted through the fog of his sleep. Words formed into sweet melodies, made even more beautiful as they bounced across the walls and echoed through the chamber of the tree. Joshua opened his eyes with a start as he remembered where he was.

All around the perimeter of the chamber were little creatures. They all had their backs to him, and were facing the tree, holding hands with one another. They appeared to be in a state of sheer ecstasy as they sang with many voices merged into one.

"Oh great tree, we adore thee, body, temple of our soul.

Let us pour our love upon you, help you grow and become whole."

This chain of small, bright creatures appeared to be hugging, loving, and caressing the inside of the tree. Joshua propped himself up on his arms to take a closer look. The chain of small, bright creatures continued their adoration of the tree.

"Oh great tree, our hearts implore thee, love us now as we love you.

Let us do our work together, create each day our lives anew."

He noticed that there appeared to be a few different types. Some were taller, about two and a half feet in height, and were more flamboyantly dressed. Most of them were much smaller, with bodies that were almost transparent, ethereal wisps of color. Some were bright forest green, others golden yellow, bright vibrant red, ice blue or misty purple. Yet others were a kind of shiny bronze; there were even crystal clear ones, black shadowy ones, and some with all the colors of the rainbow.

Joshua had never seen creatures like these, and wondered what they were. They seemed innocent enough. He certainly didn't sense he was in any kind of danger from them. So in a great loud voice, to ensure he could be heard above the singing, he shouted, "Hello, can you help me?"

At first, the little creatures ignored him, as they seemed to be in such a state of ecstasy, and completely focused on what they were doing.

"Oh great tree, we hear your message and we respond with love to you.

Let us fill you up with goodness, help you flow and flow so true."

Louder still this time, Joshua tried to be heard above the din. "My name is Joshua. Who are you, and can you tell me how to get out of this tree?"

"Oh great tree we praise your beauty, loving you is our duty. Vessel of our light and life force, bring us joy and map our course."

Joshua lay back on the floor and quietly waited. Eventually the singing quieted to a low hum as the creatures swayed from side to side in unison. The music became quieter and quieter, until they let go of each other's hands. Then they each reached out and gave the tree one last hug. With a loud whoop, they started to scatter about the chamber in great throngs, beginning to disappear into the passageways in all directions.

"Wait, stop!" shouted Joshua. "Hold on, won't any of you talk to me?"

Just then, three of the more colorful creatures nearly tripped over him, in their rush to go about their day.

"Who are you?" they shouted in unison.

"My name is Joshua, and I have come here from the garden of color and light, and from the arms of Morfar. Who are you?"

They responded in unison "Why, we are the Devas of the Midas Tree."

"The who of the what?"

In unison again, "The Devas, the mystical creatures of this tree!"

"What does that mean? Why were you all singing, and where are you all going to now?"

They answered one at a time:

"Every day at dawn, we hug the tree from the inside and send her love."

"It is our duty to take care of all of her physical and emotional needs."

"We seek to make her happy and fulfilled."

"We all have tasks that we must fulfill to keep her watered and fed, and in good humor. Right now we are going about our duties."

15

"Some of us go down, deep into the ground, within the roots of the tree."

"And some of us go up, high into the leaves and branches of the tree."

"I am Devandra. I look after the leaves that reach up to the sky."

Devandra was about two feet tall. His skin was green, like the color of the leaves he tended. He was dressed in a little jacket and pants made from leaves, sewn together with vine fronds. A strip of supple bark from the tree formed his belt, and he had pointy-toed little boots and a tiny green hat with a feather in it.

"I am Deverall. I look after the water that flows up from the roots."

Deverall was a little shorter than Devandra and, unlike the other Devas, he had skin that was an interesting shade of blue. He was dressed in a tunic made from the light inner bark of the tree. Fine droplets of water clung to his clothes, and hung from his nose like little diamonds. He also had a belt of bark, as well as a long hosepipe-like object made from tree root, which wound around his waist several times.

"And I am Devalicious. I take the sugar from the leaves, and feed it to the rest of the tree."

Devalicious was the tallest of the three Devas, mainly because she was wearing high-heeled clogs made from wood, decorated in brightly painted colorful flowers. She had on a very ingenious little dress, carved from wood and also decorated in brightly painted flowers. It enhanced the pink glow of her skin. As she spoke, she ran a finger over one of the flowers on her dress and licked it. As he looked closer, Joshua could see that the flowers were made from colored sugar.

"Does it work, talking to the tree like this?"

"Oh yes, she likes us to speak kindly to her, and tell her

how beautiful she is."

"This is what all bodies of all kinds want."

"Really? Bodies of all kinds?" asked Joshua, looking down at his own two legs and torso.

"Absolutely! All bodies need water, they need food and shelter, but most of all they need love."

"Even your little boy body needs these things. Why don't you try it?"

"Learn to love and take care of your body, like we love and take care of the tree."

"What...? By singing to it and hugging it?"

Joshua was starting to feel a little self-conscious now. It was all well and good for these creatures to make a spectacle of themselves with their tree hugging antics, but now they wanted him to do it too, and he felt foolish. What would people think? Then he realized there were no other people like him here to think anything. He wanted to go home.

"Thank you. That's a very nice idea. I'll be sure to tell Morfar all about it when I get back to the garden of color and light. Now can you tell me which passageway I should take to get out of here?"

The three creatures all rubbed their chins and looked at one another knowingly. They did not respond immediately, and the silence became quite uncomfortable.

Eventually Devandra said, "My dear boy, you cannot go back to the garden of color and light and to Morfar just yet."

"Why not?"

"Well," said Deverall, "think of this tree as a kind of school that you have come to. You need to expand your horizons and learn your lessons. Then one day, when all that is done, you may return to your home."

17

"But…"

"Look, it's all very easy really," cooed Devalicious. "You need to get to know the Midas Tree from top to bottom on a very intimate level. Understand her needs and what makes her happy. Help her to survive and flourish, and along the way unlock the great mysteries of living the best life you can."

"But how do I do that?" questioned Joshua. "I don't know where to start, and I don't understand anything about living in a tree."

Devalicious continued, "Don't worry, you are not alone. We can help to guide you. We shall teach you all about it, if you ask us and if you allow us to."

"How many mysteries and how many lessons are there, and how will I know when I have solved them?" Joshua was becoming quite concerned and daunted by all of this.

"My dear boy, there are as many lessons and as many mysteries as you need to learn. How many would that be? It's different for everyone. Nevertheless, one thing is for certain, there is a clear signal that will let you know exactly when you have achieved your goal. You will know you have learned your lessons and solved the mysteries, when you have turned the Midas Tree to gold!" stated Deverall with an air of great authority.

"Sorry, did I hear you say everyone? Have others been trapped in this tree before me?"

A new voice spoke. "Oh yes, as many people as there ever were and ever will be, have met their challenges in this tree. Each on a journey of their soul, inside the tree 'till they grow old."

Joshua turned to see another creature approaching them from behind. This one was extremely dapper, with long hair and a pencil thin moustache curled at the edges, and a little goatee. He was wearing khaki jodhpurs, a white cotton blouson, and a red kerchief tied with a flourish around his neck. This Devas skin was pinkish beige.

"Joshua, please meet our resident songsmith, and poet laureate of the Midas Tree, the great Deva and most ancient bard, Devon."

"P... pleased to m meet you" stuttered Joshua, who was feeling quite flustered not only by the poet's flamboyant entrance, but also by what he had heard him say.

"Did you just say that everyone ends up in this tree until they are old?"

"This tree is home to young and old, it harbors all both meek and bold, they will reach the end of time, when they get the tree to shine," rhymed Devon.

"What he means," added Devandra, "is that everyone that visits the Midas Tree is a unique individual with a unique journey. They are considered young and ignorant at the beginning of their journey, and old and wise at the end of their journey, no matter how long it takes them to learn their lessons here.

"Oh I see," said Joshua, though really he didn't see at all. He just wanted to hurry things along, so he could get started on his unique journey. He hoped it would be short, because he wanted to leave. On the other hand, he hoped it would be long, because he didn't want to grow old too soon. This really was quite confusing.

"You promise that if I do this, I can go back to the garden and to Morfar?"

"We promise that if you learn all your lessons and unlock the ancient mysteries, you will be able to leave the tree and return home," said Devandra.

"What do you mean by 'all your lessons'? What are these lessons, and where do I start?"

"Well, you can start by learning to love your body as we love the tree, our greater body. Learn how to work with your body and keep it happy. Every morning when we hug the tree and sing our praises to her, we help her to smile on the inside. You need to learn to smile on the inside too."

As Devandra was answering Joshua's question, the three other Devas made a whistling sound, and as they did so, hundreds of vibrant red Devas came back from the passageways in a stream of light. In a flash, they traveled in through Joshua's feet, up his legs and into the rest of his body. They whirled around inside him, until his limbs moved about and he was seated comfortably in a cross-legged position. Then they swirled around some more, until they finally settled in his heart.

"Happy heart, happy heart, happy, happy, happy heart!" they sang with great joy.

They repeated this mantra over and over again, and as they sang, Joshua could feel the corners of his mouth lifting up into a broad smile. He suddenly felt really amused, and he just couldn't help it. He could feel his heart smiling, getting brighter and lighter, and filling up with love. It really felt like his heart was smiling too, so much that it might burst with joy any second.

Just as he thought his heart might burst with joy, the little red Devas swirled out of his heart and around his body some more, and took up residence in his liver.

"Happy liver, happy liver, happy, happy, happy liver!"

Joshua smiled even more broadly, until his face ached. His liver became so full of joy he could hardly contain it. He wanted to laugh, dance, and sing, all at once. All his worries had disappeared, and he felt like he could fly, as if he could do anything.

Just as he was about to get up and dance with joy, the little Devas swarmed into Joshua's brain.

"Happy brain, happy brain, happy, happy, happy brain!" they sang, repeatedly, until Joshua's brain felt light and clear. He felt the fog and confusion of the morning and previous night lift away, like the early morning mist.

Devon, Devandra, Deverall, and Devalicious, who had been watching all of this, whistled again. On hearing this sound, the little red Devas quickly swarmed out of Joshua, and streamed back into the passageways.

Joshua suddenly felt deflated. Instantly he became concerned once again about being trapped inside the tree. He was unable to recapture the feelings of joy and happiness created by the Devas.

Devalicious continued. "You must learn to generate this feeling from within yourself, by yourself, without the little red Devas to do it for you. Then when you are overflowing with love and happiness, you will be able to share your joy with everyone around you, especially with the Midas Tree. So put a smile back on your face, Sugar." She tweaked the corners of his mouth back up.

"A smile deep inside in your heart," she patted him on the chest, "laughter in your liver, and a clear, joyful mind." She touched his liver and forehead with her index finger.

Devalicious carried on, "Learn to love yourself from the inside, so that all your troubles will disappear. Learn to treat your body as a temple, as we do the tree, and you will achieve freedom and love beyond your wildest dreams. You will even have the power and the clarity needed to easily learn all your lessons, and solve the mysteries of the tree."

"You may join us every morning at dawn for the tree hugging ceremony. You may sit in the middle of the Grand Chamber and sing praises to yourself, as we sing praises to the tree. When you have transformed each part of yourself to love and light, you will be able to leave the tree and return home."

"How long will this take?"

"As Devon so eloquently explained, it will take as long as it does," Devandra replied. "This is the Midas Tree, and while you are here, you must turn everything to gold. As you turn your inner world to light, so shall your outer world turn to light. When you turn your entire body to golden light, and when this light is reflected in the Midas Tree, then you can leave the tree and return home to Morfar and the garden of color and light."

Deverall added, "If you are lucky and you do a good job, then you will be able to take all your memories and all you have learned back home with you, and you will be able to keep them forever."

Then each of the four Devas turned in a different direction, and started to walk toward one of the passageways.

"Wait," said Joshua, "don't leave me here all alone!"

Devalicious took hold of his collar and led him to the entrance of one of the passageways. "Journey down this tunnel, Sugar, which leads to the great root. Ask for Devadne, the Deva who helps anchor the tree into solid ground, and who also helps it let go of what is no longer needed."

Chapter 3

Anchoring the Light

oshua crawled down into the tunnel on all fours, but soon the passageway grew broader and taller, and he found that he was able to walk upright. The slope was quite steep, and as he walked, the temperature became cooler. He felt like he was an intrepid traveler on an epic journey through the center-most root of the tree, in search of ancient mysteries.

Far off in the distance, he could hear a deep low humming sound. He allowed his fingers to drag along the wall, which was cool and wet to the touch. He was also aware of a light breeze brushing past his cheeks in the same direction he was headed. Eventually he caught a glimpse of light in the far distance, which grew bigger the further he proceeded.

Soon enough, Joshua found himself at the entrance to another chamber. There was a large group of little bronze-colored Devas gathered, sitting on chairs arranged in a circle in

25

the center. They were quite still, as if in meditation. He could see that a fine column of light was coming from each Deva through the base of their chair, and into the ground beneath them. In the center of the circle was another Deva who was standing, and appeared to be directing them in whatever it was they were doing.

The low humming noise that he could hear as he approached was now much louder, and it was coming from the Deva in the center of the circle. He assumed that this was Devadne, as she was taller and much stronger-looking than the others. She was wearing a grass skirt made from the fine roots and root hairs from the tree, along with a bikini top woven from the same materials. Her hair was long and curly, and it was pinned into a mountainous bun of cascading locks. Long, slender fingers adorned her hands. Her skin was of an orange hue, and her nose was quite pointy.

She spotted him as soon as he entered the chamber, and stepped out of the circle to greet him. The other Devas kept on with whatever it was that they were doing.

"Hello" she said. She did not seem at all surprised to see him.

"Oh hello, my name is Joshua, and I was sent to meet you by Devon, Devandra, Deverall, and Devalicious," said Joshua.

"Welcome to the great central root of the ancient rooting system of the Midas Tree," said Devadne.

"Thank you. I am here to learn how to get back home to Morfar and the garden of color and light. Can you teach me something that will help me to do this?"

"Yes of course, that's wonderful, Joshua. I am so glad that you asked," said Devadne, taking his hand and leading him over to a balcony overlooking a stairwell with steps going down even further into the ground. They stood and looked over the railing at what was down below. Joshua could see a massed tangle of roots reaching deep down into the earth, as far as the eye could see. Little ice blue Devas who were holding buckets were sitting along the stair rail reaching in to the roots.

"Joshua, as I mentioned, this is the center of the root system of the Midas Tree. This system is one of the most important parts of the tree, because the roots help to anchor the tree into the ground. They reach down deep into the core of the Earth, providing stability and safety for the rest of the tree, and all who dwell in her."

She placed her hand in the small of his back, and gently turned him around, so that he was once again facing the shiny bronze Devas who were sitting in the circle.

"The root Devas especially love the roots of the Midas Tree. They tend to the root system and help it to grow strong, and thereby help to anchor her firmly into the ground. Equally importantly, do you see the column of light coming from each of the burnished bronze Devas sitting in the circle?"

Joshua nodded. Devadne took his hand and gently led him over to the circle.

"These columns of light also reach deep down into the core of the earth. The Devas create these columns of light to help keep the spirit of the Midas Tree anchored here inside its physical presence. The spirit of the tree is extremely powerful, similar in a way to a strong electric current. It needs to be grounded, so that all that energy doesn't arc off away from the tree. As long as there is spirit in the body of the tree, there is consciousness and there is life."

By now, they had reached the circle. An empty chair, just the right shape and size for Joshua's body, had mysteriously materialized.

"Joshua, all life has a spiritual spark just like the Midas Tree, including you. If you are going to find your way out of here, you are going to need access to all of your power. The first thing you need to learn is how to ground."

Devadne stretched out a hand toward the chair, indicating that he should take a seat. Once he had settled in, she walked back into the center of the circle and addressed the group. "Welcome, Joshua, to our group. Now we shall all resume our grounding exercise. For the benefit of our new member, here's what to do."

"First, sit with your feet flat on the ground, and your hands resting lightly in your lap. With your eyes closed and your spine straight, take a few nice big deep breaths. Then tune in to a place in your body near the base of your spine, and create a cord of light that goes from there all the way to the center of the earth."

Joshua uncrossed his legs and sat as she instructed. He closed his eyes and visualized a cord of light, just as he had observed the little Devas displaying when he first arrived here in the great root chamber. It seemed simple enough, and he didn't have too much trouble imagining his grounding cord.

"Very good Joshua; now tune in to how this makes you feel."

Joshua wasn't sure that he felt anything. Even though he could see the cord, he didn't know how he was supposed to feel, and he said so.

"OK, so to feel the difference, release your grounding and tune in to how you feel. Then reground, and see if you can tell the difference."

Joshua let his grounding cord go, and immediately he felt light-headed. His thoughts were more diffuse, and he was less in touch with his physical body. His mind drifted off back to the garden of color and light. He remembered the sunflowers and the poppies, the bridge across the stream, and how he liked to play all day with the butterflies and beetles.

"Joshua!" interrupted Devadne, "Come back from your day dreams. Replace your grounding cord and tune back into you."

The sharp sound of her voice immediately brought his attention back into the room, and he did as she asked. This time when he grounded, he noticed that he felt more focused, more present, more inside his body. His mind was calm and his thoughts were no longer wandering. In fact, he could now see that there was a real difference.

"But Devadne, what does this have to do with turning myself to gold, so that I can go home to the garden of color and light?"

"My dear Joshua" said Devadne. "The more you ground yourself, the more your energy fills your body, and thus the more enlightened you become. This is the first step to turning yourself to love and light. The grounding helps to anchor the light into your body. The more grounded you are, the more light you can hold. This is why we love to ground our tree, so that she can be more and more present, and hold more and more light. Now come along with me. Let's take a little break and stretch our legs for a while."

They left the little Devas, who were still deep in meditation with their grounding cords growing stronger and stronger for every minute they sat there. Devadne walked Joshua back over to the stairwell, and this time they started to descend the stairs together. From this vantage point, Joshua could see a great group grounding cord coming from the ceiling, from the Devas seated above them. It flowed down the chasm, deeper into the center of the earth.

"What happens when the Devas leave their chairs in the rooting chamber? Does the tree loose her grounding and her spirit?"

Devadne laughed. "No, my dear Joshua. The Devas continue to ground the tree no matter where they are, or what they are doing. Whether they are hugging the tree, or singing, or playing and laughing, they always maintain their grounding cords. You can do this too. In fact, you must learn to stay grounded as you continue your adventures here in the tree, no matter what they entail. You can start tomorrow morning, during the tree hugging ceremony. Make sure you are grounded before you do anything else."

Joshua continued to imagine his grounding cord as they stepped down the stairs. In doing so, he lost his focus on physical reality for a moment, and almost tripped on the stairwell.

Devadne laughed again. "It takes a little practice, but believe me; you can learn to hold your focus in physical and non-physical reality at the same time. I have no doubt that you will be grounding even in your sleep, in no time at all."

They walked past a pair of ice blue Devas who balanced on the railing next to a woody hollow in the wall. They appeared to be collecting a murky, dark, sticky substance from the base of the hollow, and were placing it into their buckets. They walked on and continued their conversation. The further they went, the finer the roots all around them became.

"Let's walk a little further into the root system now, Joshua. We can work up an appetite for our supper," chirped Devadne. "Of course, as I mentioned earlier, the tree roots themselves also help to physically anchor the Midas tree into the soil. There are as many roots as there are branches in this tree."

They climbed down even more steps, passing more of the little ice blue Devas on the way, until they entered an open doorway. They appeared now to be traveling inside one of the finer roots.

"Each root has a function in anchoring the tree, and we will teach you more about this later. First, you must master the most fundamental of all lessons here in the Midas Tree, which is to be grounded."

All around them, and through the roots, were various pipes, channels, and little capillaries of flowing substances. The little ice blue Devas were rushing around with buckets, here, there, and everywhere. Some of the buckets contained what looked like water, whereas others seemed to be carrying the black sticky substance that Joshua had seen earlier. Other Devas appeared to be stuffing a solid white substance from their buckets into the walls of the roots.

Devadne must have noticed his curiosity, because she remarked "The ice blue Devas have many functions in the nutrition and cleaning of the tree. We will teach you all about this in due course. For now, I find it best to focus on one lesson at a time."

By this time, they had reached another door, which led into a chamber located inside a pipe of flowing water. They stepped inside. Joshua thought it was quite beautiful. He touched the transparent wall. It felt surprisingly brittle and stiff. It was like being inside a glass chamber inside a waterfall, except the water was flowing up instead of down.

The doors had started to shut, when three little ice blue Devas with buckets full of the white substance squeezed through and joined them. "Going up?" chirped one of the little fellows, as he pressed a button in a panel on the wall. All at once, they shot upwards in their capsule, at an amazing velocity.

When the doors opened, they found they were back in the Grand Chamber where they had all started their day. It was somehow magically taller, and Joshua found he could now stand up. He looked enquiringly at Devadne who explained, "Yes, we put the elongation Devas to work in here, to make it more comfortable for you."

"Elongation Devas?"

"They are the misty purple Devas who help grow the tree. They elongate the roots, and they grow the new shoots. They have a special magical powder that they sprinkle on parts of the tree when they want them to grow. What we have done here is a tad unorthodox, but you may be here for some time, and we want you to be comfortable."

"Thank you," said Joshua, who was feeling more concerned by the minute about how long he would be staying. He tried to take his mind off this by watching the commotion that was going on all around him. As the elevator door opened, the ice blue Devas with the buckets had rushed past them. They were now putting the contents of their buckets onto a serving dish, placed atop a big wooden table in the center of the room.

Devas from all over the tree were swarming in, and placing all manner of foods onto the table. There were honey pots, pitchers of sweet nectar, urns of hot herbal teas, overflowing salad bowls, and fruit of all kinds. There was chattering and rustling and scraping of chairs as everyone settled down.

"Please be seated at the table," said Devadne.

Joshua took a place at the table and looked around. He was seated amongst all the larger Devas. The smaller Devas were buzzing around making preparations, and placing food onto plates in front of the larger Devas, but they did not appear to be going to join them. In no time, an abundance of food adorned Joshua's plate, and his goblet filled to overflowing.

As he reached to pick up a rather delicious-looking plum, Devadne, who had sat down next to him, playfully slapped his hand. "Devon must say grace before we eat," she whispered. "This helps energize the food, and is how we thank the Midas Tree for all she gives us."

"Ahem!" Devon had appeared at the top of the table. In fact, he was standing on top of the table, so that he would be visible above all the mountains of produce.

The din started to die down, and Devon continued.

Thank you Tree for all you give

So all of us can thrive and live

We eat with grace and gratitude

All of this delicious food
So we can work another day
In your great presence, this we pray
Welcome friends old and new
Let them feast beside us too…"

The Devas were starting to shift in their seats now. Some were even raising their eyes to the ceiling.

"Unfortunately, he does tend to get a bit carried away sometimes," whispered Devadne.

"We rejoice at this food
For it is oh so good
Lovely, lovely Midas Tree…"

At this point Devalicious, who sat beside Devon, gave a sharp tug on his sleeve and pulled him to his seat.

"Bravo, Amen," clapped everyone, and immediately started to enthusiastically chomp down on his or her plates of food.

Joshua picked up a piece of the white substance brought up by the root Devas. He sniffed it, to find it smelled a bit like turnip. Joshua didn't like turnip. He bit into it and chewed. Actually, it was a lot nicer than turnip. It had a crispy refreshing texture, and tasted more like carrot, or was it beet? No, maybe celery root; yes, that was it, or…

"Joshua," said Devadne, "you simply need to imagine what you would most like to eat, and this food, which is the manna from the roots of the tree, will take on that flavor for you. The Midas Tree is a magical tree, capable of creating all manner of abundance. When you live inside the tree, you become one with her, and have the ability to co-create with her."

Lamb stew, thought Joshua, and immediately that was the taste inside his mouth. Chicken teriyaki, spaghetti meatballs, steak and mushroom pie, baked potato; each time he changed his thought, a new taste manifested in his mouth. Better not think liver and onions, or sprouts. "Yuk!" exclaimed Joshua.

"Careful what you think now, Joshua," laughed Devadne.

He settled on the lamb stew, and eagerly filled his belly, finishing off with a few selected fruits and a cup of sweet herbal tea.

There were a few more questions from the day's activities that Joshua had not yet had the chance to ask Devadne. Once he had eaten enough to satisfy his hunger, he started by asking her about the humming noise he had heard on his way into the main root chamber.

"There are many powers we can use here within the Midas Tree, to help us in our journey, and to learn our lessons. The power of visualization is one, and you used that today when you created your grounding cord. The power of thought is another, and you used that just now, when you were deciding what to eat for supper. Sound is another great power that we can use for healing, and to enhance our energies. This is why we sing to the tree every morning. I was also using the power of sound inside the root chamber, to create a vibration in the room that would help with the grounding process."

"Wow, that sounds cool. Can I do that too?" asked Joshua, who was imagining himself having fun conducting the little Devas, just as Devadne had been doing.

"You will see many amazing things while you are here in the Midas Tree," said Devadne, "but do not be in too much of a hurry. Take things at a steady pace, and don't get ahead of yourself. If you tackle advanced techniques before you are ready, you may do more harm than good. Stick with the grounding for now, and let us guide you through each step as you become ready."

Joshua felt a little put out by this comment. After all, how hard could humming a few simple notes really be? He changed the subject to take his mind off his annoyance.

"Devadne, why are only the big Devas sitting at the table to eat?"

"The little Devas don't need to eat, Joshua, because they are pure spiritual beings made from light particles. They feed from the energy and light substance that we find all about us. We larger Devas are creatures. We can live partially from the energy around us, but we also have physical bodies, and so we must nourish them - just as we work together to nourish the tree."

"Anyway, now my little child, let's get you settled for the night. In the morning, after the tree hugging ceremony, you must come back down to the central root to resume your lessons with me."

Devadne led him by the hand to an alcove in the wall of the chamber, where a comfortable-looking mattress with a feather down pillow and duvet were neatly arranged. "This will be your bed chamber for the duration of your stay. Have a good and pleasant sleep. You will need it, as we will be up at dawn, and you have another full day ahead of you tomorrow." With that she withdrew, along with all the other Devas, until the main chamber became once again hollow and empty.

Joshua climbed into the downy bed, which was the most comfortable place he had ever encountered, and fell instantly asleep.

Chapter 4

Taking Sustenance from the Earth

"OH GREAT TREE, WE ADORE THEE, BODY, TEMPLE OF OUR SOUL"

Joshua awoke with a start. The Devas were already in full chorus around the perimeter of the chamber. He jumped up out of bed and stumbled sleepily over to the center of the Grand Chamber, where he sat as the Devas had prescribed, in a chair created especially for him.

As the Devas swayed and chanted, he turned within and focused his attention on his grounding. He created a cord of light from near the base of his spine all the way down into the earth, and immediately felt more present. Then he placed a big wide grin on his face and started to wonder why he wasn't instantly feeling happy. He had a smile on his face, but inside he felt frightened. How would he ever get home? He was daunted

37

by the lessons he must learn, especially as he did not know what they were, or how many of them there would be.

He returned his focus to his grounding, but it seemed the more grounded he became, the more aware he became of his emotions. He was feeling sad, because he was missing Morfar. He was worried and scared about what the future held, and in spite of his deep sleep, he was still feeling tired. A little voice inside him was calling "Don't you worry, you'll be fine. You are fabulous and clever, and you will show them all. These lessons will be easy for someone as great as you are."

He focused on his grounding again, and then he remembered he was supposed to be smiling into his body as well. He started with his belly, but that only served to make him feel even more emotional, so in the end he settled on his feet. May as well start at the bottom and work my way up, he thought. He placed a smile in each of his feet, and continued grounding. He was beginning to feel like quite the contortionist, when he felt a light tap on his shoulder.

It was Devandra. "How did it go?" he asked.

"I'm trying really hard to do the exercises like I was told, but I don't think it is working."

"The trick is not to try at all," Devandra replied. "Now off with you down the passageway to the root chamber, to meet with Devadne. He pointed in the direction of the tunnel that Joshua was to take.

Somehow, the journey down to Devadne seemed much longer today. Joshua was feeling despondent, and kicked a few chips of bark along as he went. As he walked, he thought about his fate, and how unfair it was that he was trapped in this tree. Why hadn't Morfar looked after him better? Wasn't it Morfar's fault that he had ended up in this situation? If Morfar had looked after him properly, and kept an eye on him, he wouldn't be here at all. He started to kick the bits of bark harder and harder.

By the time he reached the main root chamber he had worked up quite a temper.

"My, oh my, Little Man!" said Devadne in quite good humor, considering the way Joshua was glaring at her, "Looks like you need to practice your grounding technique some more." She beckoned towards the empty chair.

"I don't want to have to do this again," shouted Joshua. "I learned this yesterday and I practiced it this morning. I want to learn something new today!"

"My oh my! We are in a temper this morning, aren't we? Trust me, Little Man; you do need to ground again today, and every day of your life from now on. That is, if you want to go home one day?"

Joshua slammed himself down onto the chair, with such violence that the little bronze Devas all jumped. He was sitting slumped down, with his arms and legs crossed.

"Okay!" said Devadne. "Thank you for joining us Joshua! Please adjust your posture so that your back is straight, your feet are flat on the floor, and your hands are resting lightly in your lap. Thank you!"

"Now focus on that place near the base of your spine, and create a flow of energy from there all the way to the center of the earth."

"A flow of energy?" questioned Joshua. "I thought we just made a cord?"

"Yes, a flow of energy, Joshua. Create a flow of energy that runs from the energy center near the base of your spine, and allow that energy to flow all the way to the center of the Earth."

Reluctantly, Joshua did as she asked. It seemed to be helping him to calm down.

"Now simply allow anything that is causing you disturbance to flow away down your grounding cord. Any worries or concerns you may be experiencing, any emotions that are overwhelming you, and any feelings of tension or tiredness in your body."

Joshua imagined his seething red anger, like the molten lava of a volcano, was flowing away to the center of the earth. Soon he noticed he wasn't feeling angry any more.

He allowed his fears and his worries to flow away, and soon he was feeling safe and supported again.

"Good," said Devadne. "You can change your reality in an instant, by using the flow of energy down your grounding to let go of unwanted emotions. Even beliefs that you hold, which are not helpful to you, can be released down your grounding cord."

Joshua started to let go of his belief that it was hard to ground and smile in his body at the same time, and instantly he felt more grounded. Then he imagined that both of his feet glowed with a golden light and were smiling back up at him.

"Well done, Joshua!" clapped Devadne. "Everyone look, Joshua has started to turn to golden light."

All the little bronze Devas opened their eyes and gasped. They enthusiastically joined in the clapping. Then a swathe of little ice blue Devas ran up from the stairwell, exclaiming that the tips of the deepest roots of the Midas Tree had also turned to gold.

"My, oh my, Little Man!" beamed Devadne. "I think you are ready for your next lesson. Come with me."

They walked over to the stairwell, and descended further into the root system, just as they had done on the previous day. As they walked, Devadne pointed out the little ice blue Devas with the buckets of black sticky substance.

"You know, Joshua, we all have a tendency to store our worries and our fears inside our bodies, and the Midas Tree is no exception. Every morning when we wake up, we find that the tree has placed her worries, her fears, her pain and even her hate and bitterness into these spaces in the walls of the roots here. The little blue Devas are collecting this from these spaces, to dispose of it. Here, let me show you. By the way, these little spaces are called vacuoles."

They walked down a few more steps, to a platform where some Devas were filling their buckets up. Once they were full, they walked over to the edge of the platform and tipped the buckets of black tar over the balcony into the grounding stream coming from the burnished bronze Devas in the central root above.

"You see, they are helping the tree to release her pain and sorrow down her grounding, just as you were doing in our meditation this morning."

"What will happen if they don't help her let go of this stuff?" asked Joshua.

"The same thing that would happen to you, my friend. Negativity would take up so much space; there would not be enough room for positive things, or for the light. There would be no balance, and no space to create new things, because all the space would be taken up by sadness."

Joshua understood. He must release his fear and pain, to create space to turn his body to gold, so that he could go home. If he did not do this, he would be trapped by a prison of his own making, inside his own negative thoughts, emotions, and memories.

"Here we are now," said Devadne, ushering them into the glass elevator. This time, she pressed a different button, and they headed down into the bowels of the earth. They disembarked into some finer roots, which had lots of little side branches everywhere.

"These are the root hairs." Devadne casually indicated the side branches, all the while looking all around. Her eyes searched in the dimness for something or someone.

41

"Deverall!" she shouted, "Deverall, where are you?"

They heard a squelching noise, pitter-pattering from lower down, and getting louder and closer with every squelch.

Deverall, the blue Deva, eventually appeared. He was much wetter than yesterday when Joshua had first met him. He was mopping the glistening beads on his forehead with a wet rag, which had the effect of making the beads of water turn to rivulets streaming down his forehead. The hosepipe wound around his waist was dripping quite the little stream of water.

"Ah, Devadne, our little student is here so soon? I did wonder, when I saw the glow coming from the root tips," he pointed downwards, where in the distance Joshua could see a faint golden glow.

"Yes, Deverall, our student has already turned his feet to gold, and so I think he is ready for his next lesson. I will leave him in your capable hands, and will see you both again at the supper table." She disappeared at once into the elevator, and Joshua was left alone with Deverall.

"Welcome to my domain," said Deverall, who seemed to be a little flustered.

He noticed Joshua was watching him intently.

"It's been a busy morning," he quipped. First, we had a couple of burst roots in the north channel. Then we had some slug damage to repair in the south-west channel. To top it all off, the east channel has another blockage. I've been running around like a mad plumber in a cold winter storm."

"Have you thought of grounding?" suggested Joshua. "I find it's very helpful in moments of panic."

Deverall burst into chortles of laughter. "I can see why Devadne thought you were ready for a lesson in energy management. Let me show you around a little bit.

"They walked over to a wall that was very densely packed

with side channels. "These are the root hairs," explained Deverall. Joshua nodded. "They are here to increase the surface area available for the Midas Tree to bring in water from the surrounding soil. The water flows up channels in the roots, and is distributed throughout the tree. As it flows, it also transports mineral salts which have been dissolved in the water, which are important for the tree to grow and thrive."

"Now, my little ice blue Devas have a big part to play in all of this. You may have seen them running around the root system, carrying buckets of water and so forth?"

Joshua nodded.

"Yes, well, in addition to their practical function, helping me with the physical workings of the water intake system, they also have another equally important role. This way my dear chap..."

They walked down and then across one of the root hairs, until they reached a chamber where several of the smaller roots had become fused to create a large-sized room.

This time it was the little ice blue Devas who were sitting deep in meditation. Joshua could see that they too had grounding cords, but in addition, they had energy flowing in through their feet and up their legs.

"What are they doing?" Joshua asked, his curiosity piqued.

"All in good time, my dear boy," beamed Deverall. "The best way to find that out is to experience it for yourself."

Joshua took a chair amongst the ice blue Devas, while Deverall continued his explanation in a calm, clear, and soothing tone.

"Devas and guest. You must all remember to strengthen your grounding. Tune in to that flow of energy coming from near the base of your spine and traveling to the center of the earth, and visualize it getting stronger and stronger. Good! Now tune into some energy centers in the arches of your feet."

Joshua looked with his mind's eye at the arches of his feet. His feet were still glowing gold, and he could just make out a little swirl of energy in the center of each arch.

"Imagine that these energy centers are gently opening, like a flower bud that gently opens to the sun. As they open up, they allow energy from the earth, which exists deep below the Midas Tree, to flow in. Let this earth energy continue to flow up through your legs. It will flow through channels that exist in your legs, just like water flows up through the roots of the Midas Tree."

Joshua felt the arches of his feet tingle, and he visualized them opening up like golden daffodils. He also imagined he had channels in his legs, like the ones he had seen in the roots of the Midas Tree, and he started to feel a gentle rush of energy flowing into his feet and up his legs. At first, it was a slow moving trickle, but soon it felt like a fast-flowing stream.

"That's truly wonderful, Joshua," encouraged Deverall.

"Now everyone, bring that that energy all the way up past the tops of your legs, so that it flows into that place near the base of your spine. Joshua, that is the same energy center that you learned to ground from. That's great, great. Just lovely! Now let some of the earth energy flow down your grounding cord, and notice how that feels. Let it enhance and strengthen your grounding, that's right. Just so."

Joshua could feel the flow getting stronger and stronger. He could feel himself becoming more grounded, more solid, and more real. He was really enjoying the sensation of being grounded and having his earth energy flowing. Then he felt a sharp pain and a pulsating ache in one of his knees. "Ow!"

"Keep going..."

"But Deverall, this is making my knee hurt," said Joshua.

"Precisely why, my dear boy, you should keep going. All that is happening is that the flow of energy has found a blockage that needs releasing. It's quite simple, and quite easy to solve."

"Argh! Now it's getting worse."

"Now, now, I guarantee it will clear in no time at all, if you keep on doing what I say."

Joshua tried again, but the more he tried, the more it hurt. The more it hurt, the less he could focus on his grounding or on his flowing earth energy. Moreover, the pain was now spreading into his calf muscle.

"I have to stop and stretch my leg." Joshua jumped out of the chair, and limped over to the wall. He held onto it, as he stretched out his calf muscle and his leg so that it was straight at the knee.

"Alright, carry on troops," Deverall said to the Devas, and then he came over to where Joshua was standing.

"Perhaps that is enough of a lesson for today. No sense in hurrying things. Remember to add this technique to your exercises tomorrow morning during the tree hugging ceremony, and try smiling through your knees."

The pain was starting to ease off a bit by now.

"Do you think you can walk? I'd like to take you down to the root tips, to show you what you managed to achieve this morning in your meditation."

"Sure!" Joshua was keen to go and explore the golden glow he had proudly created, and he gladly limped alongside Deverall to the base of one of the roots. As they approached, the golden glow grew stronger and stronger, until they were bathed in a beautiful golden light. It felt truly wonderful, like standing in a great golden waterfall of energy.

"Welcome, Joshua, to the root tip of the Midas Tree, to witness all your good work first hand. This is one of the places in The Midas Tree where growth occurs. Do you see here, right at the very tip, is a little cap which looks like a thimble?"

Some thimble, Joshua thought, as he crawled inside to take a closer look. Up close, he could see that parts of the cap were disintegrating, and other parts seemed new.

There were a few misty purple Devas sitting around with buckets of the white manna substance. They were molding the manna into shapes, and then placing them onto the inside of the root cap. Then they patted it down, and rubbed it in so that the surface looked smooth. Then they pushed everything forwards, so that the wall of the root cap stayed in the same place inside the tree. The result was that the root tip protruded further into the earth.

"This serves as a protection while the roots are growing. The cells on the outside are continuously worn away, as the root pushes through the soil. As this happens, new cells are formed to take their place. See this region here behind the root cap? This is called the Meristem, and it is where the new growths comes from... and see this part here?"

Deverall pointed to a region in between the Meristem and root cap.

"This is where these newly formed cells elongate. As they get longer, this forces the root to push forward and penetrate the soil."

"It's a bit like what Devadne was saying about getting rid of the old, to make way for the new growth," remarked Joshua.

"Quite so, quite so," replied Deverall. "You know, my dear boy, we all must learn to grow at a balanced pace. If we grow too quickly, we can become vulnerable, because we won't be so well protected." He looked long and hard at Joshua, as if the longer he looked, the deeper his message would penetrate his new student.

"I think that's quite sufficient for today. Let's away to the glass elevator, and get ready for our supper."

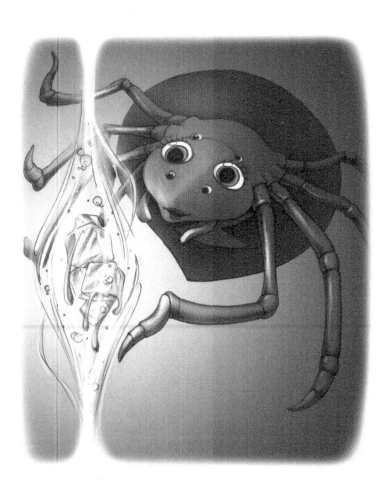

Chapter 5

Breaking the Ice

oshua was still reeling from the heady delights of supper when he awoke the next morning. He had been dreaming about what delicious tastes and smells he might experiment with creating next at the supper table. In his dream, not only did the taste of the food manifest through his thoughts, so too did smells and textures and colors of the entire meal. He was popping out sumptuous strawberry shortcakes, zingy lemon drizzle cakes, soft, decadent black forest gateaux, and silky-smooth chocolate ganache tortes all night.

Sleepily, he made his way over to the bathroom, which had recently appeared in his room, to do his wake-up routine. Next, he chose an outfit to wear from the walk-in closet, which had also materialized. The Devas had explained the night before that they were doing their utmost to make his stay as comfortable as possible. In between their other duties, they had been working on making his living quarters more livable.

Of course, the items were all made from things that were readily available from the tree. His toothbrush was made of a wooden twig, frayed at the end into a brush. His hairbrush was also made from wood, and his clothes were woven from plant fibers. He was definitely starting to feel more at home.

He wandered into the Grand Chamber, and took his seat right in the center of the hall. He started by grounding. Then he used the flow of energy down his grounding to let go of all distracting thoughts. This was particularly useful, he found, for letting go of all the dreams from the night before. Then he moved on to running earth energy in through the arches of his feet. He imagined the flowers opening again, and he let the energy flow all the way up his legs.

No sooner had he started than the pain in his knee was back. He remembered what Deverall had told him the day before about how this was an energy blockage, and he just needed to keep on running the energy so that the blockage would dissolve. It seemed the stronger he ran the energy, the more the knee hurt, so he created a more gentle flow and the pain lessened considerably. This way he found that he could also focus on releasing the pain down his grounding. He was getting quite into this, when there was a tap on his shoulder.

This time it was a Deva whom he hadn't met before. She was very beautiful. She had lovely emerald-green eyes and peachy white skin, and was adorned in a long milk white robe, with a crown of mistletoe berries in her braided flaxen hair. "Hello, my name is Devi," she said. "Didn't you notice that the tree hugging has finished for the day?"

"No," said Joshua. "I was so intent on my meditation that I didn't notice. Now what will I do? Deverall didn't tell me what I should do today. Do you know where I am meant to be?"

Devi laughed a tinkling laugh. "You are exactly where you are meant to be, of course."

"Yes, but where am I meant to be going?"

"That depends on you, I should think." She smiled, and her green eyes twinkled mischievously.

"But I have to learn my lessons. First, I was learning grounding with Devadne, then I was learning running earth energy with Deverall, and that's what I was doing this morning. I think I probably need some more practice at that, but oh dear! I don't know how to get back to the deeper root system."

"My dear, every other passageway leads deeper into the root system, and every alternate passageway leads up to the canopy. If you wish to go down into the roots, then simply choose one of the tunnels that goes down."

"Yes, but which one? Which one will lead me back to Deverall and his chamber the fastest?" Joshua was looking around the chamber from tunnel to tunnel in great confusion.

"Sometimes it can be fun to not to take the fastest route to our destination. You don't want to get there before you are ready. Sometimes it can be more fun to go on an adventure, and take time to enjoy the journey," quipped Devi in a faint and ethereal voice.

"Yes, but all these tunnels have sign posts on them. The signposts must mean something. You must be able to tell from the sign posts where the tunnels go?"

As Joshua turned to face Devi again, he realized that she had completely disappeared. Oh my goodness, thought Joshua. Whatever shall I do now?

He wasn't going to repeat the antics of his first day in the tree, where he spent hours and hours trying to figure out the markings on the bark signposts. He started walking to the nearest downward facing tunnel. He took a deep breath and marched inside.

The descent in this tunnel was quite steep, and it was very windy. Luckily, there was a handrail on the wall that he could hold on to, so he wouldn't slip down the incline. Soon, he reached what amounted to a hole in the ground. The walls were steep, and it seemed to go a long way down. He noticed a ladder on the side of the wall.

Bravely, and in the spirit of adventure, Joshua climbed down the ladder into the depths of the hole. The end of the ladder and the hole turned out to be the ceiling of another root chamber. Joshua carefully lowered himself down by hanging from his arms from the bottom rung of the ladder, so that his feet dangled closer to the ground.

As he let go, he instantly regretted it, because how was he going to get back out of here? He looked around and became increasingly panicked, as there didn't appear to be a door anywhere. Not in the walls, or even in the floor. Only the route he had entered, in the middle of the ceiling... out of reach. He sat down on the floor with his head in his hands, exhausted from his effort to climb down into this space.

Just as he thought he was doing so well, now he had to go and ruin it all! He curled up on the floor with his eyes screwed closed, and inside began to implore Morfar, "Please Morfar, please come and take me out of here. Please release me from this place. I don't deserve this. I don't deserve this." He was feeling very sorry for himself, and he started to cry. Deep sobs emerged from inside him, so that he found himself gasping and gulping for air.

Eventually, worn out from the crying, he wiped his eyes and took another look around the dimly lit root chamber. The walls were formed of earth. There were gnarled, tangled old roots peeping through the dirt, interwoven with one another. Could he be outside the tree now, he wondered? In any case, it didn't really matter, as he must be deep below the ground. The only way out appeared to be the way he came in.

Joshua walked across to the edge of the room, and slowly padded around the perimeter, touching the walls and absent-mindedly staring at the dusty floor. He had almost come full circle when he felt a fluffy, sticky substance on his face. "Yuk!"

he exclaimed, as he waived his arms in an attempt to extricate himself from the spider's web he had just stumbled into.

The harder he struggled, the more enmeshed he got. The silken fibers of the web had become wound around both of Joshua's hands like a pair of handcuffs. He could still feel it wafting ethereally, like a ghostly fine thread, on his face and neck. He blew hard out of his nose, to stop himself breathing it in.

This must be a really big spider's web, he thought, as he turned around to look behind him. He instantly regretted that, as now he had a rope of silken tendrils wrapped around his chest. He tried unwinding back in the opposite direction, but to no avail. Because his hands were tied together, he didn't have the reach to pick at it and pull it off. Still he tried, only to find that the fibers were so sticky, that his hands now became glued to the web on his torso as well.

This must be a really big spider that spun this web, he thought with a shiver. He was just about to look up, when he felt a tickling sensation on his head, and the weight of something creeping and crawling in his hair. "Aaaargh, aaaargh, get off, get off, get off!" he shouted. His main emotions, which had been frustration and anger at being all tied up like this, now started turning to fear, as he felt a set of long legs making their way down the back of his head and neck.

"All my hard work is now gone to waste."

"What?" said Joshua.

"All my hard work is gone to waste. I am not sure any of it can be salvaged. I may have to start all over again."

"Sorry, who is there? Where are you? I can't see you, but I think I have a spider on my back, can you help me get it off?"

"Oh for... Morfar, stay still and stop jiggling about."

"Yes, but you see I have this big spider on my back, and it's really scary, please can you help me get it off?"

"Look, your main problem is not the spider on your back; it's the web you've tangled yourself up in. Though Morfar knows if I wasn't in so much of a hurry to get it repaired, I should give you a piece of my mind, I really should. Now stay still!"

Joshua stopped in his tracks. Did he just hear correctly, or were his ears deceiving him? "Did you say you are the spider? I didn't know spiders could talk..."

"Oh, stay still for goodness sake! Listen, the only way to get yourself out of a tangle is to stay still and not struggle. Don't wriggle about, don't struggle, be still. Take a nice deep breath and stay calm. Haven't those Devas taught you anything yet?"

"I know how to ground, and run earth energy!"

"That's a start. That would certainly help you with your panic. Lucky for you, you're a human being and not a bug, or I wouldn't be giving you any of this advice."

Immediately Joshua grounded. It certainly couldn't hurt. Right away, he started to sense that he wasn't in as much danger as he had thought he was.

"Thank Morfar for that," said what Joshua could now clearly see was indeed a large spider, and a scary-looking one at that.

The spider instantly went to work on unraveling the mess that Joshua had managed to get himself into. She scurried round and round Joshua's body, rolling the web into sticky balls of silky thread. Joshua increased his grounding as she crawled once again over his head, neck, and face. He could feel her eight legs, and they gave him the heebie-jeebies. Finally, she got to his hands. Patiently and painstakingly, she disentangled them, so that he finally had the full use of them again.

"Thank you, I think," said Joshua, scratching his head.

"I'd like to say you're welcome, that I'm pleased to be of service, anything else I can do for you?" quipped the spider, "but given the circumstances, count yourself lucky that I'm running low and needed the silk. Otherwise, I'd have left you there to try a bit harder. See what more of a mess you could have created!"

"Sorry and thank you. Much appreciated, Mr. Spider, sir."

"My name is Ariadne, and it's Mrs. Ariadne Arachne, if you please. The full title is black widow, of many, many, many husbands, all now deceased."

"Ah… err, ah… err... do you, Ariadne, happen to know how I might get out of here?"

"Get out of here? You mean you don't like it down here, deep in the black widow's lair?" She glared at him, eight red eyes glowing in the dimness, eight shiny black legs bristling.

"Err, oh no... It's a lovely lair. Quite delightful really, I'd love to stay; only I have an appointment with Deverall to practice running more earth energy, so I can start to turn my legs gold. I'd, well, love to keep you company, but I'm already late, you see."

Ariadne let out the biggest, most amused laugh Joshua had ever heard. In fact, she was so amused, that Joshua could not help but to burst out laughing along with her.

"Look, I know you might not be thrilled about being here, but you may as well relax and settle in. You never know, you might learn something here too. Don't you think I know a thing or two about earth energy as well? I do have eight legs, after all."

"I guess that's true," said Joshua. "You mean I can learn some of my lessons here with you?"

"Yes indeed. That is, if you pay attention, I can teach you some very valuable lessons."

"…And that will help me to get out of here?"

"Yes indeed. Out of the spider's lair, and of course this will contribute to getting you closer to leaving the Midas Tree altogether. If that is what you want? You know you always have a choice in everything! Now about that earth energy, I can see you have an energy block in your knee."

"Err, yes, I have a pain in my knee, but how can you see that."

"We spiders are highly sensitive beings in many ways. We have the power of inner vision, to see deeply into all that is, and we have the power to sense the slightest movement, such as a hair's whisper. You know I run earth energy through all eight of my legs. It's very important for me to keep my energy channels clear, because I use my legs to sense my prey."

"The web I weave is very delicate, and when a bug becomes trapped it sends vibrations along the fibers, that I sense with my legs. Actually, although my inner vision is great, my physical vision is quite poor. I rely on my legs and my sense of touch to guide me to my prey, and to help me weave my web."

"So every day, many times a day, I clean my leg channels out, to keep them in good working order. My physical survival depends on it."

"Ariadne?"

"Yes."

"Could you teach me how to clean my leg channels, so that the earth energy moves smoothly, and the pain in my knee goes away?"

"It will be my pleasure, dear... what did you say your name was?"

"Joshua."

"Joshua, oh my dear Joshua!" exclaimed Ariadne. "Find a place to sit, maybe on one of those roots over there." She pointed one of her spindly legs at one of the roots in the wall, which bent into the shape of a chair.

Joshua walked over and sat down. "Don't you need to sit down to do this, Ariadne?"

Ariadne laughed. "How do you propose I do that?" She lowered her abdomen onto the ground, and raised all eight legs in the air at once, and they both rolled around laughing again. When they recovered, she explained. "Actually I run earth energy all the time; while I am walking around and when I am resting. There is never a time when I am not running it."

"Can I do that?" asked Joshua.

"Yes, of course. It's just that when you are just learning, it's best to sit and meditate, because that helps you to focus. So sit and do your grounding exercise, and then get your earth energies running."

Joshua did as she asked. At once, he felt the same sharp pain in his knee that he had felt before.

"You know, my dear Joshua, I can see with my inner vision that you are afraid of moving forwards in your life. You are fearful of an uncertain future, and you are worried that you cannot achieve your goal of turning the Midas Tree to gold. A lot of that fear of moving forwards is being stored in your knee."

Joshua sensed that what she was saying was true, but how could he become confident in himself and his ability to achieve what he was here to do?

"Yes, but how can I clear myself so I am no longer blocked?"

"Easy! I am going to teach you a visualization technique that will help you to unblock your knee!"

"Imagine with your minds' eye that the pain in your knee is a block of ice. Visualize the flow of earth energy as warm water that can melt the ice. Absorb the block into its flow, and send it away down your grounding cord."

Joshua imagined he had blocks of ice in his knee, and he allowed warm earth energy to gently flow over these ice cubes, like pebbles in a stream. As he watched, the ice cubes were slowly melting.

"Well done, Joshua, that is fantastic. Keep on going," remarked Ariadne, who was intently focused on what was happening in Joshua's knee. "Now relax, and keep taking nice, deep breaths in and out, in and out. Be patient, and know that you are giving yourself a great healing right now."

Joshua relaxed, and really got into the swing of it. Gradually he felt the pain in his knee subside, and he could see that the ice cubes had almost melted away completely.

"Lovely. You must be quite hungry by now. Would you like to join me for a bite to eat?"

"Actually, I am starving," said Joshua. "Yes, that would be very nice."

"Now, now what can I offer you? Let me see... Well, I just finished off the eleventh Mr. Arachne. None of him left, I'm afraid, but I do have a nice couple of moths, and a little bug or two. My web is becoming rather fruitful these days, I must say."

"Thank you Ariadne, that's really generous of you, but unfortunately I don't eat bugs," said Joshua.

"Don't eat bugs! Ah yes, I remember that, you humans are very peculiar in your eating habits. I think I might be able to whip up a piece of manna from one of the root vacuoles here."

"Fabulous!" said Joshua, who couldn't wait to continue his practice of imagining delicious delicacies, on the blank canvas of Midas Tree manna.

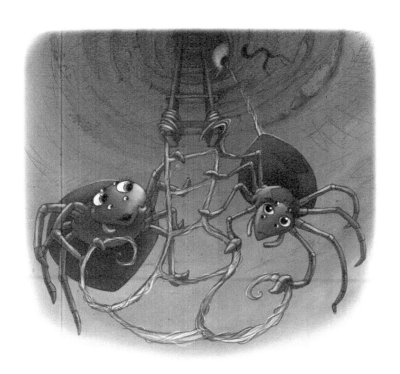

Chapter 6

Oh What a Tangled Web We Weave

oshua enjoyed lunch with his new friend. It tasted like chicken in tarragon sauce, followed by cake and ice cream. Although his lunch was tasty, watching Ariadne devour a plate of assorted insects wasn't the most pleasant part of the experience. When he was done, he felt satiated and rested, and turned the conversation back to his lessons.

"Ariadne, now that I have learned the visualization technique for melting blocks in my leg channels, can I leave the lair and go back to the Devas?"

"My dear Joshua, this was not the lesson that you came to my lair to learn. I just happen to like you, so I gave you an extra something. Call it my gift to you. No, the real lesson is a tad more complex, and has to do with the magic that we spiders weave. Make sure you are sitting comfortably, and then I will begin."

Joshua was already in a reclining position on the ground, but he shuffled his position a bit more, and rested his chin on his hand and waited intently for Ariadne to begin.

"My human friend, we spiders know a secret that few of you humans know, or manage to figure out in your brief journeys into the tree. It is that we, the creatures of the tree, are the weavers of our own fate. It is a kind of magic that we weave in each and every moment. Oh yes, it is an ancient truth that destiny is not pre-ordained. It is created in each moment through our thoughts, deeds, and beliefs."

"Spiders are the master weavers, the keepers of this ancient magic, and we show it to you humans every day. However, hardly any of you ever looks close enough to see. Most of you are fearful of us, and turn away as fast as you can. If you would only pause to watch, then you would see the wisdom in our work, and receive the knowledge that we are here to teach."

"We cast the spell of destiny as we weave our mystical webs. Every subtle stitch, every decision on whether to add a thread here or there, all lead to the final culmination, the result, the outcome, the ultimate destination, another now moment."

"Hmm. I can see how important it is for you to weave your web just so," said Joshua. "If you weave it too loosely, then the small bugs will fly through, and if your threads are too thin, then the big bugs will escape."

Ariadne sighed. "Yes, that's true, but did you really hear everything I just said to you, Joshua? Maybe the best way for you to learn is through some practical exercises of your own."

"Here, use these silk threads that I untangled you from, and see if you can figure out a way to get yourself out of here. I'm busy. I've got to get on and repair the part of my web that you so absent-mindedly destroyed. Now, as I'm so kindly letting you have this silk, I'm going to have to make some more." She scurried away, up to the corner of the room, and started creating new silk threads and weaving them into the broken web.

Joshua sat and scratched his head. How could three sticky balls of spider's silk possibly help him get out of Ariadne's lair?

"Oh, I forgot to mention," Ariadne shouted down from the ceiling. "Spider's silk is the strongest natural substance known to man!"

And the stickiest, thought Joshua, as he held one of the balls in his hands.

Joshua picked at the end of thread poking out from the ball of spider's silk. It was so fine, so delicate. He wondered how such a flimsy wisp of nothing could be as strong as Ariadne had claimed. He started to unravel the thread. It stuck to his fingers, and was extremely difficult to manipulate, because it billowed in the air and stuck to anything and everything it touched.

He looked up to the corner of the ceiling, where Ariadne was busy at work repairing her web. She was spinning new fibers and cross-weaving them into the original structure. Focused completely on what she was doing, it seemed she had entered another zone of reality, where all that existed was her and her craft.

Joshua watched as she delicately maneuvered her way across the fine bridges of silk, from one part of her web to another. She was so in tune with her environment, so present. The little cross-wires functioned as stepping stones for Ariadne to navigate her way around the structure she was creating, and yet they were also traps for her unsuspecting prey.

I wonder…, mused Joshua, stroking his chin and scratching his head. Perhaps I can use Ariadne's threads to create a ladder, so that I can climb back out of here?

He looked around the lair. He would need something to hold the silk, so it didn't billow; something that he could use as a frame while he worked with the silk fibers. He walked around the perimeter touching the gnarled old roots, until he came to a couple of them that were side by side in the wall. There were gaps between the roots and the wall, which would allow him to loop the silk around them.

He dipped his hands in the earth, so that the silk would not stick to them. He then took one of the balls and tied the end to one of the roots, then across to the other root. All well and good, but using the roots as the sides of the ladder wouldn't work, as he would not be able to remove them from the wall. Besides, they were not long enough. No, what he needed was another root somewhere else in the lair, so that he could draw out a string to create a rope ladder long enough to climb out.

He laid down the ball of silk, and continued exploring the walls. There were no other roots sticking out like the ones that he had spotted. There was one across the way that he thought might work, if only he could dig out the dirt behind it. So he set to work, using his fingers to claw at loosening the soil.

Eventually he had created another root just like those across the chamber. Now obviously, a ladder has two sides. If he was to draw a string from each of the roots across the chamber over to this one other root, he might be in danger of having the ladder get twisted and stuck together. He looked for a second root that could work equally well to do the job. With some more close examination of the lair, he found what he was searching for, albeit more deeply embedded into the wall. Interestingly enough, Joshua found he was quite enjoying the challenge, and so he set himself to work.

Once he had bored out the second root, Joshua was ready to set up the frame for his unusual rope ladder. He picked up the ball of silk that he had already tied to a root and started unraveling it across the room. The silk was so fine, you could barely see it. It seemed so fragile, even though Ariadne had assured him it was not. He began to doubt himself and what he was doing. There was no way, he thought, that a thread so fine could support his weight.

When he reached the root at the other end, he passed the ball behind the root and decided to double up the thread. He wound the ball around the suspended thread to create a spiral effect. This made the thread thicker, but not thick enough, and Joshua continued doing this repeatedly, until his entire ball of silk was used.

Every once in a while, he tested the strength of the thickening rope with his dirt-powdered hands. It definitely was getting stronger.

Once the first side was completed, he started doing the other side, being careful not to get himself tangled up in the first rope. By now, his wrists were getting sore from all the twisting, and eventually he had to take a break because they were starting to cramp.

He put the silk ball down and sat on the cool floor with his back to the wall. He looked up to see what Ariadne was up to.

Her web was now finished, but she was nowhere to be seen. He guessed that she was also resting. Weaving webs was tiring! He now knew that from first-hand experience, and he didn't even have to make the silk that he was using. Joshua closed his eyes, and went into another of his daydreams about the garden of color and light. Lately it seemed so much further away, and he found he was consciously thinking of it less and less.

Drifting past the poppies and cornflowers and floating by the stream, impressions of another life barely registered in his awareness.

"Pitter pitter pat, slide. Pitter pitter pat, slide."

Joshua yawned and turned on his other side

"Pitter pitter pat, slide. Pitter pitter pat, slide."

Joshua yawned again and rubbed his eyes. Slowly he opened them. In the middle of the floor was another black spider. He knew it wasn't Ariadne, because it was a lot smaller. It was dragging the carcass of what looked like a dead grasshopper along the floor.

"Hello," said Joshua.

The spider dropped his prey from his mouth and asked, "Who are you?"

"My name is Joshua; are you looking for Ariadne?"

"Shhhhh," said the other spider. "I'm not looking for Ariadne. I'm trying to be as quiet as possible, so she won't hear me."

"Well, you're not doing a good job of it so far," said Joshua. "You managed to wake me up."

"Oh dear!" exclaimed the spider, and he came closer to Joshua, so that he could speak a little quieter.

"My name is Araneus. I am bringing a special present for Ariadne. She is so beautiful; she is so lovely. She is the most enchanting of all. Have you seen her?"

"Oh yes." said Joshua. "She has been teaching me her magic."

"Really!" exclaimed Araneus.

"Oh, what I wouldn't do to be enraptured by her stories, beguiled by her wonders, held in the hypnotic gaze of her lovely eyes. She is so captivating; she is so enthralling; she is the most fascinating of all." Araneus rubbed the ends of his two front legs together as he spoke.

"Is that your present for her?" asked Joshua, pointing to the dead grasshopper.

"Yes, a little token, for my little enchantress."

"You might want to be careful there. You know she has had eleven husbands and, well, sorry to break this to you... She ate them; all of them."

"Listen, I know this is difficult to understand, but I can't help myself. I'm just so in love with her. It's the flirtation with danger, and the hope that I can be the one that is different from all the rest. Besides, I have a cunning plan. See that grasshopper over there?"

Joshua nodded.

"If I keep her well fed, if I provide her with all the food she could ever want, then maybe she will stop short of devouring me."

"Hmm. You know, that's not a bad plan at all," agreed Joshua. Why would Ariadne need to eat her husband, if she was completely satisfied from bugs, grubs, and creepy crawlies?

"Come here," said Araneus. "Help me lift this grasshopper and place it into her web. You can lift it off the ground and do it more quietly than I can. In the meantime, I'll scurry away and hide, and I won't call on her until after she's eaten my gift."

"Sure, why not?" Joshua picked up the grasshopper, and placed it in the center of Ariadne's web. Immediately, a long spindly spider's leg emerged from a crack in the ceiling. At lightning speed, Ariadne rushed to the center of the web, where she wound some extra fibers around the grasshopper. It was now suspended in a little bag that she could carry back to her hiding place. She carefully repaired the damaged area in the web, where Joshua had placed it, and then carried its body back to the crack in the corner of the ceiling. She was now free to begin gently nibbling at its flesh, and crunching on its exoskeleton.

Oh well, back to work, thought Joshua, as he picked up his ball of silk and continued winding the second side of his rope ladder.

Once he had completed both sides, he picked up the third ball, and started weaving it across from one side to the other to make the steps. He took the time to reinforce each and every rung, so that they were strong enough to hold his weight. As he wound and twisted, he began to take great pride in his handiwork. Just the simple pleasure of making all the twists an even size, and the sheer joy of creating; how beautiful it looked.

"Pitter pitter pat, slide. Pitter pitter pat, slide."

"Pitter pitter pat, slide. Pitter pitter pat, slide."

Joshua looked up. Araneus was back, this time with a huge copper-colored beetle.

"Joshua, can you help me again? I decided one good meal isn't enough for my beautiful Ariadne. She is a spider of insatiable appetites, and while I want her to have an appetite for me, I don't want her to take that too literally."

"Sure." Joshua stopped what he was doing to help Araneus. He placed the beetle on the web, while Araneus scurried away, and then watched as Ariadne once again rushed down from the ceiling to wrap up and carry off the captive beetle.

This time she looked down at Joshua and exclaimed, "You see how successful my weaving has been? The weaving I do in one moment leads to the manifestation of the most wondrous things, and takes care of my life in the next moment." She tiptoed triumphantly back up to her hiding place in the ceiling, carrying her prey.

Rather than watch Ariadne eating again, Joshua went back to his task. In fact, he became so engrossed, so focused on what he was doing, that he completely forgot why he was making the spider silk ladder. He completely forgot to be worried about the future, how he was going to get out of the lair, and more importantly how he was going to get back to the garden of color and light. He also forgot to admonish himself about how silly he had been to trap himself inside this tree in the first place.

Joshua was so focused on what he was doing, it took him by surprise when he reached the end of the last ball of silk, before he had completed his project. He sat down despondently. All of the worries and fears that had temporarily escaped him while he focused on crafting his ladder had returned.

"Pitter pitter pat, slide. Pitter pitter pat, slide."

"Pitter pitter pat, slide. Pitter pitter pat, slide."

Joshua looked up. Araneus was back, this time with a couple of flies and a wasp.

"Hello Joshua, here I am again, bringing even more sustenance for my darling Ariadne. She will never go hungry as long as I am here to tend to her needs. I will be more use to her alive, than I ever could be dead. She will appreciate me so much when she sees these gifts."

"Araneus," said Joshua. "You do realize that Ariadne doesn't know that it is you leaving these gifts, don't you? She thinks it is she who is capturing all these bugs in her web."

"Oh my, oh my. Then what shall I do? I cannot talk to her until she has eaten all of my gifts. I am afraid that if I speak with her too soon, that she will not be able to control her desire for me, and she will help herself to my delicious flesh too."

Just then, Joshua had a bright idea.

"I will help you, Araneus, in exchange for a favor from you. I will place these three insects into Ariadne's web, and this time I will tell her that it is you who has been bringing them to her."

"Oh, thank you Joshua, thank you from the bottom of my heart, thank you. Now do pray tell, young Sir! How may I pay you back for this most generous favor?" perked Araneus.

"Well, as you see I have been crafting my escape from this place, by making a ladder out of spider silk. But I have used up all the silk that Ariadne gave me, before I was able to complete the ladder. I was wondering whether you could help me complete the project by weaving the rest of the rungs."

"Why, certainly I will help you to do that, Joshua."

Araneus climbed up onto the ladder, and started weaving the next rung.

Joshua picked up the two flies, and wandered back over to Ariadne's web. He placed them onto the sticky threads, and gave the web a gentle shake.

Ariadne appeared from the crack in the ceiling, moving a bit more slowly this time.

"Oh my, oh my, there's more food! I don't know that I can eat another morsel. I am so full after my last meal I think I will explode. This new web of mine is proving to be too successful."

"Actually, Ariadne, the food is being brought for you by another spider. Do you see that spider down there on my rope ladder? That is Araneus, and he likes you so much. He wants you to be really happy, and so he has been bringing you lots of treats. See the wasp on the floor? He brought that along with the flies, the beetle, and the grasshopper."

Ariadne peered down at the ladder, where Araneus was busy at work in a flurry of legs and spider's silk.

"Really, he likes me so much, and he wants me to be happy, so he has brought me all these treats?" Ariadne lifted up her two front legs and started preening at her spiky hairs.

Joshua nodded.

"Well, that's wonderful. I must meet this Araneus. Won't you introduce us, Joshua?"

"It will be my very great pleasure," said Joshua, as he wandered over to Araneus, who was just finishing off the last rung of the spider's silk ladder.

"Araneus, Ariadne would like to be introduced to you."

"She would? Oh, she would! Oh, my goodness me! Oh my, oh my, how do I look?"

"You look fabulous," replied Joshua, who wasn't really sure what looking fabulous was to a female spider, but he didn't want to make Araneus any more nervous than he already was. "By the way, thank you so much for finishing my ladder. It looks fabulous too."

"You are welcome, my dear fellow, I cannot possibly thank you enough."

"Great, well, come on over and I will introduce you to Ariadne."

They walked over to where Ariadne was demurely hanging by a thread of silk from the ceiling.

"Ariadne, please allow me to introduce you to the very generous and spidery Araneus. Araneus, may I present the delightfully lovely and spidery Ariadne."

"Pleased I'm sure," said Ariadne.

"Delighted to make your acquaintance," said Araneus.

"Grasshoppers and copper-colored beetles are my favorites. However did you know?"

"Well, I decided that one as beautiful and tasteful as you would surely have an exceedingly cultured palette."

"Oh, how lovely, thank you. Would you like a tour of my lair? It's in the upper back corner of the room, as I find that gives me the best vantage point."

Ariadne led Araneus by four of his legs up the silken spindle to the crack in the corner of the ceiling. They seemed to be getting on like a house on fire, and so Joshua, his matchmaker's job complete, turned his attention back to the ladder.

It seemed very strong, as he could lean his full weight on it, and it supported him without him falling over. When he let go, it sprung back into shape. Plus, if he doused himself in the powdery dirt, he found he didn't stick to it too much. So far so good, but how would he now be able to take the ends, and connect them up to the ladder in the hole in the ceiling? He was worried that if he tried to throw it, and hook it over the bottom of the ladder in the ceiling, that it would get all tangled up again. Then he would have to start from the beginning.

"Ariadne and Araneus!" shouted Joshua, "could you please come here for a moment."

The two new lovers peered bashfully from the ceiling. "Why darling, it's our dear friend Joshua calling," cooed Ariadne. Whatever can he want now?"

"I need your help, Ariadne, and yours Araneus! I need you to take the ends of my ladder, lift it to the ceiling, and then connect it to the bottom rung of the ladder in the hole in the ceiling."

"My, oh my, you have been busy," said Ariadne, as she swung down from the ceiling on a gossamer thread. "Well done, Joshua. What did you learn while you were making your ladder?"

"I learned that when I became absorbed in my task, I forgot about everything else. It was such a pleasure to be creating something with my bare hands."

"Yes, Joshua, you learned how to be present. You have learnt that the present moment is where your creativity lies. You noticed that you had no worries when you were in the now moment; the past and the future drifted away to nothing, which is what they truly are, absolutely nothing. They do not exist. They are just thoughts in your mind. If you can be in the present moment, then you can be truly creative. Look at what you have achieved! You have created a way for yourself to get out of this predicament."

Then she looked over at Araneus. "Darling, you take that side, and I will take the other side. Let us connect the ladder to the ceiling, so our friend can be on his way."

"Certainly, my sweet, and well done, Joshua."

The two spiders gently detached the ends of the ladder from the root, and floated up to the ceiling on their silken threads. Then they carefully secured the ends to the bottom rung of the ladder in the hole in the ceiling.

"Joshua this is ready, and hopefully it will hold your weight, so come on now and away with you. We will be removing it once you leave, as everyone who enters here must learn this task in their own way," said Ariadne.

Joshua cautiously put a first foot onto the ladder and grasped hold of the side. Then he placed a second foot and hand on the other side. The ladder swayed like a swing, and he had to steady himself and wait for it to calm down. However, he found that he could climb one step at a time, and it did indeed support his weight.

When he was level with the spiders at the entrance to the hole, Ariadne spoke to him. "You know Joshua, this is how to treat your life. Go one step at a time, with no fear of the future, without looking back and being concerned about what might have been. Just be exactly where you are in the moment, and you can't go wrong. After all, it is the only place you can be anyway. Otherwise, you will be in denial of the truth, of what is really happening. Do you see?"

Joshua said he did see, and he looked over at Araneus and grinned, "I get it, live for the now moment, and don't fear what might happen in the future because that is just a thought you have. It isn't real."

Araneus looked nervously between Joshua and Ariadne. Ariadne must have picked up on this, because she said, "Darling, the joy of life is in the now. Oh, how lucky we are to know that, because poof... it can all be over in the blink of an eye."

Araneus shuffled and moved a little further away from his new partner. "Once we wave goodbye to Joshua, how about we go back into the lair and share a nice tasty wasp? Then you can have a well-earned rest, and I'll go and see what I can find for supper?"

"Oh, Araneus, for a spider you know very little, don't you? We weave our web of destiny, and then we wait for what we have created to come to us. We can both have a nap, and when we wake up, we will see what new delights have been caught in the web.

With that, both spiders floated across to the crack in the ceiling, Araneus a lot more timidly than Ariadne. Meanwhile, Joshua made his way back up the vertical tunnel through which he had arrived.

Chapter 7

Center of the Tree

As Joshua climbed up the ladder, he noticed two things. To his relief, the pain in his knee had definitely disappeared, and there seemed to be a faint golden glow coming from the walls of the root through which he travelled. As soon as the gradient became less steep, and he was able to walk upright on the ground, he bent down to brush the dirt from his clothes. To his great surprise, that same faint golden glow was coming from his legs.

Joshua leaned against the wall and closed his eyes. He tuned into his grounding and then to the earth energy running up his legs. He imagined that the flow was getting stronger and stronger, until he could tangibly feel the energy. When he opened his eyes, he was amazed that the glow all around him had intensified. When he looked down at his legs, they too were now much more than a faint glow; they were definitely shining.

With a big broad grin on his face and a skip in his step, Joshua continued on his way. The funny thing was, that although this should be the same exact route that he entered by, he did not recognize it at all. He started to become extremely doubtful. The further he walked, the more uncertain he became. His fears were validated when he came to a fork in the path. Surely, there was no such fork on his way down this root?

Joshua scratched his head. Perplexed, he first went up the left tunnel, and turned around to look back down. The angle of the root was misleading, and unless you were very present, you could easily miss the other route. It was hard to see because it was almost parallel to this one.

That explained how he missed it, but more importantly, which one was the correct one to take back? He had no idea, and so he set off up the channel on the right hand side. Soon he was facing another fork on the path. Oh, this was too confusing! He must have chosen the wrong branch. When he turned around to consider retracing his steps, he was surprised to see that there was another fork behind him.

So the only choice, it seemed, was to keep going upwards. Regardless of which path he chose, he should at some point make it back to the Grand Chamber. As he walked on, he became aware of a soft pecking sound, far off in the distance. He surmised that this was the Devas hard at work. If he followed the sound, he would at least encounter someone who could guide him in the right direction. So from then on, he allowed the pecking sound to guide his decision whenever he came to a fork in his path.

As Joshua followed the sound upwards through the maze of roots, it became louder and louder. Each time he had a choice to make, he tuned in to the sound and stepped a little way into each path. He chose the route where the noise was the loudest. Eventually though, he found that he had entered a root that was becoming narrower and narrower. This was definitely where the noise was coming from, but he had to walk sideways to keep on shuffling along.

Soon the tunnel was so narrow that the walls were touching his chest and his back, and he was walking with his head to the side to see where he was going. In due course, he came upon a low and narrow gate within the passage. He was not able to see, once he had passed through this narrow gate, whether more space was about to open up for him.

The trouble was that the handle to open the gate was just out of his reach. He needed to bend sideways in order to reach down and grasp the handle. After a few tries, Joshua eventually unclipped the fastener, and the gate swung open. He pushed himself through, gasping from exertion.

Once he caught his breath, he peered around this new environment. He appeared to be standing inside a very small chamber. It had polished wooden walls, and a smooth wooden saddle-shaped seat, which was hewn from the back wall. There was barely enough room to walk around the three open sides of this seat, and you could touch the seat with one hand and the smooth wall with the other. Joshua started to cough, as the air in the room had become full of fine particles of dust, which he had stirred up as he moved around.

Joshua collapsed into the seat, as he was exhausted from his exertions to fit through the narrow tunnel and gate. He wanted to be still a while, and let the dust settle. As he sat gathering his senses, he became aware that the sound vibration that he had been tuning into was now very loud. In fact, it was right in front of his forehead. He started to get a headache.

The front wall of this small chamber was very close to him, and the sound was actually quite irritating. As he rested his vision on the wall in front, he noticed a spiral-shaped knot in the wood, right in front of his forehead in the exact place where the sound appeared to be coming from. As he watched, a thin slither of light appeared in the center of the knot, creating a beam of light that was playing with the dancing dust particles.

As he sat in wonderment, this crack of light became larger and larger. A thin, black, pointy object was pushing backwards and forwards through the knot. As the space got bigger, Joshua could see that this was attached to something that was covered in red, white, and black fluff.

Gradually an opening appeared that was large enough for Joshua to begin to see through more clearly. He could tell that the thing on the other side was a bird of some sort, and given that it was pecking away at the tree, he surmised it must be a woodpecker.

When a thin pointy tongue started darting in and out, he felt he must speak up.

"Mr. Woodpecker? I'm sorry to tell you this, but there aren't any bugs in here just now. Only me, I'm afraid, and I'm too big and not so tasty."

A round eye appeared at the center of the hole. Then the beak once again, with a thin black tongue darting in and out.

"Mr. Woodpecker? Please stop. This isn't helping you, and it surely isn't helping me," said Joshua.

The other round eye peeped into the hole this time, followed once again by the beak and tongue.

Joshua sighed and lowered his eyes. Now there was increased light in the chamber, he could see that there was a pile of sawdust on the floor. In the sawdust were a few small round juicy-looking grubs. He leaned down and picked them up in the palm of his hand.

"If you can't beat them join them," he muttered as he picked up a grub between two fingers, and fed it to the woodpecker. He kept this going, until all the grubs were gone and he could find no more. Then he grabbed the end of the woodpecker's beak between two fingers, and gently but firmly pushed. As he did so, he noticed that the knot itself was loose. He gave an even firmer push, and to his great delight, the entire thing gave way, leaving a thick twisty-walled hole, with even more light pouring in.

"I knew you'd find 'em."

"What?"

"I knew you'd find 'em, the Midas grubs, very tasty they are, but hard to get hold of."

By now, Joshua was familiar with speaking creatures, and was not surprised at all to find himself in a conversation with a bird. He looked through the hole in the trunk, and could see the woodpecker leaning back from the hole, peering back at him.

He had thought that the woodpecker was quite stupid, but now he learned that it was actually clever. It had somehow known that Joshua was on the other side, and would pass the bugs through to him.

"How did you know I was here?"

"Because I can see you!"

"Wait a minute, the hole wasn't always big enough to see through, and when you first started pecking I wasn't here. I was somewhere else. So how did you know someone would be here, and that they would pass you the bugs?"

"Because I can see you!"

"No, yes, but see I only just got here, I wasn't here when you started. How did you know?"

"Midas to Morfar, how many times? Because I can see you!"

"Huh?"

"Look, I'm a woodpecker, right? Mr. Nicholaas Adrianus Cornelius Woodpecker to be precise."

"Right, and I am Joshua."

"Yes, pleased to meet you Joshua. Anyway as I was saying, as a woodpecker I have access to certain powers, so to speak."

"Yes?"

"One of those powers is the gift of clear seeing."

"Oh you mean like the spider, Ariadne, and how she could see inside me to see my energy?"

"Sort of like Ariadne, although she lives inside the Midas Tree and has the power to be and see in the moment; whereas, I live in the hinterland between the Midas Tree and the garden of color and light. You see, I travel in the space between the tree and the garden. As such, I have the power to see the past and the future, and the truth of all things in an instant."

"So you knew that I was coming here, and that I would pass the bugs to you?"

"Yes, I knew you would be here, in the center of the Midas Tree. Here in the hinterland, I can try out and see into all the possibilities. I knew that this was the most likely future, and so I came here and waited for you to appear."

"Woahhh!"

"Precisely."

Joshua's mind was reeling. If he could learn to see into the future, he could find out how he could get out of the Midas Tree. He could find out the solution to all the lessons that would come to him.

"Can you teach me how to do that too?"

"Steady on there, you need to learn to walk before you run. Remember, inside the Midas Tree, you create your reality from the present moment. It's just here in the hinterland that the rules are somewhat different. It's a place where we can experiment with new ideas."

"Anyway, the first thing you need to learn is another power that we woodpeckers possess, and that is the power of rhythm.

You need to learn to walk your path with a steady pace, and not go too fast. If you do, you will jump ahead of yourself. Take what you learned from Ariadne, be humble and be glad to be exactly where you are at present, and then move forwards with a rhythm that you can keep up with. If you do that, then all you need is what we woodpeckers call the power of discrimination. To be able to see what is true in any given moment."

Before Joshua could answer, the woodpecker was gone.

Joshua stayed sitting on the smooth wooden saddle, in the hollow chamber in the center of the tree. He took a nice deep breath, and grounded himself, and he ran his earth energy. Once he felt calmer, he peered out through the hole in the trunk. To his amazement, a broad view of the hinterland appeared through this new window.

So this was the space that was between him, and the garden of color and light. He could see fields, trees and flowers with such a degree of clarity it bedazzled him. He could see patterns in the yellow grain fields as the wind blew on the grasses. The clear blue sky had puffy white clouds that shifted into shapes as they passed by. He saw a woodpecker, a spider, a tree, a fish, and any number of other things he cared to imagine. He discovered that he could make the clouds look like whatever he wanted in an instant.

As he looked out through the knot to the bright and beautiful world outside, Joshua's heart opened. He thought about Morfar, and all the love they had between them. In the garden, there were no worries, no lessons or hardships, only beauty, love and light. Knowing that the garden was so close was a great comfort to Joshua, and he didn't want to leave this place. He wanted to sit here forever. He was so grateful to the woodpecker for coming into his life, and revealing this window to home.

As if on cue the woodpecker returned, and spoke once more to Joshua.

"Joshua, there is a way that you can stay in this place forever; a way that you can always carry these feelings with you. Whenever you are worried or concerned, or your life seems too hard, you can come back to the center. All you need to do is quiet your mind, and sit right here where you are now. You will be able to reach a state of stillness and balance, where you will see everything clearly, and not be bowled over by emotions or confusion. You will be able to communicate with the ones who are living in the hinterland, and even with Morfar in the garden of color and light. I will guide you, and help provide insights and answers to your questions."

"Can we not make this hole bigger? Can I not come through now, and travel across the hinterland with you? I want to once again be with Morfar, in the garden of color and light."

"Joshua, your work there in the Midas Tree is not yet done, although you are doing very well. My young friend, you are right on track, exactly where you are meant to be."

"But how can I stay in this place? I need to eat, I need to sleep, I need to find my way back to the root chamber, see the Devas and learn some more lessons."

"Let me teach you some more woodpecker magic. Whenever you feel confused, whenever you doubt yourself, and whenever you cannot see the woods for the trees and need some clarity, this is what you can do."

"Simply take the index finger of each hand. Place one finger in the center of your forehead, and another at the side of your head, just above your ear. Imagine that there is a line of light coming from each of these two fingertips. Then focus your attention at the point where the two lines cross. This will seat you in the center of your head, and that will instantly bring you back to a place where you can see clearly."

Joshua did as he was instructed, and placed his fingers, one in between his eyes in the center of his forehead, and another at the side of his head, above his ear. He visualized two golden beams of light coming from these fingers. He could see them intersecting in the center of his skull, and as he placed his consciousness here, he became aware of a bright spark of light.

"Mr. Woodpecker, I can see a light in my head."

"Quite so, Joshua and that light is you; the bright spark that came to the Midas Tree from Morfar! You are placing your awareness into a special location in your physical body, called your pineal gland. Its job is to reflect the light of truth. When you sit here, you can see the truth, for everything you need to know about."

Joshua did what the woodpecker suggested. He closed his eyes and placed his consciousness in the center of his head, and immediately he felt calm, and could see the bright spark of light. He wondered what the quickest way to get back to the root chamber was, and immediately he could see that the saddle seat was also a door, that opened into the Grand Chamber of the tree.

When he once more opened his eyes, Nicholaas Adrianus Cornelius Woodpecker was gone. He stood up and pulled on the back of the chair and sure enough, just as he had seen in his mind's eye, a door swung open. He walked straight into dinnertime, where a subtle golden glow was just starting to radiate from the walls.

Chapter 8

Messages in the Bark

After dinner, Devon pranced over to Joshua and beamed.

"You are glowing, with hidden knowing. Your head is alight, you are looking so bright. You are so bold, your head is gold. The time is now, to tell you how, to read the bark and make the marks."

"I don't know, Devon. I'm quite tired. I'm not sure I can concentrate."

"Do not fear, for every seer, must be relaxed and not hard taxed; the messages will come to you, when your brain is unglued."

"It's definitely that," laughed Joshua. "Okay, sure, teach me what you know."

Devon led Joshua over to the wall opposite his bedchamber, opened a curtain, and beckoned him inside.

"Welcome to my chambers, where I only invite my closest friends and definitely no strangers. Take a seat, because you look beat. Relax your brain, while I explain, from my abode, the secret code, the symbols and the runes of old."

Joshua sank into an extremely comfortable large armchair, and said with a chuckle, "Wonderful, please go on, my dear Devon."

Devon wandered over to his bookshelf and sorted through a few very old looking scrolls and piles of bark. When he returned, Joshua had fallen asleep, and so he laid them on the table at his side, and wandered into his own bedchamber yawning.

When Joshua stirred, it was to the sound of a pen scratching on parchment. He looked across the room to see Devon sitting behind his desk, busily scribbling away. He looked so intently focused that rather than disturb him, he reached down to the table at his side and picked up a piece of bark.

Looking down at the symbols, he felt a sense of curiosity coupled with anxiety. He remembered to relax and to ground, and then he pored over the bark. Hmm, it still didn't make much sense. He looked back at Devon, and then once again at the bark.

That was curious. The symbols looked different this time. He looked back over at Devon as if to question him, and then decided against it. When he looked back down at the symbols, once again they had shifted. Now he was totally flummoxed.

Then he remembered what Mr. Woodpecker had said. "Place one finger in the center of your forehead, and another at the side of your head, just above your ear. Imagine that there is a line of light coming from each of these two fingertips. Then focus your attention at the point." He placed his consciousness in the center of his head, and immediately saw a spark of light appear. He started to feel calmer, more neutral.

When he opened his eyes, he nearly jumped out of his skin. Here he was, once again sitting on the saddle seat in the center of the Midas Tree. He looked out through the hole into the hinterland. It was beautiful, the sun was shining, and the wind was whispering through the trees. If he held his nose close to the hole, he could faintly smell the fresh scent of flowers.

He peeked through again. Mr. Nicholaas Adrianus Cornelius Woodpecker was nowhere to be seen. He placed his mouth close to the open knot and shouted. "Hello, Mr. Woodpecker. Hello, are you there? You said I could come back here when I needed guidance, and so I'm back. Helloooo!"

He removed his mouth and replaced it with his eye. Far off in the distance, he thought he could see Mr. Woodpecker perched on the trunk of another tree. He removed his eye and replaced it with his ear. Yes, there was an almost imperceptible pecking rhythm, way off in the distance.

"You won't get him to come over until he's finished with the bugs in that hole." said a familiar voice.

"Araneus?" asked Joshua.

"Hello, my dear boy."

"Where are you?" said Joshua, looking all around inside the little chamber.

"I'm out here in the hinterland." A translucent, almost invisible version of Araneus appeared, floating just outside the hole on a wispy gossamer thread.

"What are you doing out there, Araneus, and why are you looking so ethereal?"

"She ate me!!!"

"What?"

"Ariadne, she ate me. She couldn't contain herself. She persuaded me to stay in her lair with her. Even though my instincts were telling me to go out hunting, and bring back more food while she slept. She persuaded me to take a nap with her, and when we woke up she was feeling a bit peckish, and well here I am - disembodied, floating around in the hinterland."

"Oh Araneus, I'm so sorry."

"Oh, it's not so bad really. It's lovely here. I can travel between the Midas Tree and the garden of color and light, and I can visit Ariadne any time I want to. Although the trouble with that is all the other eleven Mr. Arachne's are usually there too. Anyway, what's up with you, my dear Joshua? Why are you sitting here in the center of the tree, calling out to us here in the hinterland?"

"Mr. Woodpecker said that I could come here any time I was confused, to get my clarity back. He said that this was a place where I can communicate with the creatures in the hinterland and receive guidance from them."

"Oh really, is that right? What is it that you are having trouble with now?"

"Devon wants to teach me how to read the ancient runic scripts, so that I can better find my way around the inside of the tree. The trouble is, they are so very confusing. I thought it was bad the first time I tried, but now every time I look at a piece of bark, the symbols shift. I can't even get a stable picture of what is on there."

"Hmmm," pondered Araneus, "you know, this might be your lucky day, Joshua. We spiders are gifted with many talents, not least the gift to inspire creativity. Did you know that we are keepers of the ancient alphabets? No one can sit and meditate on a spider's web, without seeing the relationship between the patterns in the threads and writing."

"Do you know the runic script that the Devas use inside the Midas Tree?" asked Joshua.

"Weeelllll……"

"Well, do you?"

"Let's just say I do, but it's not an ordinary language. I cannot teach it to you, like I could teach you your A, B and C's. Each person must learn to read its meaning for themselves, by themselves. Its meaning is unique to the person who is reading it. What is more, there is not just one meaning, but many meanings. They depend on your perspective, your timing, and what you want to find out."

"Huh?"

"Yes, I knew that would throw you for a loop."

"But they use it in signs that label directions. How, then, can the meaning change for each person?"

"It's like this. We each have a unique path to experience, and the direction we choose to take is entirely up to us. We have access to a lot of information that can help us make our choices. The symbols act as a doorway, to help us access this information."

"Huh?"

"Let me try an example. Let's take the written word 'apple'. It's a perfectly good one-dimensional symbol. Now what if we take a picture of an apple instead?"

"Huh?"

"If I show you the picture of a juicy green apple, the meaning it might hold, for you, is something different than that of a rotten apple. An apple with a bite taken from it, or one with a maggot poking out of it, or an apple being held by a witch all evoke different meanings. Do you see?

"I'm starting to. I think" With each description of an apple, Joshua could see an image of what it might look like with his mind's eye.

"I always find, with these things, that it's much better not to think, my dear boy. Just visualize the differences. Now what about the apple being held by a witch? What masked meaning does that make apparent for you?"

"It says beware; don't eat this apple because it might be poisoned."

"Yes, exactly. Well done! And the apple with a bite out of it?"

"It depends. If it's a first bite of the apple, it may indicate an opportunity just starting. A bite right down to the core might mean it's all finished, or the core of the matter has been exposed."

"Now you're getting the hang of it, Joshua. Well done."

"Yes, but how does that relate to the runic script?"

"The runes are symbols that have meaning. They represent things, and they point to ideas. They are not just letters that evoke a sound that can be used to form words. Each rune, or combination of runes, evokes a kind of picture. Look at my body, and tell me what you see."

"Your body is shaped like the number eight."

"Yes, and it's also the symbol of infinity. So the symbol of a spider is linked with the number eight and infinity, which is everlasting life. So if you see a symbol that looks like a number 8 you might also think of a spider, or an octopus, or eternity."

"Okay, I start to get it now."

"Good, because we've already talked about it too much. The best way to learn this is to meditate and to practice it."

Just then Mr. Woodpecker appeared, with a piece of bark in his mouth. He held the bark just where Joshua could see. Written on the bark were more shifting symbols.

Joshua groaned, but he was also determined to give it a chance, and so he focused on being grounded and centered. He looked out through the hole in the chamber and relaxed, determined to just let his imagination flow.

The first symbol was two wavy lines, and it reminded him of water. The second symbol was a triangle, and it reminded him of a boat. The third symbol was... who knew what it was?

"A journey to the water" said Joshua.

"Yes, well done, this is a sign that points down to the root system."

"But what does the third symbol mean?"

"It means whatever it means to you," mumbled Mr. Woodpecker from behind his piece of bark.

It looked like a circle with a dot in the middle, on top of a stick. It reminded him of being in his center and being grounded.

"Remember to be grounded and centered along the way."

"Hey, hey, hey!" Araneus and Mr. Woodpecker cheered together.

"Now here, let me get another one." Mr. Woodpecker dropped the piece of bark he was holding and flew off a little way. He swiftly returned with another piece of bark.

"Now try this one on for size," quipped Araneus.

This time there were more symbols, and they were arranged in four horizontal lines, or four vertical lines, depending on how you looked at it. Rather like a short poem, thought Joshua. Or even like one of those puzzles where the words can appear in any direction.

"Where do I start?" he asked. "Should I read it from left to right, right to left, or up and down?"

"What do you think, my young friend? What are you drawn to do? Let your intuition guide you."

"Well," said Joshua, "I intuitively want to read these symbols in columns from the top to the bottom, starting from the one on the left hand side."

"Then that is what you should do," said Mr. Woodpecker.

"Great, so I got it right," chuckled Joshua proudly.

"Hold on a minute," interjected Araneus, "didn't you listen to Mr. Woodpecker at all? It's whatever you are drawn to do *in the moment*. This time it's this way, but next time it might be another way. Even the next time you see this same sign, it might be another way."

"Gosh, alright then," said Joshua scratching his head, but keen to give it a go. "Let's see... well I think this symbol at the top..."

"Don't think now, Joshua" said Woodpecker.

"No, don't think at all," emphasized Araneus.

"OK, well, oh, I imagine."

"Don't even imagine." said Mr. Woodpecker, "Simply SEE it and KNOW it."

"I know this symbol at the top means..." Joshua said the words, but he didn't feel he knew anything.

"Come on Joshua, you must believe in yourself and your abilities. You must believe that you know, because you do know," encouraged Mr. Woodpecker, this time in a much gentler voice.

"Oh yes, you do know," said Araneus, "and if I may offer one more piece of advice?" He looked at Joshua for permission to continue, and when Joshua nodded, he explained, "Even though you need to pull the pieces apart to pull out the meaning, also look at the entire script as though it were a pictograph, a picture within a picture. Aim to get a feel for the entire picture."

"Yes, and place your consciousness in the center of your head when you want to SEE, and at the top of your head, when you want to KNOW."

Joshua's head was buzzing. Nevertheless, he did what his friends had suggested. From the center of his head, he looked at the configuration of symbols. As he looked, he could swear they were moving around, changing shapes, and swapping places with each other. Woodpecker and Araneus were looking on expectantly. Joshua didn't want to let them down. They were being so patient with him, and so kind to take the time to help him like this, but he really was struggling.

He felt the wooden saddle in the center of the tree under his body, and he grasped the edges of this wooden seat. He took a deep breath in, and another one out. He checked his grounding cord, which had become weaker due to his anxiety. He took another deep breath and increased its flow, and he sat in the center of the tree. From the center of his head, he dropped his anxiety down his grounding cord. With another deep breath, he relaxed and engaged his eyes once more with the piece of bark in front of him. Then he moved his consciousness up to the top of his head.

He became aware that each line was a different possibility; each was a different direction he could take, an alternate path that he could choose. The lines were shifting as the possibilities were shifting. The line that he was most drawn to appeared to be the most likely choice and the most probable outcome at this time. Joshua started to read, "Travel up this path to reach the honey bees."

Mr. Woodpecker and Araneus were both in stitches of laughter.

"It looks like your next lesson is going to involve Devora."

"Who is Devora?" asked Joshua. Although he knew she must be another Deva because, as he had come to learn, all of the Devas had names that started with Dev.

"Devora is the Deva of the honey bees," said Mr. Woodpecker. "She is the sweetest little thing, always singing sweet, sweet songs."

"And she has the sharpest wit, and a sting in her tongue," laughed Araneus. "Be careful when you spend time with Devora, Joshua. She sees and knows much, but she never tells. However, there are times when she sees something dark, and the words of her song turn from sweet to sour."

"Oh my," said Joshua, as he took his leave through the door behind the seat and walked straight back into the Grand Chamber. All was quiet, and most of the creatures of the tree were not yet arisen to sing their morning praises.

Joshua walked across the room until he reached the entrance to Devon's chambers. He could hear the bard snoring loudly. He tiptoed back to the armchair that he had left earlier, and sat back down. He tried to go back to sleep, but it was no longer very comfortable. He wandered back to his own room to catch some more rest, before he had to face the challenges of another day in the Midas Tree.

Chapter 9

The Queen Bee

Next morning, Joshua quickly arose and took his place at the center of the chamber. He sat and meditated while the Devas sang their praises to the Midas Tree.

"Oh great tree with roots a'golding, in our arms with love enfolding."

"Tree of wisdom, tree of light, every day we fight the fight."

"Battle on against the darkness, every day it's getting less."

"Standing tall like a candle, then we know that we can handle."

"Every challenge, every day, even when it's hard to play."

"When we know that you are near, helps us all our course to steer."

Joshua listened to the words intently. They sounded a bit more subdued than usual. A bit less celebratory, which was odd, because hadn't he just brightened the roots with his lesson in the spiders lair? Hadn't he just helped add some light to the heart of the tree with his lesson in the center? He was pretty sure he had added a glow to the leaf tips with his knowingness.

Once the Devas had finished singing, he looked for Devon, because he wanted to apologize for disappearing from his chambers last night without a word. He also wanted to share his delight at his newfound knowledge in deciphering the symbols in the bark.

He finally spotted him deep in conversation with Devalicious, and so he casually wandered over, being careful not to be too intrusive, though he couldn't help hearing part of the conversation.

Devalicious was saying "...poor sweet thing, I don't know what she's going to do without those bees. Every day they leave the hive to collect pollen for honey, and every day a few more of them don't come back. Devora is at her wits end. She needs to keep the bee population up, so that the flowers in the tree will get pollinated."

Devon responded with a suggestion. "If every day some go away, Devora's task is to make new bees fast."

"Yes, well I know she's a queen, but honestly, it's been some time since she made any bee babies," intimated Devalicious, as she ran her hands over her delicious curves. Devon and Devalicious burst out laughing.

Joshua walked up smiling, though as soon as Devon and Devalicious saw him they straightened themselves up and took on more of a serious look.

"Morning, Little Man," said Devalicious, running a finger under Joshua's chin.

"Hello Devalicious," said Joshua, "and Devon," he said,

looking into Devon's face to see if he could gauge his reaction to his swift departure last night.

"Good morning my dear, your mind seems so clear, I trust that our session gave you such a good lesson, that now you'll be knowing where you are going." He laughed.

"Err yes," said Joshua. "But that's just it. I wasn't there because I was elsewhere. I was in the center with my mentors..." He paused as he realized that he too was now speaking in rhymes. "Mr. Woodpecker and Araneus," he added.

"You were there in the chair, all night in my sight, in a very deep sleep," said Devon.

"But, huh, how, what, huh?" said Joshua.

"You solved the puzzle, away from the muddle in your head. You consulted your guides, behind closed eyes, while you were abed. In fact you were so bold; the leaf tips have turned to gold."

"Huh?"

"What Devon is telling you, Little Man, is you solved the riddle of the symbols while you were asleep. You went to visit your guides from the hinterland in your dreams, and they helped you read the symbols. It was a way that you could get out of your intellect for a while," offered Devalicious.

"Oh, I see," said Joshua.

"Yes, you were under very deep, and you were learning in your sleep," explained Devon.

Did you find out anything of interest while you were dreaming?" asked Devalicious.

"Yes I did. My next lesson is to be with Devora," announced Joshua.

Devon and Devalicious looked a bit stunned at this news, but they quickly shook themselves out of it. Devalicious said, "Then what we are waiting for, Sugar? That's where I'm spending my day as well. Now walk this way, Sugar," and she sauntered off, hips swinging widely from side to side, tottering on her heels.

Joshua imagined trying to walk the way Devalicious walked, but he preferred his comfortable woven sandals, and he wasn't sure his hips could swing that wide. He followed Devalicious to one of the entries, where the ground sloped upwards. For the first time he was going to climb up into the branches of the tree.

"Hold on a minute," he called to Devalicious, who was striding on ahead. "I want to read the sign."

"OK, Sugar!" Devalicious paused a little way up the passage.

This time there were five symbols on the sign, arranged in a kind of circle, or even a star. He was drawn to focus on the uppermost symbol, which looked to him like a bee.

The symbol next to it was a leaf. "Bee Leaf," muttered Joshua out loud.

The next three symbols were not so apparent. One was a diagonal arrow, another was a circle, and the third was a triangle on top of a square. All three symbols had a vertical line running through them on the left hand side.

Joshua scratched his head, puzzled. One thing they all had in common was these lines crossing through them, as if to indicate an error of some sort. He really didn't have much more of a clue than that, which was disappointing, because he had expected that he would easily decipher all of the signs in the bark from now on.

"Come on, Sugar. I'm sure it will all become clear in no time."

Joshua ran up to Devalicious, and they continued weaving up the branches in the tree to find Devora. Joshua noticed that there was a different quality to the walls on the path upwards through the branches, compared to the walls of the roots. At first, the walls were quite thick, but as they went further they got thinner, and the atmosphere felt lighter and more airy.

Devalicious noticed Joshua running his hands over the structures in the walls. "Soon you'll spend time with Devandra, no doubt, and he will be able to explain all about the processes that take place in the leaves and branches of the Midas Tree. Right now though, we must hurry to get to see Devora."

She quickened her pace, and Joshua skipped a few steps to catch up with her. "Why are we in such a hurry to get to Devora? Is it because the bees are not coming back?"

"Why Sugar Man, were you eavesdropping on Devon and I this morning?" she frowned.

"Not on purpose. I tried not to pry, but I just couldn't help overhearing your conversation," said Joshua.

"Hmm, well, it is true that every day some of the bees leave the tree to collect pollen from flowers in the hinterland, and then they return and pollinate the blossoms on the Midas Tree. They also take pollen from the Midas Tree, and use it to pollinate the other flowers they visit."

"The Midas Tree is very special. You may have noticed that it bears many types of blossoms, and so many types of fruit. It depends on the endless creativity of the bees. They search out new forms, and make new combinations so that the infinite possibilities of creation can be explored. Devora's job is to take care of the bees. She's kind of a devic beekeeper. She's also a prophetess, and a magical queen bee."

The cogs of Joshua's brain were turning, "If she is a prophetess, why couldn't she see this coming and plan for it? If she is a prophetess, can't she see how it will all turn out? If she is at her wits end, like you said, it must be bad?"

"Devora never shares her visions. She never tells us the future, because she knows that we create what will happen in the future from the now. She wants to empower us all, including the bees, to create our reality in the moment. Our only clue is to listen to her songs. She is always singing sweet songs, but sometimes if she is at a loss about the choices people are making, those songs turn sour."

Joshua could hear a buzzing noise in the far off distance, and he gathered that this must be coming from the bees. The passage inside the branches was becoming steeper now, and he had to focus on his breathing and be careful not to lose his step.

Eventually they came upon a series of structures in the wall that looked like catacombs. Some of them contained little white bullet-shaped objects.

"Well good," said Devalicious, "Devora has gotten to work and started to make new bee babies, and that's important to replenish the ones that have disappeared."

Joshua looked more closely, and could see the shapes of big huge eyes and spindly legs in some of the pupa. He thought they looked strange, like beings from another world outside of the Midas Tree.

"Now let's not dilly-dally, Sugar. We are almost there." Devalicious hurried him along, but the buzzing was now so loud Joshua could hardly hear her speak.

"There she is now! Yoo-hoo. Devora! Devooraaa!"

Off in the distance was either a very small female Deva, or a very large female bee, with a very long and pointy nose. She was wearing tight black pants, and a fluffy yellow and black striped sweater. She carried a worker's belt around her waist, with two pouches at the side of each hip, full of what appeared to be pollen. Her dark hair was tied up in a bun on the very top of her head. She had finished off the coiffure with a few sticks of white cherry blossoms to hold it all together.

"Devaliciouzzz, what on earth are you doing here? Come to help, I hope? And who izzz thizzz you have brought with you?"

"My name is Joshua, and I am very pleased to meet you," interjected Joshua, extending his hand towards her.

"Pleazzzed to meet you too I'm sure. Now let's get you to work immediately." Devora was unhooking her work belt as she spoke, and was fastening it around Joshua's waist.

"Now go and stand over there, and collect the pollen from the bees as they come in, and place it in these pouches." She ushered a slightly stunned Joshua over to an open knot in the wood. Bees were lined up outside, and as Joshua stood next to the opening, they started coming in one by one, bending over so that Joshua could see behind their knees. He looked down at the first bee in line, not quite sure what to do."

"Oh mercy me," cried Devora. "You have to take the pollen from the back of their kneezzz and put it in the basket!" Then she added, "As fast as you can."

"Oh!" Joshua timidly leaned down and took a palm full of pollen, and placed it in the pouch on his hips. As soon as the bee's knees were empty, the bee turned and flew back out of the opening in the trunk, and the next bee stepped in and took its place.

Devora and Devalicious were talking, and at the same time were tending to the bee babies in the wall. Joshua did what he could amongst the din of the bees to listen to their conversation.

"Where are those nursing Devazzz!" exclaimed Devora. "I sent them off for the Royal Jelly hourzzz ago, and I haven't seen them since. Meanwhile, I've had to collect the pollen, and I haven't had time to take it to the flowerzzz. Look and see for yourself, it's piled up over there. I was up all night long making new baby beezzz, and trying to take care of them all."

"Where are all the other helper Devas?" asked Devalicious. "You shouldn't have to do all of this on your own. Why, there must be hundreds of babies here to look after."

"Over one thouzzzand baby beezzz, to be exact, and that's not enough. I need to get cracking and make some more, as soon as those Devazzz get back."

"Devora," called Joshua, "the baskets are full. What should I do?"

"Run them over to the blossom branchezzz, soon as you can."

"But I don't know where the blossom branches are. I might get lost," said Joshua.

"Never mind, give them to me, I'll do it. Oh, but the bee babiezzz..."

"Now, everybody stop for just one minute," said Devalicious. "Devora, I am surprised at you. Where are all your helper Devas?"

"I sent them to look for the lost beezzzz," said Devora.

"Don't you know that help is limitless, all we have to do is ask? Why, I bet you we can get some more helper Devas in here in a jiffy. Let's all just stop what we are doing, and take a moment to calm down."

"Joshua, you come over here too, Sugar."

Joshua did what Devalicious asked, but he couldn't help being concerned at the backlog of bees that was building up outside the window.

"Now, let's take a moment to ground and center," said Devalicious, "especially you, Honey Child." She looked over at Devora, who was by now almost in tears.

"There are so many Devas and spirits in this world. Let's ask the great creator spirit, Morfar, to send us some more!"

Morfar! Joshua hadn't thought about Morfar in quite some time, and the garden of color and light was a fond yet distant memory. He thought about how much he loved Morfar, and if he loved Morfar so much, then Morfar must love him too. If this was true, how could his plea for help possibly be refused?

Joshua calmed his mind and spoke to Morfar. "Morfar, please send help to the Midas Tree. We need Devas to tend the baby bees, Devas to collect the pollen, and Devas to carry the pollen to the blossoms. Please send them to us now."

No sooner had he opened his eyes, when a swarm of golden yellow Devas, wearing white coats and carrying baby bottles, came along the passageway.

"So sorry, Devora," said the one at the front. "We had to make a new batch of Royal Jelly, and it took so long. We're here now, and don't you worry, we'll take good care of all those babiezzz."

"Thank you Matron, I'm so happy to see you." Devora sighed, and she seemed to be starting to relax a little.

The golden yellow Devas, along with the nurse bees, set to work tending to the bee babies and feeding them the Royal Jelly. Then another set of golden yellow Devas, wearing work belts like the one Joshua had on, swarmed in through the open window.

A number of them immediately formed a receiving line, and started collecting the pollen from the bees.

The others came over to Devora and spoke. "We couldn't find the lost beezzz anywhere, and we looked everywhere. We asked a few of our kin to keep on searching, and then we came back to help you.

"Thank you," said Devora. "I appreciate your hard work and your concern. Now if you wouldn't mind, pleazzze start taking this pile of accumulated pollen up to the blossomzzz."

Immediately the remaining Devas set to work, and Joshua, Devora, and Devalicious remained seated.

"You see Honey! I told you," said Devalicious to Devora. "You need to learn to balance your giving and receiving, Mama. I can't believe after all these years of motherhood, you haven't learned that one yet. Those little golden yellow Devas looked well rested. They probably had a little vacation out there in the hinterland, and meanwhile you're run ragged."

"I know, I know," said Devora, "but I love them all so much. If I can do it for them, then I will."

"But you can't do it for them, Devora. We need you to conserve your energy, so you can focus on the things that you are here to do. Let everyone be who they are meant to be. Let everyone serve their own unique purpose, and then the Midas Tree will thrive. If you try to do it all, that won't help any of us, least of all you."

"I know, I know, but my heart is so big, and some of them are so young and inexperienced."

"How do you think they will get their experience, Mama?" asked Devora in a kind but firm way. "If you mess your job up, then that influences the rest of us too. What's more, if you are overwhelmed like that, then you lose sight of all your amazing gifts, Honey. Then none of us can benefit from that either. Why, I haven't heard you sing one note since we've been here."

"I do see your point, Devalicious, honestly I do, but..."

"There are no butts, Sugar, except this big ol' delicious one here!" Devalicious pointed to her rear end and laughed a big hefty laugh. "Allow yourself to receive the help from your little army of golden yellow Devas. You need all your energy for making those babies right now. Now off with you to the birthing chamber. Joshua and I will take over the investigation of the missing bees, while you get all caught up. Come now, Little Man, I'll show you around the rest of this joint." Devalicious prompted Joshua to stand.

"Here, give me one of those pouches; we may as well make ourselves useful."

As Joshua helped Devalicious fill her pouches, he could hear a sweet song echoing through the birthing and nursery chambers.

"See, now she's happy, now she's free to make more babies. She'll be back to her old self in no time."

"OK, so, Little Man, you may have gathered most of the story, but in a nutshell here it is. The bees collect pollen from the hinterland, and bring it to the golden yellow Devas in the Midas Tree. These Devas collect the pollen from them, and then send them back into the hinterland for more. There's a little factory line of these Devas, filling up their pouches, taking the pollen to the blossom Devas, and coming back here for more."

"Devora is the guardian of the bees, and she watches over them. Usually she guides the golden yellow Devas in their tasks, as typically she only has to make about a thousand bee babies a day. Now, unfortunately, because the bees are disappearing in much larger numbers than usual, she is devoting herself to making more bee babies. Any questions, Sugar?"

"No, I don't think so..."

"Well, of course when Devora gets out of balance, then all of her little golden yellow Devas don't get good guidance and the whole system breaks down. I bet those Devas were out there in the hinterland enjoying themselves, not thinking what kind of an impact they were having on Devora. If someone else will do it for you, why should you bother, right? She should have asked us for help. Instead we had to take it on ourselves to come up here and see what was going on."

By now, they were walking further up into the branches. As they walked, little golden yellow Devas swarmed by with full pouches in one direction and empty pouches in the other.

"So I guess we all need to remember to ask for help, and to keep our giving and receiving in balance?"

"You got that right, Sugar!" Devalicious ruffled Joshua's hair. "You're pretty smart and quick off the mark for a human, Honey Child. You see how her energy and lack of grounding was contagious? Where was her swarm of helpers? Because she was in a panic, then everyone else around got into a panic, no doubt. No one wanted to be there with her, because it felt much nicer to be somewhere else."

"So the golden yellow Devas deliberately took a long time?"

"Well, not exactly. I'm sure it wasn't conscious on their part, but hey, where would you rather be? In a flummox and panic with Devora, or chatting with your buddies in the hinterland or the kitchen?"

"So do you think that might explain the missing bees?" asked Joshua.

"I'm not sure, Little Man, but of one thing I am sure. We'll get to the bottom of this in no time. The sooner we get to the blossom Devas the better."

Chapter 10

The Power of a Rose

A beautiful aroma filled the air - the sweet scent of cherry blossoms, jasmine flowers, roses and more. It seemed that Joshua could smell every flower he could remember from the garden of color and light. They mixed their scents into a heady perfume that delighted the senses, and sent him into a reverie of delight. His head felt hazy with sweet daydreams, and he continued along the upper branches in a vacant and trance-like state.

Devalicious noticed that he had stopped talking, and his eyes appeared glazed over. "Hey Sugar! Wake up Little Man. Increase your grounding. The higher up the tree we go, the finer the energy, and the more we need to ground. Ground some more, so you can stay in your body and pay attention to the here and now. We need all our senses about us to figure out what is going on."

Joshua tried to do what Devalicious asked, but for some reason he still felt lightheaded. "Devalicious, I feel funny," he mumbled "I don't feel like I am in my body."

"I can see I'm going to have to pause a while and teach you how to deal with the higher energy at the top of the tree. Here Sugar, get comfortable like we've taught you to do when you meditate."

"Now Sugar, tell me all the techniques that you have learned so far."

"Let's see. I know how to smile from inside my body. Devadne taught me to ground, Deverall taught me how to run earth energy, Mr. Woodpecker taught me how to go to the center of my head. Ariadne taught me to be present and to give my knees a healing, and Araneus taught me unconditional love. Oh, and Devon and Woodpecker and Araneus taught me about knowingness, when I learned how to read symbols."

"My, you have come a long way since that first day in the middle chamber. Although it appears that you skipped a few important lessons along the way. Your education has a good few gaps that need to be filled in, and we need to get you to the upper leaf chambers with Devandra to learn about cosmic energy as soon as we solve the mysteries of the bees."

"In the meantime, the least I can do is to teach you about creating and destroying roses"

"Creating and destroying roses?" What is the point of creating something and then destroying it, thought Joshua, and why roses? Seemed like there were plenty enough flowers around here anyways.

"Now settle in Sugar, and get yourself as grounded as you can in this moment. Run your earth energy, as that should help you increase your grounding. Now be in the center of your head, and then create the mental image picture of a rose about six to eight inches in front of your forehead."

Joshua thought this was very strange, but he went along with what Devalicious was instructing him to do. He imagined that he could see a rose in front of his forehead. It was a beautiful pink rose with lots of petals, and a lovely aroma. The stem was long and there were thorns, leaves and a few little green aphids, which were a bit bothersome."

"OK, got that." Joshua nodded.

"Great, now get the rose to disappear. You can explode it, or allow it to fade away into nothingness, or any other way you choose. Just make it so the rose isn't there anymore."

Joshua could see how he might want to get rid of the pesky aphids, but why delete such a lovely creation?

Then Devalicious said, as though she had read his mind, "Now don't you worry Sugar, you can create another rose anytime. As much as you need to learn to create using energy, you also need to learn to let go of energy."

Joshua exploded his rose into a million pieces and watched them fade into space.

"Good job, Little Man. Now create another rose, and once again admire your creation."

This time Joshua's' rose was a blue rose bud. That's odd, he thought, I didn't know there was such a thing as a blue rose.

Again, as though she had read his mind, Devalicious said, "We can create anything we want from energy. A rose is just the start of it. However, in order to make room for new creations, we need to let go of old ones. So once again, let go of your rose."

Joshua chopped it into pieces, set it on fire, and watched as the smoke wafted off into the ether.

"That's marvelous, Joshua," encouraged Devalicious. "Now sit and practice a few more times."

Joshua created and destroyed a bunch of roses, a rose bush, a green one, a red one, an orange one, and even a silver one.

"OK, now let's take this lesson one step further. Create another rose, and this time let the rose represent anything that would prevent you being as grounded as you can possibly be right now. Then explode the rose."

Joshua understood the concept. He created a deep red rose and placed the energy that stopped him from grounding inside it. Then he let it go. Immediately he felt more grounded.

"Way to go, Little Man. Keep on blowing up roses to increase your grounding."

Joshua did as Devalicious asked, and in no time at all he was feeling back to normal.

"Remember to use this technique the further up the tree we go, so that you stay grounded at all times."

"Wow, thank you Devalicious. I feel so much better."

The pair set off again, in pursuit of the blossom Devas.

"Does that work for other things too?" asked Joshua as they walked. "And why roses?"

"Well, you really are a smart cookie! Yes, you can use it to create or let go of anything. Though right now, I suggest you get familiar with it by practicing using it to increase your grounding, and to let go of anything that's in your way of being very present. We need all our faculties about us if we are going to solve this mystery."

"You can do this exercise with any symbol you like. The reason I like to use roses is that it's a neutral symbol, and I like to be reminded that I can create beauty at any time."

Satisfied with this answer, Joshua kept on creating and destroying roses, until he was doing one every time he took a step forwards. In no time at all, they had reached the upper branches where the blossoms were. The passageway they took ended up at the apple blossoms. However, Joshua could also see other fruit from this vantage point, and he remembered how he had seen all this before, the very first time he saw the tree, when he was in the garden of color and light.

There were other branches with different types of blossoms, and further around he caught glimpses of the plums, oranges, pears and other fruit that he remembered seeing from the ground.

"Devalicious?"

"Yes, Little Man?"

"Why is the Midas Tree not just one type of tree? Why does it have all these different types of flowers and fruit and buds and leaves?"

"Well, as you must know by now, the Midas Tree is a very special tree. You can almost think of it as a tree of life. Every branch represents a choice you might make, and at the end of every branch is the result from that choice. Just like you, the tree is infinitely creative. There are countless possibilities."

"But what if you make the wrong choices, and end up in the wrong places? Like you said before, I have missed a few steps. I must have made the wrong choices, since I don't know some things that I should know by now?"

"Oh, Joshua! By saying that, I didn't mean to infer you had made incorrect choices, because there is no such thing as a wrong choice. All there is, is the choice that you make. All that you can do is take your journey through the roots and branches, and see what you manage to experience and learn along the way. You cannot experience everything the tree has to teach you in one journey. You will learn everything you are meant to learn, at the time you are meant to learn it. Hopefully you will have some fun along the way."

"So what are we here to learn now?"

"I like your style, Sugar! Well, first let's seek out those blossom Devas." Devalicious put two fingers in her mouth and let out a shrill whistle.

Immediately the most delightful little creatures surrounded them. They looked like little blossoms themselves, and they were all colors of the rainbow, but in ethereal, pastel hues. Joshua thought they looked like little faeries.

"Hey ma babies. How's things goin' wit y'all?" asked Devalicious.

"Hi Devalicious, are we glad to see you! We've not been able to pollinate as many flowers as usual, because the pollen supply has been low, due to the bee shortages."

"So I hear, ma babies. What do you all know about that?"

"Not a lot, but we can tell you that the creativity of the tree is down as well. We seem to be getting a lower variety of pollen than usual, and so we have more flowers and fruits of certain types than others."

"No kidding? Do you have any idea why that is?"

"No. Not yet, but we are glad that you are here, and we are open to your guidance and your suggestions."

"Hmm, well, don't let me interrupt your work any longer. Give us a few moments to catch up with our thoughts, and I'll see what we can come up with. This is Joshua, by the way."

"Hello, Joshua," they all chimed in unison. Joshua thought they were lovely, very pretty.

"Devalicious?"

"Yes, Sugar?"

"Why don't these blossom Devas have one of the bigger Devas in charge of them?"

"Why, Sugar, there is a guide that oversees the blossom Devas, but you see, these blossom Devas are quite highly evolved, and they are so very creative. We don't like to put too much pressure on them, because we want that creativity to flourish and not be limited. We like to think of them as our co-creators."

"Oh, I see, so you come and help them when they need help like now, but otherwise you let them get on with things."

"Exactly right, Sugar!"

"So what do you think it means, that the variety of pollen is more limited than usual?"

"I don't know yet, but I'm gonna find out. Come on Sugar, sit with me and we'll meditate on it a while. Now once you ground and center yourself, do as you did before, except this time let the rose you create represent the problem we are having here. Got your rose?" Joshua nodded. "Now look at that rose and tell me what you see, and I'll do the same."

"I don't see anything, but I just get the feeling... it's a kind of knowing, that the bees that are missing are all in one place."

"That's cool, Sugar. Well, I'm seeing that there's a barrier between my rose and the missing bees. It's as though for some reason they cannot see the Midas Tree any more. They cannot see the tree, and they cannot see the way back to the tree."

"Oh yes, I do see that," said Joshua. "There is a black line above the top of my rose." Then he remembered the symbols he had seen when they entered the passageway to the bees. "Devalicious, all the symbols that I could not read on the sign had lines through them. Do you think that is connected?"

"Well, there are no coincidences, Sugar. Can you visualize the symbols now and tell me what they looked like?"

"Yes, one was a diagonal arrow, another was a circle, and the third was a triangle above a square. All three of them have a vertical line running through them on the left hand side."

"Hmm, that's a very clear description. Thank you, Joshua. Now if I remember, the first two symbols were a bee and a leaf."

"I think it's something to do with beliefs," said Joshua. "Perhaps the bees have stopped believing that they know their way home?"

"Well that's possible, Little Man, because you create through your beliefs, and so if they believe they can't come home, then they won't come home. But what has caused this? You know, I think it's time we spoke to one of the bees." Devalicious let out another whistle, and in response, a couple of the blossom Devas showed up. Devalicious asked them to go and get a bee for them to talk to.

In the meantime, they continued to look at the roses and the symbols.

"You know, the arrow could indicate the way home, and the line that the way home is blocked," said Joshua.

"Yes, and I can't help thinking that the triangle above the square looks like a little house."

"Hmm. I wonder if they got trapped inside a little house?" said Joshua.

Just at that moment, the blossom Devas returned with a bee.

"Thank you very much Devas, you may go back to work now." Devalicious turned to the bee, "and thank you for agreeing to talk to us, Mr. Bee."

"No problem, I am glad to get a break from all that buzzing around," said the bee.

"As you are probably aware, we wish to understand where all the missing bees are. Do you have any idea Sug... Mr. Bee, where they could be?"

"Not really, although I did get knocked off the trail yesterday. I wazzz on my way to find an amazzzingly abundant new crop of flowerzzz. Bob had told us about it and danced directionzzz to us the night before, and I wazzz following his trail, or so I thought. He said it was around the outside of the Midas Tree, about thirty degreezzz from the sun."

"Wait a minute," said Joshua, "Bob danced directions for you?"

"Yes, that'zzz right. We always dance directions to each other when we find a new source of nectar. We like to share our good luck with the other community members, and we're so happy to share that we dance the directionzzz to them."

"Wow, that's so interesting, I've never seen a bee dance before. Can you show me?"

"Sure, I'll show you the exzzzact dance that Bob did."

Devalicious was just about to stop him, as she didn't want to waste any time, but her intuition told her to let him continue.

Mr. Bee started his dance. First, he went round in a circle. When he finished he paused to say, "That meanzzz it's not too far away from home." Then he wagged his tail, walked straight up and back to the center and then he walked in another direction at a thirty-degree angle to the first line he had drawn.

"So if you didn't get that, then to clarify, that meanzzz it's a bit further away and at a thirty degree angle from the sun. Now what I took that to mean izzz that the new flower patch started close to home, but that it stretched out for a wayzzz in that direction."

"Oh my goodness!" said Joshua "Mr. Bee has just drawn two of those three symbols with his dance!"

"Oh, my! You are right," said Devalicious, "except for the crossing lines, they are the same as the circle and the arrow.

"What's that?" asked Mr. Bee.

"We saw five symbols along our path. A bee, a leaf and your 'near to home' and 'thirty degrees from the sun' symbols. Except the last two had lines through them," said Joshua.

"Indicating faulty directions no doubt," said Devalicious. "Mr. Bee, there was a fifth symbol. I wonder if you know what this means?"

She went on to describe it, but the bee did not recognize it at all, although he agreed that it did look like a house of some sort.

"So what happened when you tried to follow Bob's directions?" asked Devalicious.

"That's the funny thing, there wazzz nothing there. Literally nothing, except cut stalks. It looked like there had been plants there before, but there weren't any more. The big crop I expected wazzz not there. I kept on flying further and further out, but I got an uncomfortable feeling, and so I turned around to come back. I felt so disoriented, I barely recognizzzed where I wazzz. I still feel a bit peculiar now."

"Thank you so much for your help Mr. Bee," said Devalicious. "You can be sure that we are doing everything we can to solve this problem."

The bee took his leave, and Joshua turned to Devalicious and said, "Devalicious, is there any way that we can go out there and investigate this for ourselves?"

"Well, Sugar, once inside the Midas Tree, in a way you are inside her until you complete your full journey. Think of the tree as though she is your body, your school and your playground. You exist inside her space, and you depend on her for survival, and for learning your lessons."

"But what about the bees and Devas? They are coming in and out of the Midas Tree."

"Well, that's true Sugar, and it is possible to consciously cross the bounds between two worlds. Devas are pure spirit beings, and as such they are not limited by time and space, and so they can travel outside of the Midas Tree at will. However, they choose to focus their attention here because they love the tree and they wish to help her grow."

"But does that mean that I am not spirit?" asked Joshua, "because I used to be in the garden of color and light all the time. I remember it."

"No, Joshua, you are spirit," said Devalicious in a tender and compassionate voice. "You are an eternal spiritual being, and you must never forget that. Many who come to the Midas Tree completely forget who they are. It's as if they take a pill that erases their memory. The difference between you and the Devas is that you now have a physical body, and they do not."

"Okay, I can understand what you are saying, Devalicious, but I still don't see why I cannot leave the Midas Tree? The bees have physical bodies... how come they can go in and out?"

"Bees are the keepers of many secrets. They are a long-recognized symbol for accomplishing the impossible. Did you know that their bodies are very large in comparison to their wings? It is a great mystery that they can fly at all? In actuality, they fly because they move their wings at such a high rate of speed. They are here to show us that anything is possible when you raise your vibration."

"So if I raise my vibration, I can leave the tree?"

"Why yes, Sugar. In fact, your goal here in the Midas Tree is to raise your vibration to gold, so that you can leave should you choose. Although let me share another lesson from the bees, Sugar, that might help you understand your present situation better. While you have your physical body, a part of your energy and focus is here in the tree at all times. That's also true for the bees, because their Queen never leaves the tree. You see, each bee is a member of the hive, rather like your cells are part of your body. Because the queen is always in the tree, then a part of the whole is always here. Of course, even though only a part of you is here, you have access to all the information you will ever need to learn your lessons, unlock the mysteries of the tree and regain access to your spiritual abilities."

Joshua looked down at his body and then over at a group of shimmering blossom Devas, over in the corner, who were picking up sacks of pollen to take to the blossoms. So many more questions flooded his mind he almost became dizzy again.

"How is it that I can see them if they don't have a body?"

Devalicious laughed, "My, oh my, Little Man, you are so full of questions today. Maybe the best way will be to show you how, and at the same time we might get closer to solving this mystery."

"Let's take a seat right here. That's right. Get yourself nice and grounded and focus your attention into the center of your head. Close your eyes and create a rose, and once again let it represent the story of the missing bees."

Joshua did as she asked.

"Now do you see the rose clearly?"

"Yes," replied Joshua.

"Now reach out your hand to where you put the rose and feel its energy. Got it?"

"Yes," replied Joshua. He felt the density of energy change when he placed his hand where the rose was.

"Now open your eyes, Sugar, and look at where the rose is with your physical eyes."

Joshua opened his eyes. "There's nothing there!" he exclaimed.

"Well, I wouldn't say that Sugar. Close your eyes again."

Joshua closed his eyes and the rose was still there. He scratched his head.

"You see, Sugar, your physical eyes are constructed so that they can see dense physical matter. Everything is energy, and your physical eyes can see energy within a certain range of wavelengths only. But you also have spiritual sight, Sugar, and you can use that to see other vibrations outside the range of your physical eyes."

"Now many people when they come to the Midas Tree forget their spiritual senses, as well as losing their memory of the garden of color and light. But it seems that you have such a strong connection with Morfar, that your spiritual vision stayed open."

"All I am helping you do with the rose technique is to validate that you have spiritual sight, and can use it at will. You can also manipulate energy to make creations, let them go, and use your spiritual sight to observe this process."

Joshua was still looking at the rose he had created to represent the missing bee's story.

"Thank you, Devalicious. Although, if I am creating this rose, then how am I creating it as the bee story?"

"My, oh my, Little Man, you are on fire today! Well, you see, you can use energy to create anything you want to create. You can use your spiritual sight to see anything you want to see. As every particle of energy in the universe contains a reflection of the whole, you can create a symbol out of energy, and use it to obtain information about anything else you want to know about. Make sense?"

Joshua nodded. He was still looking at his rose, and was now keen to see what it would tell him about the missing bees.

"OK, so now let's get on with the task at hand. Tell me what you see inside your rose?"

"My rose has some dark energy in between it and the sun, and it is stopping the light of the sun from reaching the rose."

"That is exactly what I am seeing," said Devalicious. "The sun represents guidance from Morfar and connection with our life purpose. The bees are unable to receive guidance, and it is blocking them from their purpose, which is to collect pollen for the Midas Tree."

"Yes and it reminds me of the lines through the symbols that I was reading earlier," Joshua added.

"Quite so, my Little Man! So let's take a closer look at the energy in the rose, and at the dark energy above it. What are the bees learning about, by having this experience?"

Joshua answered her question. "The dark energy looks to me like it represents greed, and a concept that there is not enough to go around."

"Exactly, there is an outside force, which looks to me like those who have forgotten that they come from Morfar, who believe that they have to own and control everything. They fear that if they don't, someone else will, and then they will be left with nothing. This is affecting the bees, because they need to learn about abundance too."

"How do we know this, Devalicious?" asked Joshua, shocked and excited at the same time.

"We're using our spiritual abilities, Sugar. Now don't you go all scared on me, because there's nothing to be scared about, and lots of reasons to be joyful. Now take a look at that rose. See if we can discover more about what the bees are learning about. What color is your rose?"

"Mine has a light green glow around the outside, but the rose itself is tangerine orange."

"And what shape is the rose, what does it look like?"

"It's about a third of the way open, and there are lots of petals, except it seems as though there is a gap in the middle where there aren't any petals. You can see right down into the center."

"OK, great, now see if you can get a word to describe what those colors mean?"

"I feel that the green represents newness and growth, and it is what the bees are learning about. The orange represents their creativity and their joy about creating. The hole in the center means they have lost sight of who they really are, and they have lost their joy."

"Oh my! That is a sad state of affairs. Let's see if we can give them a hand with that. First, let's move off the dark energy that's between the bees and the sun."

"How do we do that?" asked Joshua.

"We simply use our will and our desire that the energy be moved, and so it will move. Have a go, Sugar. What do you have to lose?"

Devalicious and Joshua worked together, until all the dark energy was gone.

"Now let's bring some of that bright sunshine back onto the rose."

Together they connected the sun with the rose, and brought a stream of sunlight through the rose. As they did this, the rose changed. The petals in the center reappeared, the color became brighter, and the rose became stronger.

"Now don't forget to ground the rose, so that all of this healing can be made manifest."

Joshua did as she asked, and created a grounding cord from the rose to the center of the earth.

"Now there's one more thing we can do."

"What is that?"

"Why, we can speak to the bees, of course."

"But how can we speak to them if they are not here?"

"We speak to them as spirit. As spirit, we are not bound by space and time. As spirit we are pure energy, and so we can use our spiritual communication to talk to them wherever they are; even if we don't consciously know where that is."

"So let this rose you have been working with disappear. Tune into your light, and tune into the light of the bees that are missing. Then create a bridge of light between you and the bees. Now let's send them love, and let's explain to them that they live in a loving universe that supports them and where there is an abundant supply of energy for all to enjoy. Tell them they can use this beam of light to find their way home, and we look forward to seeing them soon."

"Now Sugar, while we wait for our healing to manifest, I think it's time I introduced you to Devandra..."

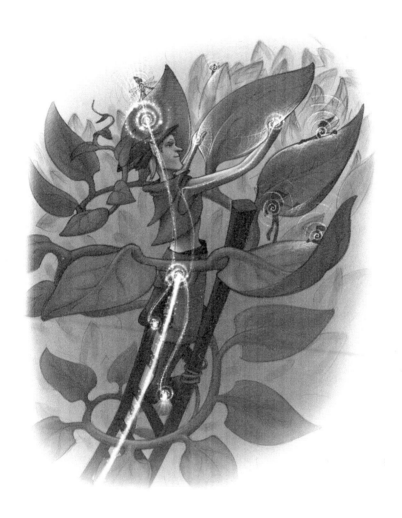

Chapter 11

Bringing in the Light

evandra was poised on one foot on the upper rung of a wooden ladder, stretching up as high as he could into one of the topmost branches. He appeared to be manipulating the direction in which the leaves were pointing. As he moved his little branch, a thousand little green Devas moved all the other branches to match.

Joshua and Devalicious didn't disturb him, as what he was doing seemed important, and so they patiently waited at the bottom of the ladder until he was finished. Joshua hadn't talked with Devandra since his first day inside the Midas Tree, but he remembered that he was the Deva that looked after the leaves. If he hadn't remembered, then he could have easily guessed. If what Devandra was doing wasn't enough of a clue, there was also his attire, made from leaves and supple, sappy green bark.

"My Darling Devalicious, to what do we owe this pleasure?" Devandra hopped down from the ladder and planted an affectionate kiss on the cheek of Devalicious, who responded by putting an arm around his waist.

"Well Sugar, I feel it's time, no I feel it's past time that our young pupil, Joshua, spend some time with you up here in the tree canopy. He's already learned so much; we need to catch him up on cosmic energy, and the suns' life-giving rays. Plus, I've got some work to do, and so I'm going to leave him with you for a while. I'll be back later to see how you're getting along." With that and another peck on the cheek, Devalicious made her exit.

"Why don't you take a seat over here, you look exhausted. You can watch the sunlight Devas and I work, and I'll explain to you what we are doing as we go along."

Joshua was grateful for the break. All of the new things he had learned from Devalicious had left his mind reeling. He sank into the sun-speckled, cushioned wicker chair that Devandra had pointed to and relaxed.

"Up here in the branches, the leaves are one of the busiest parts of the tree," started Devandra. "You see, the tree gets most of its energy by converting sunlight into sugar, and all of this happens inside the leaves. They are like little sugar factories. So the leaf Devas and I are very diligent about ensuring that our sugar factories are operating at maximum capacity. One way of doing this, is to ensure that the leaves are always at the best angle to the sun. Because the sun moves across the sky every day, we must continuously alter the angle of the leaves. That is what we were doing when you first arrived."

"Of course, that's only one of the important operations that take place here. As well as controlling the direction of the leaves, the little green Devas also work inside the leaves, where they help to capture sunlight inside little catalytic converters called chloroplasts. The chloroplasts absorb photons from the sun, and through a process called photosynthesis, they convert carbon dioxide from the air and water to form sugar molecules.

A side product of this reaction is oxygen, which is in the air we breathe."

As Devandra was speaking, Joshua could see everything he was explaining in his mind's eye. It was as though there was a screen in front of his eyes, and Devandra was projecting images onto it, to illustrate what he was saying. He could see the leaves become magnified until all the little chloroplasts inside them were visible. He could see all the busyness and activity going on in the process that Devandra was describing.

"Carbon dioxide in the air enters the leaves through pores in the leaf's surface, called stoma. The water comes in from the roots, and is transported up to the leaves, via a process called translocation. It's all extremely fascinating, and we operate it, of course, like a well-oiled machine," Devandra looked at Joshua, who was trying to stay awake.

Joshua didn't want to be rude, so he sat up straight and tried to appear more alert. It was very nice of Devandra to give him a biology lesson like this, and all very useful information he was sure, but he was already over-loaded and all he wanted to do was take a nap.

Devandra continued for a while longer about the structure of chloroplasts and the wavelength of light, and all the chemical reactions involved in photosynthesis. Eventually though, he said, "There, there Joshua, why don't you take a break? Have a nice nap, and when you wake up, I'll teach you what you really came here to learn about."

Oh no, not more chemistry, biology and physics, thought Joshua. "Thank you, Devandra, I am feeling tired. I'll just take a nice little nap here on this comfy chair while you go about your business."

"Just so, dear boy, just so."

Joshua drifted off, amongst a sea of mathematical symbols and equations. When he woke up, he found himself sitting in the room in the center of the tree. He was looking out through the knot in the trunk into the hinterland. It was night time out there now, but the sky was clear, and he could see thousands upon thousands of stars in the sky.

Each star was a bright shining light, and he wondered how many trees there were in the universe, all feeding on the light of those stars. They were so very beautiful, each one unique with its own position in the sky in relation to all the other stars, and each one a brilliant source of energy and light.

"Tap, tap, tap, tap, tap..."

"Tap, tap, tap, tap, tap..."

"Mr. Woodpecker!"

"Pause...Tap, tap, tap, tap, tap..."

"Mr. Woodpecker! It's me, Joshua. I'm back."

"Tap, tap, pause..." Mr. Woodpecker appeared on the other side of the knot.

"Hello, Joshua. It's a fine clear evening, so lovely, so pretty, and the air is crisp and clean." Mr. Woodpecker was breathing in and out deeply as he spoke. "Tell me, what adventures are you up to now?"

Joshua recounted all of his adventures since he had last seen Mr. Woodpecker, starting with the missing bees, and finishing with the biology lesson from Devandra.

"Hmm, no doubt Devandra is leading up to teaching you about cosmic energy."

"Yes, cosmic energy, that is what they said they would teach me next. What is it exactly?"

"It's the energy of the cosmos, and it's a source of energy and light for all of us."

"Oh, so when the leaves use the light to make sugar, they are using cosmic energy?"

"Quite so, young Joshua, quite so. Just as the leaves are using cosmic energy, so can you. Devandra is a master of cosmic energy, and so we'll leave it up to him to teach you. All in good time."

"But...,"

"Not to worry," said Mr. Woodpecker. "You and I still have plenty of important things to talk about. I'm very interested in what you have to say about those bees."

"Actually, Mr. Woodpecker, you fly around in the space between the tree and the garden of color and light, don't you? Have you seen a long field of stubble? The bee who we spoke with told us there is a place like this in the hinterland."

"Actually, no, Joshua, I tend to stay in the forested areas, where I can tap on the trees and feed on the grubs, but I do know someone who flies all around, especially at night." Mr. Woodpecker let out a long shrill whistle, and within moments, a bat appeared at the window next to him.

"Hello, Mr. Woodpecker!" exclaimed the bat, "And hello, eye inside the tree," he laughed.

"Bertie, this is my friend Joshua. He's living inside the Midas tree right now, and he needs our help solving a mystery of missing bees, low pollen supplies, and declining productivity. Have you noticed anything strange on your midnight flights lately?"

"Yes, especially at a thirty degree angle from the tree to the sun?" added Joshua.

"Err...?" said Bertie.

Mr. Woodpecker laughed. "We'll have to orient Bertie in another way, Joshua, because he doesn't come out in the day time."

"Oh yes, I see. Sorry, Bertie. Well, there is a long field of stubble that stretches from near the tree, far away off into the distance. We believe that the problem lies somewhere in that area."

"Oh, really?" exclaimed Bertie. "I know that area quite well. I have been going there a lot recently, because it's easy to see the moths. They are in plain sight, and they seem not to have their wits about them, so they are very easy for me to catch and eat. Although I have to say, I have been getting a bellyache recently, after I eat them. I don't know if it's that I'm eating too many, or there's something wrong with them. I was actually thinking I should go hunting somewhere else tonight, to see if it will make a difference."

"Thank you, Bertie. That is really interesting and useful information," said Mr. Woodpecker.

"Yes, thank you," said Joshua. "It seems that there is something about that tract of land that is disorienting all the insects - not just the bees, but the moths as well."

"Yes, and whatever it is, it must be poisonous, because it's making Bertie Bat here sick too."

"Oh my goodness me," said Bertie. "I knew there was something wrong. I'd better avoid that area in future."

"Hmm, well, this confirms our suspicions, but it doesn't really get us any closer to finding the cause. Have you noticed anything else, Bertie?"

"I did wonder why the moths were attracted into the field in the first place. I noticed lots of tiny dew-like crystals sticking to the stubble. They reflected the moonlight, and sparkled like little tiny faerie lights. I thought it might be the light that was attracting them."

"I wonder what these crystals are." Joshua scratched his head.

"You know, in the forest there are many types of plants and insects, birds and other creatures, and we all help each other along in our own way. Bertie and I eat insects, but then we digest them and release nutrients back into the soil for the plants and other insects to feed from. There are only ever as many woodpeckers and bats and bugs and worms as there needs to be, for everyone to live in balance and harmony. The difference I see, in this huge field, is that there appears to be only one type of plant," offered Mr. Woodpecker.

"Yes," said Bertie, "and that cannot be in balance with the natural laws of nature. If there was one type of bug that liked to feed from that one type of plant, then the population of that one type of bug would grow out of proportion to what is usual for that creature."

"Yes," said Mr. Woodpecker, "and whoever is growing that plant crop is probably doing it for food, or for some other survival need, so they would not want the bugs."

"So they kill the bugs!" shouted Joshua.

"So they kill the bugs," agreed Mr. Woodpecker and Bertie in unison.

"And they do it by putting poison on the crop, and that poison effects all the insects, not just the ones that they are trying to kill." surmised Joshua.

"Precisely," added Bertie, "and it may not be killing them, but it is making them sick. What is more, it is making any creature that feeds on them sick too."

"And it's making the bees so sick and dizzy that they don't know where they are, and they cannot find their way back to the Midas Tree."

"It sounds like a very plausible explanation," said Mr. Woodpecker, "but it still doesn't help us find the bees and bring them home."

Joshua responded, "Devalicious and I did some work communicating with the bees from a distance, as spirit. We provided them with a cord of light that they could follow, to find their way back home."

"You truly are becoming a master of the mysteries of the tree, Joshua. I hope that will work, and in the meantime Bertie and I will do some more reconnaissance. Bertie, you take the night shift, and I'll take the day shift. We should be okay, so long as we don't eat while we're near the field. We'll fly around and see if we can locate the bees, and if we do, we'll help guide them home."

As Mr. Woodpecker was speaking, Joshua felt a tap on his shoulder. He opened his eyes to see Devandra standing over him. "I trust you had a good sleep, Joshua?"

"Yes, thank you, Devandra." Joshua rubbed his eyes.

"We're just about to get started with our cosmic energy meditation, so if you don't mind, please come and join us over here." He pointed to the other end of the room they were in, where there was a circle of the bright green Devas. They surrounded a chair placed in the center, which Joshua assumed was waiting for him.

Joshua walked alongside Devandra to the meditation circle, and took his place in the center. He sat with his feet flat on the floor, and his hands resting lightly in his lap. He closed his eyes.

"Devas and Joshua, we will now begin our meditation. Joshua, I want you to use all the techniques that you know, so before we run our cosmic energy, please take a few minutes to become grounded and centered, and to run your earth energy."

Joshua tuned into the energy center near the base of his spine, and he created a flow of energy from there all the way to the center of the earth. He let go of his thoughts about the bees, and his conversation with Bertie and Mr. Woodpecker, by releasing them down his grounding cord. He wanted to give this new lesson his undivided attention.

Once he felt really grounded, and had secured his grounding cord to the center of the earth, he focused his attention in the center of his head. That allowed him to be fully present in his physical body, and be receptive to everything that Devandra was about to teach him.

Then he opened the energy centers in the arches of his feet, and allowed energy from the earth to flow in through his feet, and up through the energy channels in his legs. He allowed some of that energy to flow down his grounding cord, to enhance it and to strengthen it.

Devandra intuitively knew when he was ready. "Wonderful. Now I want you to create, in your mind's eye, a clear ball of cosmic energy above the top of your head."

Joshua did as he requested. He imagined that there was a ball of transparent energy floating about a foot above the top of his head.

"Now allow some of this cosmic energy to start to flow towards you. Allow it to flow into your energy system, down through the top of your head. Let it stream down the back of your head, into the energy channels that exist on either side of your spine."

Joshua used his mind to move the energy in the clear ball in through the top of his head. He could feel the energy flowing down the energy channels beside his spine. It was tingly, and it felt really good. It reminded him of when he lived in the garden of color and light, when he was completely bathed in light all the time; when he *was* light.

"Now bring that cosmic energy all the way down to that energy center near the base of your spine, and when it reaches that place, create your own unique blend of earth and cosmic energy."

Joshua could feel the two energies mixing and blending together.

"Bring that blend of energy up through energy channels that exist in the front of your body, until it reaches the top of your head. Allow it to flow out of the top of your head, and to fountain all around you. Let it flow through your entire energy field, a beautiful shower of energy."

Joshua felt the cosmic energy traveling up his torso, as though a light wind was blowing up the front of his body. He felt like he was standing in a shower of starlight and moonlight and sunlight all at once.

"Remember, any excess or unwanted energy will simply flow down your grounding cord and be released."

"Now as the cosmic energy flows up the front of your body, allow some of it to branch off just above your breastbone, below the base of your neck. Let this flow down your arms, and out through the palms of your hands. Sit and enjoy being grounded, being centered, and having your earth and cosmic energies running. Just like earth energy, cosmic energy will clear blockages in your energy system as it flows."

Joshua sat and enjoyed this wonderful cleansing. He felt really good, as though all of his cares were being washed away.

"Cosmic energy is the flow of energy from the cosmic consciousness. We can use this energy to cleanse and clear our energy field, and to energize it. As we bring this energy into our system, we are also helping anchor the flow of cosmic energy here into our home, the Midas Tree. There are an infinite number of cosmic energies, because it is what all things are made of - from the denser, slower vibrations in physical matter, to the higher, faster vibrations in the light from the sun."

Joshua could see that light was pouring into the tree, being channeled through the little green Devas. The room they were sitting in became so light and so bright. The energy became very high, as they sat and ran the cosmic energy.

"Now change the vibration of cosmic energy that you are working with to a bright light green energy. Let go of the clear ball of cosmic energy, and create a new green ball, and then allow this to flow through your energy channels."

Joshua brought the green energy through the top of his head, and allowed it to flow down the channels on either side of his spine and back up the front of his body. He allowed it to fountain out of the top of his head all around him, and to branch off near the cleft of his throat. He felt like he became the canopy of the tree, surrounded and penetrated by this beautiful green energy. Everything felt new and exciting.

"Now change the vibration of cosmic energy that you are working with to a bright light sky-blue energy. Let go of the green ball of cosmic energy. Create a new blue ball, and then allow this to flow through your energy channels.

Joshua changed the cosmic energy vibration that he was channeling to a lovely, light bright blue. Now he felt calm, peaceful, and very relaxed, as though he had no worries or cares in the world.

Devandra talked them through meditating with every color of the rainbow. Joshua was able to feel how he could change his energy, and the way he experienced the world, by shifting the vibration of cosmic energy that he was running.

"Wonderful. Now let us complete our meditation by running a clear gold vibration of cosmic energy." Devandra paused to allow everyone to shift their energy. Then he said, "Now that you are in this state of being grounded and centered and running your energies, take a moment to be in communication with your energy source."

Joshua took a deep breath and relaxed. He sat in the center of his head, and felt light pouring into his body and extending down all the way to the center of the earth through his grounding. He became connected with a higher force of energy, and instantly he was full of love and light.

"Morfar, where are you? Why did you lead me here to the Midas Tree, and out of the garden of color and light? Did I displease you in some way? Why did you lead me from my home and cast me away here, where I don't know how everything works, and where I don't know how to get home?"

Joshua felt his confusion melt, and his heart swell with love and light, and he knew that Morfar had not abandoned him. He knew that Morfar was always here. It was he who had been focused away from Morfar, not the other way around. He knew that he could contact Morfar whenever he wished. All he needed to do was be still in meditation, just like now, and then he could feel the presence of Morfar.

He also knew that he was here because Morfar loved him, and wanted him to grow and learn new things. Being in the tree allowed him to separate things out, and focus on them one by one. He felt happy and comforted, now that he knew his separation from Morfar had been an illusion all along.

"Well done, everyone," said Devandra. "Joshua, remember now to add this technique to your daily meditations, and remember that you can run different colors of cosmic energy, depending on what is most healing for you at any given time. So right now, adjust your cosmic energy to one that is most comfortable for you to resume your activities."

Joshua chose a bright yellow sunshine vibration, because it made him feel happy and joyful. He opened his eyes just as Devalicious returned from her errands.

"Hi, Sugars. I'm here to collect Joshua so we can get back to those bees!"

Joshua was really pleased to see her, and couldn't wait to recount his most recent conversation with Mr. Woodpecker and his new friend Bertie.

Chapter 12

Branches of Wisdom

"So you learned all about the flow of cosmic energy, Sugar?"

"Yes," said Joshua, "and I also learned how the leaves convert sunlight into sugar."

"That's right, Honey Child, and then the sugar is transported from the leaves all over the tree by my little sugar Devas." Devalicious let out a shrill whistle, and a gang of clear crystalline Devas appeared at her feet. Each Deva carried a long, thin, transparent pipe. "Let's show our friend Joshua what we're made of," she said.

All the little crystalline Devas tinkled over to the leaves, and formed an orderly line along one of the channels running down from the leaves into the branches. The Deva closest to the leaves inserted his pipe into the base of a leaf, and sucked on the other end.

A clear liquid was drawn from the leaf into the pipe. He continued with a few leaves until his pipe was full. Then he did a one hundred and eighty degree turn until he faced the next Deva in line, who drew his pipe up to connect with that of the first Deva.

Deva number one held the pipe with one hand, and used the other hand in a kind of sending motion along the length of the pipe. Meanwhile, he gently blew the clear liquid into the pipe of Deva number two. Then Deva number two turned to Deva number three, and deposited the liquid in the pipe of the next Deva.

"See how my little sugar Devas so carefully and delicately transport the sugar from the leaves, into the other parts of the Midas Tree?"

"Yes, I do see that Devalicious, but the Midas Tree is such a big tree. Isn't there a lot of sugar for such a small number of Devas to handle?"

"Oh, this is just one of the teams of crystalline Devas. There are many more all over the tree. They line the phloem channels, which are the passageways that deliver the sugar around the tree. You may not see them unless you look carefully, especially because of their transparent crystalline nature."

"Oh, I see," said Joshua, and then in curiosity he added, "Do they have a special meditation that they do?"

"My, my, Sugar Man, you really are catching on quite well. Yes, they do, as they are masters of energy flow, and it's just about time to start, Walk this way, Sugar!"

Joshua followed Devalicious into a beautiful chamber of light, where the walls were made of long thin sugar crystals. There was a meditation platform in the middle, with a beautiful chair carved from sugar in the center, and smaller chairs in a circle around it.

Devalicious let out another shrill whistle, and all of her little crystalline Devas swarmed into the chamber and took their meditation positions.

"Now Joshua, as we journey through the tree, we always build on what we have already learned. So before we learn a new technique, we always use what we already know as a foundation on which to build."

"So everyone close your eyes, and we will start by grounding."

Devalicious took the whole group through grounding, centering and running earth and cosmic energy.

"Now feel the energy flowing down your arms. This is your creative energy flow, and you can use it in creating new projects, and in healing. So right now, take one hand and run it over your other arm. See if you can feel the energy."

Joshua did as she said, and he could definitely a feel a difference in the density of the space above the length of his arm. He could feel a tingling along the length of his arm as he brushed his other hand over it. He could literally feel the energy flowing.

"Now allow the energy to flow out of the palms of your hands, and create a ball of energy between your two hands."

Joshua could feel the energy accumulate between his palms, until it felt like a bouncy elastic ball. Devalicious had them play with the energy ball, passing it from one hand to the other, and making it bigger and smaller. It was a lot of fun, but Joshua had to ask, "Devalicious, what is the purpose of this meditation?"

"We are practicing working and creating with energy. Did you see how my crystalline Devas used their hands as well as their breath to get the sugar solution to flow through their pipes? They were using energy coming from their hands, to help the energy flow down the phloem. They were also charging the sugar solution by adding cosmic energy to it."

"What can I use this technique for?"

"Well, you can use it to heal yourself and others. If you notice a pain or some tension in your body, you can run your hands over the area to clear it and get the energy flowing again. If you notice a friend is having trouble grounding, you can simply place your hands underneath their chair and help the energy to flow, for example. Once you know how to do this, there are many ways you can use it."

"Oh, I see," said Joshua.

"As you know by now, Sugar Man, everything is energy. Developing a sensitivity to feel energy will help you tune into all manner of things."

"Ahh!" said Joshua, still not quite sure how this could be applied practically. He trusted Devalicious, and so he decided to quit asking questions and wait and see how things evolved.

Once the meditation was completed, the Devas returned to work, and Joshua and Devalicious started walking back towards Devora's chambers. Joshua recounted his conversation with Mr. Woodpecker and Bertie Bat.

"Well, Honey Child, it sure seems like we are getting closer to solving this mystery, and having the missing bees return to the Midas Tree."

When they returned to the place where the bees were hard at work, they found Devora in a tizzy again. "Oh my babeezzz, they're growing up too fast. They have had to take on responsibilitiezzz too soon. Only yesterday they were pupae, and today they are out in the fieldzzz, and here I am expected to make more babeezzz so they can go out into the world and never come home." She was sobbing.

"Oh dear, Joshua, it's time to put what you just learned into action. Please give Devora a little healing. I'll talk you through what to do. Now, you don't need to touch her physical body at all, but you can use your hands positioned above and around her body to help her energies flow. You can start by helping her to get her grounding back."

Joshua walked over to Devora, who was sitting sobbing in her birthing chair. He crouched down and placed his hands near where her grounding cord should be. He could feel that the energy flow was weak, so as he held his hands there, he willed that it increase in strength. As he did, he could feel it getting stronger.

"Now Joshua, how about you help her get her earth and cosmic energies flowing too?"

"How do I do that, Devalicious?" he asked.

"Well, much like you saw my little crystal babies encouraging the flow of sugar through the phloem, you must encourage the flow of earth energy up Devora's legs."

"Joshua, hold your hands over Devora's feet, and imagine the energy centers in her feet opening up to allow the flow of earth energy into her leg channels. Then sweep your hands over her legs to clear any blockages, and encourage the earth energy to flow up them."

Joshua followed Devalicious' instructions attentively. He imagined he was using his hands to help the energy centers in Devora's feet open, and to guide the flow of the earth energy up her legs. He could feel the energy catch and clear as he hit little blockages along the way.

"Well done, Sugar Man. See how she is calming down? Now do her cosmic energy. All you have to do is guide the energy to flow in through the top of her head, and down her back channels all the way down to near the base of her spine."

Joshua imagined he was helping the cosmic energy flow in through the top of Devora's head, while sweeping his hands in a downwards motion. He brought the energy all the way down, near to the base of her spine, by sweeping his hands all the way down her back.

"Now allow the cosmic energy to blend with the earth energy, and help it flow up the front of her body."

Joshua imagined he was helping blend the earth and cosmic energy near the base of Devora's spine, while holding his hand over it. He swept his hand up the front of her body, to help her energy flow upwards until it fountained out of the top of her head.

"Don't forget the arm channels."

He traced the route of energy from near the cleft of Devora's throat, at the base of her neck, so that it flowed down her arm channels and out through the palms of her hands.

"Well done, Joshua. See how you have helped Devora to calm down? Congratulations, Honey Child, you just gave Devora an energy healing!"

"Wow, really? That's amazing!" said Joshua, pleased that he could be of help.

"Thank you Joshua," said Devora.

"Now we have some news for you, Devora," said Devalicious. "We believe that the bees are becoming disoriented by poison on some plants, which they have been flying to in the hinterland. They recently discovered a large crop, which they thought would be an abundant source of pollen. However, we now realize that this crop is of only one type of plant. We believe it helps explain the reduction in variety of pollens, fruits, and flowers we are seeing here in the tree."

"We have some friends who have offered to scout the area, and see if they can find out more about what has happened to the bees. We have given the bees a long distance healing, and have communicated with them as spirit, and we have provided a guiding light to help them find their way home.

We have no doubt that we will have this solved, and be back to normal soon."

"Thank you, Devalicious," said Devora. "That's quite the story."

"Now I suggest you try to get a little rest, and we shall do the same. I'll find something for us to eat, and we will stay here tonight in case we get any news."

After some delicious nectar tea and honey cakes, Devalicious and Joshua bedded down on some cushions in a comfortable corner of the room. It was a fitful sleep, and they were both tossing and turning, mainly because the work in the tree never seemed to stop. Even at night, Devora was making new bee babies and watching over them. They could hear all the nurse bees and the golden yellow Devas bustling around taking care of them.

In the early morning hours, a fluttering and a tapping noise awakened them. Mr. Woodpecker and Bertie Bat were perched over in the window, where the bees deliver the pollen. Devora, Devalicious, and Joshua rushed over to greet them.

"We have some excellent news. We have found the missing bees!" said Mr. Woodpecker.

"Yes! I flew over the suspected area during the night, and I used my sonar to locate a swarm of little bodies. They seem to be fine, and they're all together." Turning to Joshua, Bertie added, "We bats hold the mysteries needed to hear sounds of the unseen world, and we also have the ability to navigate and locate objects by sound vibration. We transmit sounds which hit objects and bounce back at us, and we can discern the location and size of the object by the vibrations that return to us."

"That sounds fantastic," responded Joshua.

"Yes, Joshua, if you quiet yourself and listen, you may be surprised at what you yourself are able to tune into," added Mr. Woodpecker.

"So where are my babeezzz?" inquired Devora.

"They're in a small house, the size of a bee hive, at the far end of the stubble field. I managed to get close enough to speak with some of the bees inside. They confirmed that flying over the field of stubble had disoriented them. Then in their attempt to find their way home, they picked up on the scent of Devora, and followed it."

"But they didn't end up here, they ended up inside the little house with a piece of paper soaked in a substance that smelled like Devora, but wasn't her. The little house felt like a beehive inside, but it wasn't their home inside the Midas Tree. They were confused and disoriented. They didn't know what else to do, or where else to go, and so they stayed where they were."

"Where are they now, why didn't you get them to come back with you?"

"Both Mr. Woodpecker and I tried, but they didn't trust us. They said they thought it was a trick, and we would eat them like we do to other bugs."

"Oh my, they really are disoriented. If there is one thing I teach all my bee babiezzz, it is to usezzz their sight to see the truth. They must have been through quite an ordeal if they have forgotten thizzz. But I also teach them there is nothing they cannot achieve. They need to believe this; otherwise they would never be able to fly, as they have such big bodies compared to their wingzzz. They would never get off the ground unless they believed they could."

"So what can we do now?" asked Joshua.

"It's going to take someone they can trust, to lure them out of there and back to the Midas Tree," said Mr. Woodpecker.

"The only person they truly would trust would be Devora, and a queen never leaves the hive. If she did, it would cause all the other bees to swarm," said Devalicious. "It would be very dangerous, because she would be leading them to precisely the place where she does not want them to go."

"Could we cover someone else with Devora's pheromones, and get them to lead the bees home, along the path of light we sent to guide them?" Joshua asked. "If that was what lured them away in the first place, perhaps that is what will bring them back?"

"What a fabulous idea," clapped Devora, "but who can we uzzze for this purpose? They have already met Mr. Woodpecker and Bertie Bat, and they might be suspicious of them, and yet they are the only onezzz who know where the beezzz are."

"Yes, so it needs to be someone small enough that they can travel on Bertie or Mr. Woodpecker's back," added Devalicious.

"Let's send the crystalline Devas," offered Joshua. "We could put Devora's scent into one of their pipes. Bertie and Mr. Woodpecker could carry them to the beehive. Once there, they could transfer the pheromone from one to another along the path of light we created, and the bees would follow them home."

Devalicious was not convinced. "That's a great idea, Sugar, but aren't the bees confused by all the other chemicals in the air out there?"

"Yes, but I think Joshua has a point," said Devora. "The dose of pheromone in the Devazzz pipe would be much more concentrated. It might be strong enough to tune out all the other chemical signalzzz. Your path of light to guide the beezzz home was a great idea, but they won't follow it unless it smellzzz right to them."

"Over here, Sugars," Devalicious whistled to a nearby group of clear crystalline Devas. She instructed one of them to place their pipe at the side of Devora's abdomen. Once it was in place, Devora expressed a clear liquid into the tube.

Meanwhile, Devalicious explained to the crystalline Devas what would happen next. "Now listen carefully, Sugars. You will take a ride on the back of these two creatures, to where the missing bees are holed up. When you get there, you will form an orderly line along a beam of light that we will transmit to you, that leads straight back here. You will transfer the pheromone from one pipe to another along the line of light. Act as a tag team, so once you empty your pipe, you can run to the front of the line and wait for the next transfer. Keep on going until you reach the Midas Tree."

"What if the bees don't follow the pheromone, or what if something else goes wrong?" Joshua asked.

"The beezzz will follow my perfume, I have no doubt about that," said Devora.

"I will stay in constant telepathic communication with my little crystalline Devas the whole time. If something goes wrong we will know, and we'll deal with it then," added Devalicious. She whistled again, and the cohort of crystalline Devas climbed up on the backs of Bertie and Mr. Woodpecker.

They waved them off at the window and wished them good luck.

"Now let's sit and work with the energy of this mission, while our friends do the physical part of it," instructed Devalicious.

They pulled their chairs into a semi-circle and followed her instructions.

"Everyone ground, center and have your energies running." She paused to allow them to prepare themselves. "Now create the mental image of a rose, and allow it to represent our team of creatures and Devas. Help them to ground, and connect them to the source. Surround them with a waterfall of golden light to keep them clear and safe."

"Now let's do the same for our bees," she paused in between each direction to give them time to do as she asked.

"Tune into the communication cord we created to light the way home. Create another rose, and use it to give the line a good dusting, so that it stays bright and clear for them."

They continued controlling the energy around the situation, and at the same time monitored the two roses that represented the team of Devas and the bees to see if there were any changes.

After what felt like hours, but was probably much less time than that, they started to hear a humming noise in the far off distance.

Devora became excited. "It's my babeezzz! My babeezzz are coming home, I just know it!"

The humming got louder and louder, until it became a buzz. A swarm of bees appeared at the opening to the chamber, and Devora ran to greet each and every one of them.

Devalicious whistled until her Devas gathered at her feet, and she congratulated them all with hugs. Then she turned to Joshua. "Well done, Honey Child, well done! You certainly have earned those golden arms and hands you have."

Joshua looked down to see that his fingertips were aglow with golden light. He beamed with happiness for the return of the lost bees to the tree, and for his journey bringing him closer to returning to Morfar, in the garden of color and light.

At that moment, Devandra appeared at the door to remind them it was dinnertime, and also to excitedly share with them that the outer branches of the Midas Tree were shimmering with bright golden light.

Chapter 13

Lured By a Healing Cup of Tea

oshua woke up early with a terrible toothache. He stumbled over to his meditation chair, before any Devas arrived for their morning ritual, and sat down. He tried to ground and release energy down his grounding cord, but still he was in pain. He tried to center, so at least he could be neutral about it, as otherwise it was making him feel quite grumpy.

He tried to run his earth and cosmic energy through the channels in his legs and torso, and he tried to run his healing energy down his arms and out through his hands. He created and exploded roses, as a way of trying to increase the level of healing energy that he was running through his arms and hands. Then he ran his hand over his jaw, with the intent that he would clear whatever it was that was causing this pain.

By the time the Devas all arrived, he was feeling quite frustrated, because nothing he tried seemed to be working. He sat through the chanting, and he tried to open his heart and feel full of love, as he imagined this was how the Devas felt. The pain in his jaw kept throwing him off center. He could see a light in his chest, and his heart open for a fleeting moment, and then it was gone and replaced by his frustration.

Then he remembered to sing to his tooth and jaw, "happy tooth, happy jaw, happy tooth, happy jaw," just as he had been taught on his first day in the Midas Tree. Alas, this too only seemed to provide temporary relief.

When the Devas had finished their own chanting, he looked for one of his friends in the crowd. Eventually he spotted Devon and ambled over. "Hello Devon, how are you? I'm frustrated through and through. I have a pain in my jaw, and try as I might it still feels sore."

"My dear chap, you've lost the knack. When you try then, my, oh my, you won't achieve pain relief. Looks like you are caught in much effort, and that won't do to heal you."

"Oh, I see," said Joshua, though he really didn't. He was in a hurry to get on with his day. He felt he had been making good progress, and he wanted to turn as much of himself to gold today as he possibly could. "Do you know where I am to go next?"

"My dear boy, with great joy; I say to thee, explore the tree."

"That is what I do every day, but do you know in which particular direction I should go on this particular day?" he asked, still rubbing his jaw.

"It's up to you, to get a clue and to know where to go."

"Yes, Devon, very helpful, thanks a lot. Not!" Joshua turned to walk away, when Devon added, "I always find when I'm below par, it always helps to have a nice cuppa char." He walked away from Joshua, before Joshua could walk away from him.

Within moments, he was left alone in the Grand Chamber, staring once again at a myriad of choices. "Which way today," thought Joshua, "up or down, sky or ground," he quietly rhymed to himself.

"Energy up." Joshua heard this in his left ear, and so he swung around to the left to see who had spoken, but no one was there.

"It does seem like good advice, when you're feeling down you should lift yourself up," he said again to himself.

"To the left." Joshua heard this in his right ear this time. He still could not identify who was providing these instructions, but in the absence of any better direction, he wandered over to the passageways on his left.

"Good Job!"

He looked at the signs on the first three passageways, until he spotted one with the image of a steaming cup of tea on it. "Cuppa Char," he mouthed.

"Up you go!"

"Who are you?" There was no answer this time, but Joshua instinctively felt that this was indeed the direction that he should take today. He stepped into the passageway, and made his way up into the branches of the Midas Tree once again.

This time the tunnel felt humid and steamy, almost tropical. He had to remove his shirt and tie it around his head, to stop the beads of sweat that were forming on his brow from dripping down into his eyes.

The further he went, the hotter it became, and yet it wasn't uncomfortable. If anything, it felt very healing, as if he was expelling unwanted energies through the pores of his body.

He still had a strong intuition that this was the right thing to do, so he kept on going.

Eventually he reached a transparent door. He could not see through it, because there was so much steam on the other side and it was clouded up. He pushed the door open, went inside, and took a nice deep breath of the humid air.

"Turkish Delight?"

"Pardon?" It was the same voice he had heard earlier.

"I said, would you like a Turkish Delight with your tea?"

Joshua wafted the clouds of steam to disperse them, and he continued walking further into this steamy chamber. Eventually he identified the source of the steam as a huge open cauldron in the center of the room. It was filled with boiling liquid, and a mixture of leaves and other plant parts.

"Is there a window we can open?" Joshua shouted, still not sure of who he was sharing the room with.

"Oh, would you like me to put the fan on?"

"Yes please!"

"Absolutely, hold on just a moment..."

Joshua heard a click, and then a thrumming and a throbbing, and within a few minutes the air started to clear. He coughed, and in the absence of anything else to do, picked up the huge stirring stick that was in the cauldron and began to stir the pot.

"They were all picked by the light of the moon," the voice once again broke the silence.

"Pardon me?" Joshua had trouble hearing above the thrum of the fan.

"The leaves and herbs were all picked by the light of the full moon. It is the most potent time to harvest them, if you want their medicinal properties to be maximized."

"Oh, I see," said Joshua.

"Try some." A beautiful goddess-like Deva emerged from the mist, wearing harem pants and holding a golden chalice in her hand, arm outstretched towards him. "You will find a ladle hanging there on the side."

Joshua reached down and picked up the ladle. Mesmerized, he dipped it into the cauldron and poured a ladle full into the golden cup."

"I recognize you," he said to his companion. "Weren't you the Deva that sent me off to the spider's lair? What was your name again?"

"Yes, that's right. My name is Devi. I am the Deva of the goddess energy, of the Yin, and of the moonlight. I keep the knowledge of the healing properties of all the herbs, fruits, and seeds that are found in the canopy of the Tree. Also those of the barks and roots that can be found in the depths of the Midas Tree."

"I sensed that you were in need of a healing draft to cure your toothache, and so I led you here, right to the source of what might help you."

"I know, I heard you," said Joshua, "but how did you know I had toothache, and how could I hear you when you were so far away?"

"I was communicating with you as spirit."

"Oh, I see, Devalicious taught me to speak to the bee spirits. Is that the same thing? You saw my light, and talked to me from your light?"

"That is a great way to communicate Joshua, but this is not precisely how I was communicating with you today."

"But how then?" asked Joshua.

"I was projecting my thoughts directly at you and you were receiving my communication using your clear hearing. This is a spiritual ability to hear beings without bodies, including your spirit guides. You can also use it to communicate with friends over long distances. It allows for communication without the limits imposed by time and space. This is how we were communicating when you heard my voice in your ear, even though I was not close by."

"My friend Araneus doesn't have a body any more, and I can still talk to him."

"Yes, and so when you hear his words, you are hearing them as spirit and not with your physical ears."

"What about Bertie the bat with his sonar?" he asked.

"There is another spiritual ability that we can use to communicate over long distances that does not require language. This ability is called telepathy, and is more akin to Bertie's sonar."

"Oh, now that you mention it, I do remember Devalicious talking with her crystalline Devas using telepathy," said Joshua, who was starting to sort out all things in his head a bit better.

"Precisely so, Joshua. Now drink your tea. It will cure your toothache, I promise you."

"What's in it?"

"There are some cloves for the pain. Then there is Echinacea for your immune system, yarrow for the inflammation and to prevent infection, and a little valerian and chamomile to calm you down. Plus a few other herbs that grow only in the Midas Tree."

She sounded like she knew what she was talking about. Joshua gingerly sipped his tea. It was so hot that it burned his lips, but he blew on it to cool it down. Soon enough it was cool enough to drink properly.

In between sips he asked Devi, "Why did you send me to the spider's lair, when you must have known how difficult it would be for me to find my way back? Especially as I had barely learned to ground and center at that time?"

Devi laughed a tinkling laugh, "Why, Joshua I always like a good challenge. Don't you?"

As she spoke, the fog in the room had started to reform in misty, swirly clouds around them, and Devi was becoming fainter, and more difficult to see.

"Yes, but it's much nicer when I have a Deva to teach me. What can you teach me, Devi? Will you be able to teach me about the healing herbs of the Midas Tree?"

Devi let out a tinkling laugh again. "Oh Joshua, I will provide you with the opportunity to learn much more than that..." Her voice faded away as she spoke, and by the time she had finished her sentence, Joshua could neither hear nor see her any more.

"Devi, Devi! Where are you?" Joshua was still holding the chalice in one hand, and with his free hand he reached out all around him, but felt nothing.

"Devi, can you please put the fan on again? I can't see anything! Please help me, Devi, Devi..." When Devi did not respond, Joshua bent down and placed the chalice on the floor so both hands were free. He stood up and felt around in the dark, both arms flailing around in the mists.

He took a couple of steps and felt the heat of the cauldron. He didn't want to get burned, and so he turned around and walked slowly and carefully in the opposite direction. He reasoned that he should eventually reach the chamber wall, and then would be able to feel along the wall around to the door, and let himself out. However, it seemed no matter how many steps he took, he was still in empty space.

He turned around a few times and tried different directions, but he did not bump into any objects, and he became extremely disoriented. He began to wonder about Devi.

Both encounters he'd had with her had led to unfortunate circumstances. He wondered if she really was a Deva, or some trickster spirit trying to lead him astray.

Oh well, he had beaten the challenge of the spider's lair, and so he determined he could get himself out of this befuddlement too. He sat down on the floor, as this seemed the only solid surface he was able to make contact with. He took some deep breaths in and out, although the steam made him cough a bit. He started to meditate, using all the techniques he knew.

"Joshua, Joshua," he heard Devi's faint voice once again.

"Devi, where are you? Turn on the fan, Devi, so that I can see you."

"I'm over here Joshua, come over and join me. I think the fan is broken, so follow my voice?"

Joshua stood up and walked towards the sound, "Keep talking Devi, so that I can get myself oriented."

"Keep walking, over here," she replied. "I'll sing for you so you can follow my voice."

Devi had a beautiful singing voice. It was quite entrancing, light, high pitched and almost tinkling, like her laugh had been.

Joshua followed the sound, yet it never seemed to get any louder, and he didn't seem to be getting any closer.

"Are you moving, Devi?" he asked. He was starting to get annoyed, and he really didn't trust her.

She laughed her tinkling laugh. "Over here, Joshua, just a little further," and then she continued singing.

As he didn't feel he had much choice, Joshua continued walking towards the sound. He trod as carefully as he could, as he still could not see what was in front of him.

Suddenly he hit a new surface that was no longer horizontal, but downward sloping. It was slippery and wet, and caused both feet to slide from under him. He fell backwards, and hit his back and his head on the hard slippery surface.

Within seconds, he was hurtling downwards at breakneck speed, with the fog and Devi's laugh fading into the distance, until he could see and hear them no more. This scary fun fair ride seemed to go on for an inordinately long length of time, but at least he could see where he was going again. His surroundings had taken on an almost surreal quality.

The walls and floor of this slide-like tunnel were highly polished wood, and they seemed to be coated in a very oily, slippery substance. The walls were so smooth there was nothing to hold on to. The slope was so steep that it was impossible to stop, and so Joshua had no choice but to keep on sliding.

After what felt like forever, Joshua was spat out from the end of a chute into a new chamber. He was conscious just long enough to realize that he was back in the root system of the Midas Tree, before he hit the hard ground with the back of his head and was knocked unconscious.

Chapter 14

The Masks We Wear

oshua woke up with a thumping headache. He was lying on his back. He groaned, and then propped himself up on one hand, and rubbed the back of his head with the other. Oh well, at least he could not feel his throbbing tooth anymore. He reached to feel his chin, and to his surprise, what he felt was a hard piece of wood stuck to his face.

"Huh?" Joshua sat up and felt his face with both hands this time. It was as though he was wearing a wooden mask. "What the..." He tugged at the bottom of the mask on either side of his jaw to see if he could remove it, but he could not pull it off.

He tugged at the top and at the sides of the mask, also to no avail. How bizarre! Who could have placed this mask on my face while I was unconscious? At least this meant that there was someone else down here with him.

He looked around the room that he found himself in. It was quite small, and all around him on the walls were hundreds of wooden masks. He stood up and walked closer, so that he could examine them in more depth.

Each wore a unique expression, and they were all shapes and sizes too. Some looked angry, others looked sad, and they all made him feel uncomfortable. Some had a supernatural quality about them, and these were the most scary and frightening of all.

As he explored the walls, he noticed one empty space where a mask had been. This must be the mask that he was now wearing.

"Devi, Devi. Are you here?" he called, and in return he heard laughter, but not Devi's tinkling laugh. No. It was a much deeper laugh, with a jeering quality to it, and it sounded like it was coming from an adjoining chamber just behind him.

He timidly walked over to the open door and peered inside. It opened up into a large, office-like root chamber. There were many little ant-like creatures inside, all working at desks, and all wearing masks. They mostly appeared to be fighting and arguing with each other. Or they were shouting down hollowed out roots to yet more creatures, which Joshua imagined were listening at the other end of the pipe. Even the ones who were not engaged in discussions looked serious and miserable, and did not appear friendly at all.

One of the creatures walked over to Joshua and shook his hand. "Welcome, welcome my dear chap. You must be the new clerk? Well done, it's not easy to get a job here you know." He patted Joshua on the back as he congratulated him. "It's very competitive, we get hundreds of applications for every job, and we only employ the best. So you must have impressed the management," he looked Joshua up and down as he said this.

"Is that what you're wearing?"

Joshua looked down at his Midas Tree tunic, pants and sandals, "Err yes…"

"We prefer you to be in business casual. It gives the best impression to the clients, and impresses the management no end. They can imagine you as one of them then, you see." Joshua's companion looked down and ran his hand over his own suit as he said this. "This suit is made from the finest silk that silk worms have to offer, and sourced from the best part of the tree. I got it at a steal, from a pal of mine who works there. No one else in the department has a suit as high quality as this, and if they did they couldn't carry it off anyway," he sniffed.

"Now you're starting at the bottom, but you know what they say, a foot in the door and all that." He led Joshua across the room, "Ahhh, here we are. Here's your desk."

"Thank you, my name's Joshua, and you are?"

"Employee 56789."

"Oh, hello, 56789, pleased to meet you."

"No, *you* are Employee Number 56789, and I'm one hundred and twenty five."

"Well, you don't look it …."

No, I am Employee Number 125, and you are Employee Number 56789. We don't use names here, except for the management team, and we call them by their surnames. You know, as a sign of respect for their authority and position."

"I should be management soon, and then you will be able to call me Mr. Entwistle, but until then it's 125 to you, and everyone else in here."

"Ah," said Joshua, "well my name is Joshua. Actually, I didn't apply for a job here. So you can still call me Joshua, and if you'll tell me how to get out of here, I'll be on my merry way."

"Get out of here? Get out of here? You'll be lucky if you see the other side of 65, they work you so hard. Or do you think you're management material? Think you're going retire early with your stock options, do you? Keep on dreaming, 56789!"

"You don't seem to understand," said Joshua. "I drank a potion in a misty room, served by a beautiful yet mysterious Deva. It completely disoriented me; so much so that I fell down a chute and accidentally ended up down here. I banged my head when I landed, and lost consciousness for a while. I don't want to be here, and I'd like you to tell me how to get out."

The creature looked straight at him. One of the eyebrows on his mask appeared ever so slightly raised in sneering disbelief. "Look, I don't want to be here either, but we all have to earn a crust. We've all got bills to pay. We've all got families to look after. We have annual vacations to pay for, and neighbors to keep up with. Making up crazy stories to get off work on sick leave just won't fly, especially on your first day. Look, get your head down, do your work and I promise it will seem like the day flies by. Sit down here and read through those papers. Your supervisor will be along shortly. I've got things to do," and with that he walked away.

Joshua sat down and looked at the stack of papers on his desk. He picked the top one up and read it over. It seemed to be an invoice for items purchased by Employee Number 3879 over the last month. It also included the taxes levied against this employee, and then offset against his income, with a balance being due by the employee to the company.

He looked at the next few papers and saw that they were all quite similar, but that each pertained to a different employee number. He looked across at the creature working at the desk next to him. The sign on his desk read Employee Number 56788.

"Hello," said Joshua, "you must be new too. Do you know what we are meant to be doing?"

The little ant creature looked across at Joshua, "Accounts receivable," he said.

"Thank you, and do you know exactly what we are supposed to be doing with the accounts receivable?" he enquired.

"Receiving them."

"I gathered that, but how do we go about that? Are there any guidelines that we should follow?"

"Make them feel ashamed of themselves."

"Excuse me. Make them feel ashamed of themselves?"

"Yes, for not paying on time, and then if that doesn't work, make them feel afraid."

"Really, but these people all seem to be employees of the company?'

"That's right."

"...and they all seem to owe the company more money than they earned."

"...and your point is?"

"Well, doesn't that strike you a little bit odd?"

"Why?"

"I don't know, but, well, what is it that this company does? What does it do, that they all spend all their money here?"

"It does everything."

"Huh?"

"It does everything, caters to your every need, and provides you with everything necessary to live."

"So what kinds of things does it make? For example, what is Item Number 565 or Item Number 729?"

"Battery powered toothbrush with multiple attachments for all those household jobs you've been putting off, and a root phone with a pop up communication screen and sensors embedded in the handle for monitoring 23 vital signs as you hold it in your hand. Oh, yes, plus monthly three-year subscription to the magazine of your choice. Crib sheets in the file in your top drawer."

Joshua reached into the drawer and pulled out a thick file. There were thousands of products listed in there, and most of them seemed completely unnecessary.

Yet he looked at his thick stack of accounts receivable, and could see that most of the customers had purchased multiple items. Many of them even seemed to be purchasing different versions of the same things, over and over again.

"Why do people buy these things?" he asked 56788.

"Ask 34297 over there," he nodded towards another creature sitting on Joshua's other side.

Joshua stood up and wandered over with his file.

"Excuse me, hello. I'm Employee Number 56789, and I've just started in Accounts Receivable, and I wondered if you could help me understand something?"

"What is it you want to know?" snapped 34297.

"Why do people buy all these things in this catalogue, and why do they keep buying multiple versions of the same thing?"

"Because we're good at what we do," he snapped again.

"What is it you do, exactly?"

"Sales and Marketing..."

"And once again, why do people buy all these things that they can't afford?"

"Because we make them feel lesser than."

"Lesser than whom?"

"We tell them they are lesser than their neighbors, their bosses, and everyone else, of course. We tell them these people have a lot more than they do. We make them feel they need these things to be successful. We make them believe that in order to be somebody, they need to have the latest version of everything. If that doesn't work, we make them feel afraid. Afraid they will lose their job if they don't appear to be successful, and then that will be worse, because then they won't be able to pay for the things they already bought."

"But what if they already can't afford to buy these things?"

"Then we send them over to Advances and Loans," 34297 nodded his head in the direction of another section. Joshua thanked him, and wandered over there. He stopped by the desk of a creature, wearing an angry-looking mask. The creature was rubber-stamping application forms. Joshua politely asked him to explain what he was doing.

"Who are you, coming here disturbing my work?"

"Josh..., Employee Number 56789."

"Oh, another new boy, humph."

"Yes, and I'm just trying to learn the ropes, learn everything I can about the company, you know, so I can do a good job."

"Humph, it's a bit early to be getting ideas above your station, isn't it? Just do your job, earn your money, and go home." The frown in his mask seemed to deepen, then having thought about it he added, "do come see me if you need an advance on your paycheck. We only charge 15% interest... per month." As he finished, the ends of the lips on his mask seemed to curl ever so slightly into a smile.

Joshua moved over to the next desk, where a female ant in a frightened-faced mask was sitting with another stack of application forms.

"Oh, hello. I don't know whether you overheard our conversation, but could you help me out at all?" Joshua asked most politely.

Her eyes looked out timidly from behind her mask. "We help finance people for the purchases they need to make, so they can remain within their current socio-economic group."

"But how does that make sense, if they can't afford it, and if you are increasing their debts even further?"

A flicker of understanding shot across her eyes and she lowered her voice. "This is the world we live in. Everyone wants to be somebody, and the only way others believe you are someone is if you have the best of everything. For most of us, the only way to do this is by borrowing money. You see, no sooner have you bought the latest gadget, then they bring out another version with added benefits that we simply must have. Then the race is on to be the first to get it. My husband Anthony is up for a promotion, and so he insists we make a good impression. That's why I'm working three shifts round the clock: one here, another on the production line, and a third one taking minutes for the executive meetings."

"Although I must admit it is starting to get to me. I had heart palpitations last week, and so my doctor put me on these pills." She showed Joshua the pill bottle. "They're very expensive. My husband was quite annoyed really." She looked away and then added, "Of course we are very happy. Perfect relationship our friends always say, beautiful well-behaved children, perfect grades in school, great careers here at OmniTree ahead of them." She went back to work as though she thought she'd said too much.

Joshua arrived back at his desk to find a rather short, rather irritating little ant wearing an impatient mask, and tapping on his 3-D communication device while waiting for him. "This is not a good start to your career. I have been waiting a full three minutes. That is time that could have been spent making calls, and raking in money."

"But I was introducing myself to the staff, and finding out how all the departments work," said Joshua.

"Oh for goodness sake! Not another one with ideas above his station. Look, it's the job of management to understand how it all fits together. It's our job to collect the payments from our customers."

"I'm your supervisor, so you'd better pay attention to what I say. Get your head down, do your job, don't stir the pot. In a few years or so, maybe, if you are lucky, you will get a promotion from trainee to junior collector. I'm not making any promises, mind."

Joshua sighed. Until he worked out how he was going to get out of this predicament, he decided that he'd better play along. "Great. Perhaps you can explain the ropes to me."

"Right Oh. You must go through each of these sheets, one by one, and contact the customer to remind them that they need to pay their bill. There is a crib sheet in your drawer, with a script for you to follow when you call them. Once you make contact, you must make a date entry in the master list, with a note about the result of the call. At the end of the day, you send your files to data entry, to be recorded in the filing system overnight."

"I see," said Joshua, "and how do I contact the customer, and then how do they make a payment to us?"

"By Morfar, I can see you are going to be a lot of extra work for me. You contact the customers using the root phone. Here..."

Joshua's supervisor handed him the end of a hollowed out root that was sitting on his desk. "Blow down it to clear the channels, and then tap the client employee number on the outside using your fingers. One tap for one, two taps for two and so on, pause in between numbers."

Joshua held the root phone in his hands gingerly, while the supervisor continued, "They can make an automatic transfer from their acorn account to ours through the root phone, or they can drop it off at the office here. If it comes in through the root phone, you tip the acorns into this basket on the floor here."

Joshua looked down at his feet, where there was a woven basket, half-full of acorns.

"Once your call is registered on the master database, accounting will know to check for the incoming payment. If it doesn't arrive within a week, we will issue another invoice, and you should place another call. Works like clockwork. Well, what are you waiting for? If you collect more than fifty payments a day, there's a nice little bonus in your pay packet for you."

Joshua pulled out the crib sheet and read it over. Then he tapped the first number at the top of the first sheet on his desk. "Hello, may I speak with Mrs. Antimony please?"

"Who wants to know?"

"This is the customer service department from OmniTree. This is a courtesy call; may I please speak with Mrs. Antimony?"

"This is her husband speaking. She's not here, she's at work," and he slammed the root phone down.

Joshua reviewed the sheet of paper, and noticed that there was another number, and so he decided to try that one next. As he tapped, he caught the eye of the lady he was speaking with earlier. Oddly, she picked up her root phone just as he heard his call being picked up.

"Hello OmniTree, Advances and Loans Department, Employee Number 27954 speaking," said a polite voice.

"Hello, may I speak with Mrs. Antimony please?"

The tone changed and became quieter, more defensive, and wary. "This is she, how may I help you? Look I'm at work, I can't speak for long."

Joshua cleared his throat, "Mrs. Antimony, are you aware that your account with OmniTree is overdue? Our records show that you owe eight thousand acorns plus taxes and interest. How would you like to pay?"

Silence...

"Mrs. Antimony, how do you propose to pay for your debt?"

More silence, then subdued weeping.

Joshua continued reading from his script, "Mrs. Antimony, you must pay your debt, on threat of possession of your assets and a court case."

Sobbing...

Joshua looked across at the creature he had been talking to in loans. She was still holding the root phone, and although he could not see behind the mask, he could tell by her demeanor, and by the fact that her shoulders were shaking, that she was the person he was talking with.

He looked down at his script. His next words were to be, "Mrs. Antimony, you have 5 minutes to consider this further, or we will send the debt collection team to your house."

"This isn't right," he muttered under his breath. "This place is nuts," and he got up from his seat and walked back over to Mrs. Antimony.

"Mrs. Antimony?"

She looked up at him through the holes in her mask, "employee 23654," she corrected him softly.

"Mrs. Antimony, I'm Joshua and I was just talking with you on the root phone."

Whimper...

"I was just thinking about our conversation earlier. Maybe you don't need all of these items you bought from OmniTree?" He waved the invoice that was still in his hand.

She looked at him from behind her mask. "That's true. Half the products we bought last month haven't even been taken from their packages yet."

"Yes, and I'm sure the older versions of things work just as well as the newer ones. Perhaps you could sell the newer versions to some of your colleagues, at a lower price than they can get them at OmniTree. You could make some acorns before the bailiffs come round."

"That would be fantastic, but my husband will never agree to it."

"Why not? If he hasn't used these things so far, they can't be all that essential to his life."

"I guess not, but with him it's all about appearances. It's about having the latest gadgets, so that he can appear to be on the top of his game. So other people will look up to him, and think he is somebody. His promotion depends on it, and we need the extra acorns to pay for the medical bills."

Joshua sighed, "Mrs. Antimony, this doesn't make sense to me. If you didn't buy so many things, you would need fewer acorns, and then you wouldn't have to work as hard. If you didn't have to work as hard, then you would not be so stressed, and could probably come off your medication."

Mrs. Antimony sat up in her chair and looked Joshua square in the eyes. "I do see your point! You know, I am sick and tired of how things are in this place." She pulled her designer handbag out from her drawer and stood up. "Come on, let's go. It's almost time for my shift to end anyway." She grabbed Joshua by the collar of his tunic, and dragged him along behind her. "By the way, call me Anthea."

They walked along the root system, past a myriad of ant chambers. As they walked, they talked, and soon enough they had hatched a plan between them to have a yard sale. They would sell all the excess goods that Anthea and her husband had purchased. When they reached the place that Anthea called home, she ushered Joshua inside, and showed him piles of unopened boxes.

"Take these out front and line them up by the side of the passage. My husband is at work now, but let's be as swift as we can, and get through this before he gets home."

While Joshua was doing this, she found a piece of bark and wrote a big 'Sale' sign, which she planted on a post next to the goods. The she wrote another one that said 'Prices Slashed!'

Then she and Joshua sat on a couple of deck chairs, and waited for the rush hour commuters to pass by, on their way home from work.

Pretty soon, the swelling crowd of commuters appeared at the end of the passage. Anthea and Joshua stood up and started shouting. "Come and get it. Cut price goods. Brand new, never used, straight from OmniTree to you..."

The first few commuters looked, and then quickly looked away as though this were something illicit, but eventually the first curious ant did stop to look more closely. At first, he was quite shifty. He avoided their gaze, and just looked down at the objects before him. He picked up a clock and played around with it a while. Then out of the corner of his mouth he whispered, "How much for the clock?"

"Let me see," said Anthea. "We bought it for 18 acorns two months ago, and as you can see it is brand new, never been used, not even once. It's the highest quality of course, we never accept anything less than that, and it's the latest model with all the bells and whistles. I'll take 15 acorns."

"I'll give you 10."

"I couldn't possibly go as low as that. My husband would be most irate."

"11 then..."

"14."

"12."

"14."

"Oh alright then, I'll give you 13, but that's my highest offer."

"I'll take it!" chirped the delighted Anthea Antimony.

As soon as they made the exchange, the shifty ant stuffed the clock under his raincoat, and rushed back into the crowd. Joshua shoved the acorns into an acorn sack.

By now, another three curious ants had gathered, and were poking around in the piles of goods.

"How much is this?" said one of them, pointing to a self-cleaning toaster oven with a detachable nut grinder and vegetable chopper.

"That'll be 30 acorns," said Anthea.

"I'll give you 35," said a fourth ant who was peering over the shoulder of the ant holding the toaster.

"37," said the original ant.

"38."

"39."

"40."

"Sold!" exclaimed Anthea, who knew full well she had only paid 32 acorns for it.

The purchasing ant seemed happy enough, and the one who didn't get the toaster was readily distracted by a multi-attachment vacuum cleaner, made from roots and basket weave.

Soon there was a crowd of ants gathered all around them, pushing and shoving to get a look in. In no time at all the yard was cleared, and Joshua and Anthea were dragging sacks and sacks of acorns back into the house.

Once inside, Anthea jumped up and down for joy. "I feel so free," she chirped, "so free from my cares, so free from obligations. There must be enough acorns here to pay off all our debts, and pay off the medical bills with change left over."

As she jumped, her mask began sliding up and down on her face, until it crashed down to the floor. "Oh my goodness, what has happened?"

Joshua looked at Anthea. She had such a pretty face when all the fear and worry had been lifted off.

Just then, before he had the chance to say anything to her, the front door opened and her husband Anthony Antimony walked into the room.

He looked at his wife and appeared stunned. Then he looked down at the sacks of acorns and appeared in shock. Then back at his wife, then the acorns again, and finally Joshua.

"Who are you, where did all these acorns come from, and what have you done to my wife?"

"I'm Joshua, and I have been helping your wife to sell all your unnecessary items so that you can pay your bills."

"You did what!" Mr. Antimony shouted at Joshua. "We need those things. We need them to get ahead. I need them so I can get my promotion. You have just ruined our chances completely!" He stood up to his full height, and started to take a swing at Joshua.

"Anthony, No!" screamed Anthea.

"Joshua works for collections, and he was only trying to do his job. If we had not done this, then it would all have been taken away, and we would have nothing for it. I take full responsibility for this decision. I take responsibility for my part in creating this mess, and now for getting us out of it. There is enough money here for us to pay all our debts. Don't you see? That stuff is not empowering to us. It's actually the opposite. This is our chance to take back control of our lives. We don't need all of that stuff. We don't even use most of it, and who needs a promotion if it promotes more misery?"

Mr. Antimony was looking at his wife, still in shock. "What have you done to your face? I told you we could not afford a new mask until after the promotion, when you'll need it to mix with the other executive wives."

"This isn't a mask, Ant. This is me. This is the real me. No more hiding behind mediocrity and expectations. No more keeping up appearances. This is plain old Anthea Antimony. And you know what? I'm handing in notice at all my jobs. I'm going to set up a business, recycling all the old products. We can sell them, or lease them, or barter them with those who can't afford new, or who have had their possessions repossessed."

Anthony Antimony collapsed back into a chair, head in his hands, defeated. His wife walked over and rubbed his back. "Come on, Ant. Where's the ant I first married? We didn't need anything except each other back in those days."

As she spoke, Ant rubbed his face, and then an amazing thing happened. His mask just came off in his hands, and he looked up at his wife and started to cry.

"Shhh, everything will be alright," she comforted.

Joshua was beginning to feel too much like a third wheel.

"Anthea," he whispered, "I am so glad I could help you, but I'd best be going now."

"You'll do no such thing. You'll stay for supper, and meet the children."

Joshua realized how exhausted he was feeling, and also that he had no home down here in this place. He had no idea how to get back to his chamber in the center of the tree, so he reluctantly accepted.

After a lovely supper with the Antimony family, he found himself relaxing on a makeshift bed in the living room. His mask was still firmly attached to his face, and he was still trying to pull it off. He could not understand what it was that had allowed Anthea and Anthony to let go of their masks. Hadn't he been equally instrumental in helping them sell their excess products, and change their lives for the better? Hadn't he given his all to help heal them and their situation? Wasn't he the real hero of the day? So why then was he still wearing his mask?

Chapter 15

Balancing the Flow

oshua woke up in the middle of the night, in the dark, in the center of what he assumed was still the Antimony's living room.

On closer inspection, it seemed very different from before. Over by the far wall was a large wooden bowl, surrounded by a faint glow so that it stood out in the darkened room. Joshua was certain that this bowl had not been here when he first arrived, so he walked over, curious to see what this was all about.

Big droplets of water were dripping from the ceiling into the bowl. As fast as they could enter, they were dripping out through a hole in the bottom of the bowl, leaving the bowl empty and creating a muddy pool below. Oh no! The ant's living room was getting soaked.

Curious, Joshua reached under and plugged the hole with his finger, and the bowl started to fill up. As soon as he took his finger away, the water poured out of the bowl.

He walked around the bowl and noticed that there was an inscription written in runes, similar to what he had seen on the signposts in the Midas Tree. Somehow, this seemed more complex. That is just great, thought Joshua, I have no idea what this means. But he imagined it was one of his lessons, and that the message was some sort of instruction that might tell him how to get out of here, and back to the Grand Chamber.

He was quite thirsty, and he wondered if the water was potable. He caught a few drops in the palm of his hand and tasted them. It seemed fine to him. In fact, the water seemed to have a strange crystalline quality, and once he had tasted it he felt rejuvenated, and he had to have more.

The bowl was very deep, and so once again he plugged the base with a finger, so that it would fill enough that he could lean in and reach the surface of the water with his lips.

However, as soon as the water reached the half-way point, it started to spurt out through numerous small holes that had been drilled higher up in the walls of the bowl. To Joshua's amazement, as this happened, a bunch of funny little creatures that looked like chipmunks appeared from out of the ground where the water was falling. With open mouths, they gulped up the water as it streamed out.

Joshua took his finger away so that the water dripped out of the bottom, and the little creatures disappeared as if they had been absorbed back into the ground.

"Hey, come back, I want to talk to you. Hey little creatures, come back. I want to know what this is, and how to get out of here."

They didn't return, and so he decided to plug the hole again and see if they would come back once the water spouted again. Indeed this was the case. As soon as the streams of water returned, so did the creatures. Joshua tried to engage them in a conversation, but they were so busy gulping down the water, they would not stop to talk to him.

Eventually he reached out with a spare hand and tried to grab one of them. It was a cunning little devil, and easily managed to duck and dive out of his way. He momentarily caught one of them by the tail, but it turned and bit him so hard that he instantly let go.

He decided that he needed both hands to catch these creatures. The trouble was, no sooner did he remove his finger from the hole, then the water spouts stopped. Then the creatures disappeared again. All this while, he hadn't managed to get a drink himself.

Eventually, after five or six tries of diving into the wet mud, he managed to grab one of the little pests. He held onto it for dear life, while it squealed and squirmed and bit into his flesh. Joshua wasn't letting go this time.

"Tell me who you are!" he demanded. The creature just squealed louder, and squirmed harder.

"Who are you, what is this place, and how can I get out of here?" Eventually after what felt like an hour of tiring struggle, the creature settled down, obviously realizing that struggling was not resulting in its release.

"We are the poor little creatures livin' in the mud at the bottom of the tree."

"What does that mean – *'poor little creatures living in the mud'?*" Joshua was losing his patience.

"We are poor little creatures, who rely on the charity of good people like you, Sir, to provide sustenance through the waters of life, Sir."

"What do you mean, sustenance through the waters of life?"

"You see that bowl, Sir? The water what it captures is what keeps us alive, Sir. Wivout it, we are reduced to dust. It's an 'ard life, full of trials and tribulations, we live in 'ope that someone such as yer-self, Sir, will come an' 'elp us, give us a drink from the fountain of life so we can be rejuvenated, innit?"

The creature paused." I beg ya Sir, block the 'ole again, so me and me bruvvers can have a good guzzle?"

"Why don't you drink from the hole in the bottom?"

"Couldn't do that, Sir, there's too many of us to share, innit? If we have to do that then we get in a fight. Ooh an yer don't wanna see that, Sir, ew it's an 'orrible sight to be'old."

"Have you ever thought of taking turns?"

"Well we did try that, but them lots a greedy bunch, always taking liberties wiv it, always taking longer than they should, and that just gets the rest of us real mad."

"I'm quite thirsty too, you know. How about you all take a break, and let me take a turn?"

"Oh no, Sir. I couldn't do that, Sir. It's the rules, innit?"

"Yes, but I am helping you by plugging the hole in the first place. If I wasn't here doing that for you, you wouldn't be able to have a drink anyway. So why not do us all a favor and give it a rest, so that I can fill the bowl up enough to take a drink myself?"

"The best I can do, Sir, is take your request to me bruvvers an' see what they 'av' to say about it, innit? So you just let me go, an' I'll see about your request."

Joshua let the creature go, and it instantly disappeared into the ground again. I could just lie under the bowl and let the water drip into my mouth that way, he thought. But under the bowl was a slimy, slippery pool of mud, and he was not about to get even more dirty.

He waited and he waited, and nothing happened. Then he realized that perhaps he would have to plug the bowl again, before the creatures could come back. So once again he placed his finger over the hole, and soon enough the screaming, squirming creatures were back, all guzzling the water. What was worse, he couldn't tell one from the other, so he didn't know which one he had been talking with earlier.

"Hello, poor little creatures living in the mud. Will you please cease your activities and allow me to have a drink from the bowl?" asked Joshua loudly.

None of them stopped what they were doing until he removed his finger, and then they instantly disappeared. He tried a couple more times, and then sat down in the dirt dejectedly. This was very frustrating, and he was beginning to feel exhausted. The thought of another battle to catch one of the little fellows was almost too much to bear. So reluctantly he took to lying underneath the hole, in the mud, with his mouth open. This allowed the water to drip into his mouth. This was hardly the best solution, and although it really was refreshing and rejuvenating, he was starting to feel cold because his clothes were sopping wet.

He walked away from the bowl and sank dejectedly to the floor shivering. Perhaps, he thought, I should remove my clothes and try to find some way to hang them to dry. He took off his tunic and pants, and walked over to the dining room and threw them over the backs of a couple of chairs.

He was just about to do the same thing with his shirt, when he had a bright idea. He could stuff the hole using his tunic. Then he would have two hands free to catch one of the little creatures. He picked up his tunic and ran over to the bowl, but realized his tunic was filthy. If he placed it into the bowl, it would make the drinking water dirty. Plus the hole was not so big as to need an entire tunic to plug it up.

Joshua ripped a small square piece of fabric from the pocket on his tunic, and held it under the hole until he was convinced it was clean. Then he scrunched it up and stuffed it into the hole. As planned, the other holes started pouring water out, and the little creatures returned. This time grabbing hold of one of the little fellows was much easier.

"Gotcha," Joshua exclaimed.

"Woah, woah, woah, what on earth do you think you are doing? I have rights, you know, let go of me!"

"Are you the creature I was talking to before?"

"I don't know what you are talking about. Kindly release me!"

"I caught one of you creatures before, and he said that he would talk to you all about helping get me out of here."

"I don't know anything about that, I'm sure." Joshua could tell that this was a different creature, because its elocution was superior by far to the creature he had held previously.

"What do you know about?" asked Joshua. "For example, do you know what the inscription on the side of the bowl says?"

"Oh, well now, you've got the right man for that job. Right here, sitting captive in the palm of your hand," said the little creature. "I'm the most literary of the bunch. If I tell you what it means, will you release me from this enforced and cruel captivity?"

"Absolutely," agreed Joshua.

The creature cleared its throat, "Ahem."

Fill the bowl and drink its waters
It is then that you ought to
Feel replenished and renewed

Fill the bowl, but give too much
It is then you're out of touch
And quite frankly you are stewed

Fill the bowl to feed you first
Otherwise you'll be cursed
You must balance your giving

Fill the bowl to overflow
It is then that you will know
The joy of receiving is part of living

Share your bounty when it's right
Then the tree just might
Release you from this plight

Joshua thanked the little creature, and as he had promised he let him go.

The fabric plug was still working, and all the little creatures were guzzling away. Joshua sat and watched them, as he pondered on the poem he had just heard recited.

It seemed that the message was about balancing the flow of the waters. Replenishing and healing yourself first, and then giving to others from the overflow. He got it, he really did, but the funny little creatures were drinking so fast that the bowl didn't get the chance to fill up or overflow. Balancing the flow was out of his control, because these little creatures just kept on taking.

Joshua lifted his hands to his mask and tried to pull it off again, but to no avail. He wondered why not. The Antimony's physical masks had fallen off when they let go of their psychological masks - their concepts and beliefs about how they had to live their lives. Joshua wanted to know what his stuck concept was. Maybe it was related to his current predicament, he mused.

He thought about his latest adventures at OmniTree. He had been more interested in solving everyone else's problems than his own. He had spent his time at first by trying to do his job, and then by helping the Antimonys. By virtue of that, he had also started to change how their system functioned, because he enabled a different choice of how to live.

He could see that it was now time to help himself, but how was he going to make this work? Was it too much to expect that he could plug all of these holes? There were so many of them. Plus they were much tinier than the hole in the bottom of the bowl.

He reached through the swirling mass of creatures to take the handmade plug out, so they would once again disappear. He needed the time and space to think, and he needed to get out of here quickly, as by now he was really shivering.

As he pulled out the plug, he slipped on the mud and went crashing face down into the slime. His fingers dug into the cold slippery wetness, and as he pulled himself to his knees, his hands clawed around a thick dense ball of slippery earth.

"This is clay!" Joshua exclaimed to no one in particular. "I can use this to stop the water from being given away to the greedy little creatures, and then I can sustain myself first as the poem instructs."

He pulled a big glob of clay into his hand and started smearing it on the outside of the bowl, across the myriad of little holes. He pressed the clay, so that it filled the little tunnels. As it appeared through to the inside of the bowl, he smoothed it off and wiped it with his tunic, so that it wouldn't contaminate the waters.

When he reinserted the plug, immediately the bowl started to fill up without leaking water. The little creatures did not show up to siphon it off, and Joshua was able to take in huge gulps of the healing crystalline liquid, by burying his face and his mask in the bowl of water. As he drank, he felt rejuvenated and renewed. He felt full of life and love, and ready to take on the world.

Then all of a sudden, as he drank in the waters, and as he gave to himself, his mask fell from his face into the bottom of the bowl. He felt the cool water against his skin, and with great joy he scooped up handfuls and splashed them onto his face.

He felt like he was recovering from a trance, as if he had been in an alternate reality. Perhaps it had been caused by the potion that Devi had given him, or the knock on his head when he fell down the chute. Either way, the water in the bowl was reviving and refreshing him.

Once he had drunk enough, and splashed enough of the cool waters on his face, he felt recovered enough to think of the chipmunks again. Now that he was taken care of, he could just forget about them and get on with his task of finding a way out of here.

However, his heart was full of gratitude for the healing powers of the water, and for the fact that his face was now free of the mask. He wanted to do something to help them as well. He looked around the chamber he was in. There was a tangle of old roots lying in the corner of the room like rope.

"I wonder," thought Joshua. He wandered over, and picked out six that were fairly wide in diameter and very sturdy. He split each one in half, so that the root looked like an open channel. Then, using some more clay, he fashioned twelve little bowls and placed them on the floor in a circle around the font. Again using the clay, he fixed one end of each of the twelve channels to the lip of the font, and the other end to one of the bowls.

He watched as the water in the bowl became so full that it overflowed. As it did, instead of spilling over the edges, the water flowed down the channels he had constructed. He watched as the little bowls also became full, and then as they too began to overflow, a remarkable thing happened. The chipmunks once again emerged from the mud, but this time there was space for all of them to drink from their own bowl, without fighting and screaming and competing with one another.

Joshua watched them drinking with great joy, and he chuckled to himself as they drank.

"Well done!" a smooth, deep, melodious voice said behind him.

Joshua turned to see whom it had come from.

Standing behind him was another Deva, one who Joshua had seen across the dining table, but to whom he had not yet been introduced. This Deva was rather swashbuckling in appearance, with his moustache and goatee, his long hair, boots, belt and earrings.

"Greetings Joshua, my name is Devlin, and I am the Deva of all courageous acts that take place inside the Midas Tree. I am here to congratulate you on passing a particularly difficult lesson."

Devlin whistled, and a myriad of little gold-colored Devas appeared, each carrying a fleck of pure gold. They placed the specks of gold into Devlin's left palm. When they were all done, he closed his fist and passed his right hand over it. When he opened his hand again, he held a gold medal, and he reached over and placed it around Joshua's neck.

As he placed the medal Devlin pronounced, "I hereby award you, Joshua with the Golden Heart, one of the highest honors of the Midas Tree. This is in service to the tree in balancing the flow of energies in the heart, so that giving and receiving occur in harmony with each other. You have learned to operate from your heart and from your own information, regardless of what silly nonsense is going on around you. You have learned the biggest lesson that all healers must, which is to give to yourself first. Fill yourself up until you overflow, and then you have plenty left over to give to others.

The medal hung over Joshua's heart, and as it fell into place, Joshua felt his heart opening up and filling with golden love and light.

"Did you know that little creature left a verse off the end of the inscription in the bowl?"

"Really? What did it say?" asked Joshua.

Fill the bowl to feed the tree,

And the tree will sustain thee,

Love is the answer you see.

Devlin beckoned that Joshua follow him.

They left through a panel in the wall, and into another clear elevator tube.

Devlin punched in a code on a panel on the wall, the door closed, and they sped upwards at an extremely fast pace. The elevator opened into a small chamber about the same size as the one at the center of the tree. The chamber was brightly lit, and in the center was a column of solid gold that pulsated. It emanated a high-vibration, bright gold energy field.

As they stepped into the room Joshua felt a warm tingling sensation all over his body, and he felt an overwhelming sensation of love, like nothing he had experienced before.

"This is the heart of the Midas Tree," said Devlin, "and this is its heart wood," he said, reaching out a hand and touching the gold column.

"Through your good deeds, you have helped create an opening in the heart energy of the tree. Her vibration has increased, and this new higher vibration is now available to everyone who lives here. You have helped create the greatest opportunity of all time. All creatures in the Midas Tree can now learn to operate in balance and harmony, and from a place of love. Now let's go and celebrate, everyone is waiting to congratulate you."

"*Congratulations, for accompanying Joshua on his adventure. You have also been awarded The "Golden Heart." Go to* **www.themidastree.com/readers** *and collect your certificate.*"

Chapter 16

What Gall!

oshua woke up very early, his head still buzzing from the fabulous party that was thrown in his honor to celebrate the heart opening of the Midas Tree. He felt proud and happy, and his own heart was still bursting with joy.

Then he remembered his chat with Deverall and Devalicious during the party.

He had wanted to know if he was ready to go home to Morfar and the garden of color and light. He had asked them, "Now that both the tree and I have a heart of gold, is it time for me to leave?"

They had pulled him over to a quiet corner and explained. Now that he had learned his lessons and balanced his energies, he was free to choose to return to Morfar. However, he was at a pivotal juncture in his development because he was no longer an apprentice. Instead of leaving, he could choose to remain in the tree as a teacher. This would allow him to help other creatures learn and develop as he had done.

They had explained that this would be a great way to be of service to Morfar, because the brighter the souls in the Midas Tree, the more beautiful the garden of color and light became.

Joshua was torn. All he had wanted when he first entered the tree was to return to Morfar. Yet now, he was so very grateful to all the Devas and creatures of the tree for what they had taught him. It would be nice to be able to help them, as they had helped him.

He got himself up, washed, and dressed in the still cold light of dawn. Instead of going to the Grand Chamber for morning meditations, he made his way to the center of the tree. He needed some guidance and clarity, and this was the best place he knew of to get it.

As he arrived at the narrow gate, he paused for a moment on the threshold, as he heard some tinkling voices coming from inside the central chamber. One of the voices was familiar, but the other was not. He was concerned he might be headed for another encounter with Devi, and so he paused to ground and center himself before entering. At the same time, he was curious to identify the source of the new voice.

As he entered the chamber, he saw that one of the voices was indeed Devi, and she was currently seated in the saddle seat looking out into the garden. Standing beside her, with both hands placed on Devi's head, was a Deva he had never seen before. She was just as beautiful as Devi, but while Devi had long flaxen hair, this one had long, straight, jet black hair.

She turned her head towards Joshua, so that he could see her piercing blue eyes.

"Hello," he ventured. "I was just coming here to do some quiet meditation. I have an important decision to make, and wanted to seek guidance. Being here in the center is the best way I know how to do this, but I see it's occupied and so I'll come back later..." and he turned as if to leave.

"No, don't go, stay awhile. We can teach you many things, including how to keep the center clear for when you want to use it to make important decisions," the new Deva laughed a tinkling laugh not unlike Devi's. "We also know a lot about the balance between both sides of anything, also important to know when you are making decisions." Devi herself remained silent and motionless.

"Oh, well, I don't know about that," Joshua said. "You know I am no longer an apprentice here in the tree. I am a teacher now."

The new Deva burst out laughing, "Then how is it that you have forgotten that you can clear your head by sending your confusion down your grounding?" This time Devi could not contain herself, and broke her trance to join in her laughter.

"Oh, Joshua, you are so funny," said Devi. "Don't you know you never stop being a student for so long as you are in the Midas Tree? As long as you are here, you will continue learning and expanding yourself. That doesn't mean you can't assist others as well, but do not be so proud as to assume that there is nothing more to learn."

"Absolutely," said the dark-haired Deva. "I learn more now from my students than I do even from my teachers."

"How can that be possible?" asked Joshua.

"My dear Joshua, we are all one under the eyes of Morfar, and yet each of us is only a piece of the divine presence. In this way we are none of us perfect, and never can be. If you are not perfect, then there is always something new to learn," laughed Devi.

Joshua scratched his head. "OK...," he said, still feeling bewildered. He thought, how could they say I have graduated, and give me a medal and celebrate my achievements one moment, and the next moment humble me by telling me I am not so great after all?

As if she had read his mind, the dark-haired Deva gently put a hand on his shoulder and said, "I can see this is confusing for you, and we are not telling you that you are not great, but just think...

Wouldn't life be boring if there was not something new to learn about every once in a while?"

"I guess so," he ventured.

"By the way, my name is Devany. Devi and I come here together every so often; especially when the moon is full and bright, or at dusk or dawn. We like to meditate together, and help each other see the truth and heal ourselves. We especially like to keep a watch on our egos, because being as fabulous as we both are; it is very difficult not to get carried away by our own power and brightness." Devany laughed, as if she found what she had said rather amusing. You may join us, if you like."

"Sure I'd like that," said Joshua. He was still uncertain, but in spite of his reservations about Devi, he really liked Devany.

"What are you the Deva of, exactly?" he asked.

"I am the Deva of the night, whereas Devi is the moon goddess. We work together in partnership. Devi reflects the light of the sun into the darkness of the night, so that the un-manifest can receive the power to come into form, and so the hidden can be brought to the surface for examination and transformation."

"Really," said Joshua fascinated, yet feeling rather out of his depth, "and what are you doing now, exactly?"

"Ah, do you see how the sun and moon can both be viewed through the opening right now?" Devi leaned to one side as Devany spoke, so that Joshua could have a glimpse outside. As she had pointed out, the deep orange sun had just risen in the east and was filling the sky with a pale early morning light. Over to the right, also in the sky, was a pale white shadowy moon.

"Yes," said Joshua, leaning back and standing up so that Devi could straighten up again.

"In the daytime, the moon almost becomes invisible in the light of the sun. In the night time it is the brightest object in the sky, and the only place that reflects the light of the sun."

"Yes," said Joshua still not understanding the point of all this.

"Just because you can't see something, doesn't mean it isn't there, or isn't real."

"Or does it?"

"Huh?"

"Just because you do see something, doesn't mean it is there, or is real."

"Huh?"

"Or is it?"

The two Devas laughed in unison. Obviously, Joshua's confusion was quite hilarious to them.

"Joshua, take a seat here." Devi patted the seat as she stood up, and Joshua did as she asked and sat down on the wooden saddle, and peered out through the opening.

"Psst, pssst, don't let them know I'm here. Just blink to acknowledge me."

Mr. Woodpecker was perched precariously off to the side, and sideways on to Joshua.

Joshua blinked.

Devany continued. "Everything you see at its surface level is illusion, and everything you see is a projection that reflects both dark and light."

"Yes, that's right," added Devi. "Everything has two sides, night and day, light and dark, day and night, male and female, manifest and unmanifest. We need both polar opposites you see, to remain in balance."

"Yes," added Devany, "and when both sides are validated and honored, then there is harmony and balance; looking at the sun and moon together reminds us of this."

"Oh!" said Joshua. He hadn't heard anything they were saying, as he was squinting to get a better look at what Mr. Woodpecker was doing. Mr. Woodpecker had turned his back to Joshua, fanned out his tail feathers, and was wafting them up and down.

"We meditate on the sun, the moon, and stars and we ask for harmony and balance, as well as protection from the temptations of our egos."

"Fascinating..."

As Mr. Woodpecker fanned his tail up and down, Joshua kept getting a glimpse of a lump on the side of the tree trunk.

"Now, Joshua, we will leave you in peace for a while to contemplate our words. When you make your decision, remember there are two sides to everything here in the Midas Tree."

"OK... Bye..."

The two Devas squeezed out from the central chamber, and Joshua could hear their tinkling voices petering out in the distance.

"Hey Mr. Woodpecker, they have gone now. Why didn't you want them to see you?"

"First of all, they bore the tail off of me with their long explanations and their verbal meanderings, but secondly I didn't want them to spot this until we figure out what it is." He lifted up his tail so Joshua could see the lump a bit more clearly.

"What what is?"

"I'm not sure, but it has been growing bigger and bigger; I stabbed it with my beak, and it's got sticky, smelly, gluey stuff inside. Here, smell my beak!"

Mr. Woodpecker pushed his beak through the hole in the trunk.

"It's actually quite a nice smell, like pine needles," said Joshua.

"You think?"

"Hmm, but I wonder if it is a good or bad thing? It definitely wasn't there before."

"No, definitely not."

"Do you think you can reach into it from that side?"

"I don't know, maybe. It's probably very close to the side wall in here. This is a really small room. Do you have anything I can poke it with? I don't have a sharp beak like you do."

Mr. Woodpecker passed a stick with a pointed end through the hole to Joshua. "Here you are."

Joshua used the stick to poke around in the general area of the growth.

"No, it's pretty solid in here. Oh, hold on a minute. Ah no! That's not it... wait, yes, there is a small area that feels a bit softer."

Joshua placed the pointy end of the stick into the soft part, and turned the stick as though it were a drill bit, watching as it bored into the wood.

"How would you like it if I drilled a hole in your home?"

"What?" inquired Joshua.

"I didn't say anything," said Mr. Woodpecker. What's going on in there?"

"I don't know. I thought I heard someone speak to me."

"I hope it's not those two Devas again!"

"No, it wasn't their voices."

"Look! Take the stick out now, and I won't have to retaliate!"

"What?"

"Take the stick out now, and I won't have to retaliate!"

Joshua took the stick out, and a little sticky white grub with saliva dribbling from its mouth poked his head out of the hole.

"You won't have to retaliate? It is you who is hurting the tree!"

"What?" a spray of saliva issued forth from the bug's mouth as he spoke. Some of it landed on Joshua's cheek.

"You are hurting the tree," said Joshua. "By building your home in the tree, you are causing her to swell up in a big lump," he wiped and scratched his cheek.

"Now hold on a minute. I have just as much right to be here as you do. I'm not hurting anyone. I was minding my own business, until that great lump of a bird started interfering by poking its beak in."

"Mr. Woodpecker was concerned about the welfare of this tree, as I am," said Joshua, still scratching.

"Now settle down, as we have a few questions for you."

"Oooh hark at youuuuu!" Bubbles of spit exploded as the bug spoke.

'Where did you live before you came here?"

"Ohhhoooh, where did you live before you came here?"

Joshua pinched the bug around the head and pulled him out of the hole, keeping one hand free to continue his absent-minded scratching.

"Listen to me you meddling creature, where did you live before?"

"Nowhere. I was a twinkle in Morfar's eye; where did you live before you came here?"

"Why are you living in our tree?" Joshua was finding it increasingly uncomfortable to hold onto the bug, because now his fingers were feeling hot and itchy too.

"Where else should I live? Like I said, I have just as much right to be here as you do."

"Yes, but are you living in harmony with the tree? Or are you putting the tree out of balance? Why is she reacting to your presence in this way?"

"How should I know? Ask her?"

Joshua could stand the irritation on his check and fingers no more, and he threw the bug back at the hole in the wall. He watched it slither inside as he scratched his face and fingers for dear life.

"Told you I would retaliate," the bug spat more saliva back out of the hole. It then continued spitting inside the hole, and chewing merrily away at the bark that its saliva had landed on.

"What on earth is going on in there?" Mr. Woodpecker poked an eye in to look at Joshua.

"My Dear Chap, what on earth has happened to you? Your face is all swollen."

Joshua could feel his face expanding, and he looked down at his hand to see the fingers that he had held the bug with were also swelling.

"Joshua, oh dear, you are starting to look just like the swelling on the tree."

"That bug is a nasty piece of work. Its slime and saliva must be the irritant that has caused the tree to swell up."

"Yes, and your face and hands too."

Joshua wiped his face and hands with his tunic as best he could.

He whispered cautiously through the hole to Mr. Woodpecker. "What shall we do? Clearly we must do something to save the tree from being damaged by its reaction to this little invader, but when we get involved we seem to get burned too."

"Yes, it is a dilemma indeed."

There was silence as the two friends mulled over the issue.

Mr. Woodpecker was the first to speak. "When I was training to be a guide that walked the hinterland, Morfar explained to me that it was very important, when helping others, not to invade their space. Each one of us has our own unique energy field that is comfortable for us, but it can be disruptive if we force it into someone else's field."

"I guess it's like the little white grub's saliva. It probably serves a purpose for the bug, but when it touches my skin it causes a reaction."

"Just so, young Joshua, just so..." The friends lapsed into silence.

Joshua broke the silence. "Yes, but at the same time, we all do need somewhere to live, and look how many creatures live in the Midas Tree together without causing harm to the tree."

"Just so, young Joshua, just so..." The conversation paused once again.

"Maybe it's the grub's attitude?" offered Mr. Woodpecker.

"I think I see what you are saying. Everyone else we know loves living in the tree. It could be that the grub has such a negative attitude that it doesn't care about the wellbeing of the tree, and just wants what it can get for itself?"

Joshua thought about his experience with the ants, which had also been operating from greed. Their greed was fueled by their fear of not being enough or having enough.

"Mr. Grub, what is it that you are afraid of, that makes you so angry?"

The grub poked its frothy-mouthed head out of the hole. "Idiots like you and that bird coming along and disturbing my peace."

"We would not be disturbing you if we weren't concerned about the impact you are having on the Midas Tree. Look, she has swollen up in response to your invasion."

"Invasion you say! Invasion! I thought you had to be an army to have an invasion. I'm the innocent party here, and you two are the invaders."

"Look, I acknowledge that Mr. Woodpecker and I may have poked around a little into your grub hole, and I apologize if that disturbed or frightened you. However, we do need to get to the bottom of the way your saliva is causing this unfortunate reaction. It seems as though the Midas Tree is growing an extra thick layer of cells to protect herself from you."

"We all have to eat to stay alive!"

"Yes, and I'm not saying you should die, but is there a way that we can get you to stop spitting everywhere?"

"Look, this is how I eat. I need to use the saliva to break down my food, so I can digest it, and I rather like this effect that it's having of growing me more food faster."

"Yes, but you know, most of the other creatures in the tree like to live in harmony with her. By the way, do you need to eat this particular part of the Midas Tree?"

"No, but I do prefer to eat bark."

Joshua whispered through the hole to Mr. Woodpecker. "Where does the bark we use to make the signs and to make our clothes and baskets come from?"

"That's a good point, Joshua," said Mr. Woodpecker. "Let me see, the Midas Tree does naturally renew and let go. So I believe the Devas collect the bark they use for their runic scripts from the oldest part of the tree, where the bark is naturally starting to peel away."

"I wonder. Could you go there and get a piece for me?"

"Certainly, my friend! I'll be back in a jiffy." Mr. Woodpecker flew off down towards the base of the tree.

While he was gone, Joshua sat back down in the saddle seat and meditated. He grounded and centered, and he ran his earth and cosmic energy, and created and exploded roses. This helped him cleanse his body from the irritation brought on by the bug's saliva.

Then he remembered how he had learned to clean off the communication line to the bees, using a rose. He created a rose, and in his mind's eye, he used the rose to clean out the inside of the growth in the tree caused by the bug.

He had just finished exploding this last rose, when Mr. Woodpecker returned with a few old pieces of bark in his beak. They were just about small enough to pass to Joshua through the hole in the wall.

"Mr. Grub."

"What is it now?"

"I have some tasty pieces of bark for you, from another part of the Midas Tree, and I wonder if you would like to try them?"

"Humph. Well, I don't see why not."

Joshua handed him a piece and he started to spit all over it. After a few chomps he lifted his head and said. "It's not quite as fresh as the bark up here, but it's not bad. It seems the flavors intensify with the age of the bark. It's rather a delicacy actually. Do you have another piece?" He nodded towards the other pieces in Joshua's hands.

Joshua gladly gave the bug all the little pieces of bark, and he laid them on the floor of his chamber, where he slimed them up with saliva, ready to be munched on.

"Do you think, Mr. Grub, if Mr. Woodpecker continues to bring you these pieces of bark, that you could just eat those and not continue to eat inside the trunk here?"

"Aww really, he would do that for me?" A tear came into the little bug's eye. "No one has ever done anything for me before. I've always had to fend for myself. Yes, I would agree to that, and perhaps Mr. Woodpecker, we could have a little chat every now and again? It gets ever so lonely in here all by my lonesome."

"Of course, little grub," said Mr. Woodpecker "I'd be delighted to, for so long as we stick to our agreement."

"Yes, and I hope that you learned a thing or two here?" prompted Joshua.

"Err yeah; I learned to educate my palette with a more mature piece of bark."

"I guess also that it's possible to live together in harmony, and be in balance with your environment, and you don't always have to be defensive and afraid and assume the worst in people?"

"Oh yeah, that too…"

"Joshua, may I have a word with you?" whispered Mr. Woodpecker

"Yes of course."

"I saw what you were doing cleaning out the grub's energy from the tree's space using the cleaning rose. That was very well done."

"Thank you."

"Would you like to learn another technique that might also help?"

"Why yes, I would, Mr. Woodpecker. What do you have in mind?"

"Sit tight for another couple of minutes, and I'll be back with something else."

Joshua sat and waited, and in no time at all Mr. Woodpecker was back, carrying lots of fresh rose petals in his mouth. He passed them through the open knot to Joshua and said. "See if you can line the floor of his hole, so these are in between him and the tree."

"Yes, of course," said Joshua, understanding that Mr. Woodpecker wanted to create a barrier between the grub and the tree, so that the tree would be protected from its saliva.

"Mr. Grub, Mr. Woodpecker has brought you some lovely soft bedding for you to lay on the base of your new home. Can I pass it to you?"

The sticky white grub peered out through his hole, still munching on a piece of old bark, saliva dripping from his mouth. When he looked at Joshua and the rose petals, tears started pouring from his eyes again. "For me? What pretty colors, no one has ever given me a gift before. I will lay them all around the floor and walls of my gall. It will look so luxurious. Thank you so much, my new friends."

Joshua handed the petals to the bug, and after the bug disappeared back inside to arrange his gift, Joshua resumed his conversation with Mr. Woodpecker.

"He really liked it. He's going to place them everywhere between him and the tree. What a fantastic idea, Mr. Woodpecker."

"Yes, Joshua, and you know there is another meditation technique that I want to teach you, that can achieve the same result."

Joshua shuffled in his seat and readied himself. "I'm all ears, Mr. Woodpecker, and ready to learn. Please teach me this new technique."

"First of all, you need to be grounded and centered and have your energies running, which I see you are doing. Then create and explode some roses."

Joshua was already doing all of this, and he was happy to continue until Mr. Woodpecker was ready. "Now create another rose, but this time do not explode it, but leave it on the edge of your energy field."

Joshua paused. "What is my energy field?"

"Well, everything is energy, even your physical body, and there is a further field of energy that extends beyond it, which is called your aura. You need to leave this rose at the edge of your aura."

"How do I know where that is?"

"Do you see where you created the rose? That is the edge of your aura."

Joshua noticed where his rose was and left it there.

"You can leave a rose here at all times. It will act as a protection, and will mark the boundary between what is you and your energy field, and what is not."

"Just like the rose petals formed a boundary between the bug and the tree."

"That is right, Joshua. Now every once in a while, I will bring the bug fresh petals. You should also keep track of your protection rose, and renew it with a fresh one on a regular basis. You can use your inner sight to see when this needs to be done. For example, if you see that it has withered or wilted, then you need a fresh rose."

"Thank you, Mr. Woodpecker. I am truly grateful for all that you have taught me and am blessed to have you as a friend." Nicholaas Adrianus Cornelius Woodpecker nodded his head, and then flew back into the hinterland in search of some juicy bugs.

Chapter 17

Appearances Can Be Deceiving

oshua was filled with inspiration at his experience with the sticky white grub. He was elated that he had been able to serve the creatures of the Midas Tree, and the tree herself, by working with Mr. Woodpecker to come up with a solution for everyone. The Midas Tree was no longer being harmed, and the grub was being fed and was starting to feel better about things, which could only enhance the energy of the tree.

So when he left the central chamber to go to dinner, he decided on what his answer was going to be to the Devas.

After dinner, Devon banged on the table with his stick and the chamber became silent.

"Fellow Devas of the Tree,

Please stand up and cheer with me,

Joshua has chosen to stay

And be a teacher every day!"

He held his hands out and started clapping, and soon everyone was on their feet clapping their hands and cheering Joshua.

Devalicious, who was sitting next to Joshua, prompted him to stand and address the crowd.

"Thank you all for your loving kindness and support during my journey in the Midas Tree. I have learned so much from each and every one of you. I have decided that even though I could choose to go back to Morfar now, I would like to stay and help you and all the creatures of the tree in whatever way I can."

"I hope that if there are others like me who stumble into this wondrous world, that I will be able to offer them guidance, just as you have offered it to me. Then they may also turn to gold, and in doing so help the Midas Tree grow ever brighter."

Joshua sat back down to applause that was even more thunderous.

He stayed behind after dinner for a chat with Devalicious.

"You know, you still haven't met all the Devas of the tree."

"Really? I thought I knew you all really well by now."

"No. Actually Joshua, there are at least two more Devas who I would like to introduce you to tomorrow, so get a good sleep tonight.

Joshua woke up early; he had been tossing and turning all night, wondering whom these new Devas could be. He went to his meditation chair, grounded, and centered himself. He ran his earth and cosmic energy, and he created and exploded roses.

Then before the morning chorus started, he had a private conversation with Morfar. "Is this really what you want from me? To serve you, by serving the creatures of the tree?"

Joshua could feel Morfar's love pouring over him and through him, and he knew that it was. He also knew that this was what he most wanted to do.

"Yet who am I to teach others what I only recently came to understand myself?"

"Who are you not to do this?"

Joshua started a little, but kept his eyes closed.

"But even still, I have so much yet to learn myself."

"Yes you do, and what better way to learn than by teaching others?"

"It seems such a daunting task."

"Well, what are you waiting for? Let's get going," said a familiar tinkling voice.

This time Joshua did open his eyes, and when he did, he saw the beautiful Deva of the night, Devany.

"Come on, Joshua. Devalicious has unfortunately been called away to deal with some issues with the sugar transportation system, so she has asked me to take you to see Devina and Deval."

"Devina and Deval," repeated Joshua. "Who are they?"

"Come along, let's go. We can talk as we walk, as we have a lot of ground to cover."

"I thought I had already been into the canopy and roots as far as you can go?"

"Not quite," Devany led him into one of the passageways he had not yet followed.

"We will start by visiting Deval. He is the divine male essence of the tree, and he oversees the male aspect of creation, which is the impregnation and fertilization of the ovules in the flowers so that the fruit will grow and mature. He also oversees the pushing forth of the germinating seeds as they reach for the sunlight, ready to start their journey into new life. He watches over all creativity, such as fruit that will be formed by new combinations of pollen and flowers."

"And he lives at the top of the tree?"

"His domain is throughout the Midas Tree, but I am told this morning he is overseeing the creation of new fruit, and he has asked for you to come and work alongside him."

"And what about Devina?"

"She is the divine female essence of the tree, and she oversees the female aspect of creation, which is incubation, maturation, and ripening of the fruit. As well, she oversees the proliferation of the new plants as they grow and mature. She also nurtures the choices that each new plant makes about how it will express and manifest the potential it has within it."

"And where does she work?"

"Her domain is also throughout the tree, but she will probably join us at the top of the tree. Deval and Devina work in very close association with one another."

"And why do they want to see me?"

"Now you are a teacher, they want to share with you some of the deeper secrets of creation, including how to manifest your ideas into reality."

"Wow!"

"Yes indeed, Joshua, wow! This is a lot of fun, let me tell you, but it's also not to be taken lightly, as you will be wielding a lot of power."

They fell silent for a while, as they trundled higher and higher, at first through the thick old branches of the tree, and then through higher and lighter branches. Joshua remembered to keep increasing his grounding the higher up they went. Then as they started to reach some of the very thin light branches, he struck up a new conversation with Devany.

"Devany, what is it about Devi that she always leads me into a difficult lesson? Sometimes I think she has fun tricking me, and luring me into sticky situations."

Devany laughed. "She is the Deva of the moon, and as such her role includes showing us our dark sides, to help us shed light on that which is hidden, but needs to be brought to the surface."

"Yes, but why couldn't she just tell me and show me like the other Devas do?"

"Some things we only truly understand by experiencing them. One of the most difficult things for us to see is the power of our own ego, and how we get in our own way. The other Devas have been teaching you ancient spiritual techniques that provide you with a tool kit that you can use to help you go through your journey here in the Midas Tree. Devi has been providing you with opportunities to learn some very deep lessons about yourself."

"Hmmm. What kind of Devas are Deval and Devina, and you for that matter?"

Devany laughed her tinkling laugh again. "My role, as I explained to you that day in the central chamber of the tree, is also one of creation. I help bring the unmanifest into reality. It's a job that requires a lot of power and focus, but I like to think I do it in a very gentle way, as is my nature. As for Deval and Devina, you will see Joshua, you will see."

By now, they could see the leaves in the canopy of the Midas Tree. They walked past Devandra and his bright green Devas, who were busy positioning leaves to catch the early morning sunlight. Devandra waved, but quickly resumed his task.

As they continued, Joshua could hear a faint chirping sound.

"Devany, can you hear that?" he asked.

"What's that, my young friend?"

"A chirping sound…"

"Oh, yes," and as she spoke a little black Deva scooted by and whispered in Devany's ear."

"Joshua, it looks as though we are not in such a hurry to get there. My little antimatter Deva here tells me that Deval has another matter to attend to, and would like us to join him a little later than originally planned."

"Let's see, it's not worth going all the way back down, so would you like to investigate this chirping sound?"

"Sure," said Joshua. "It sounds very cheerful."

They took a side branch off in the direction that the sound was coming from. Soon, nestled amongst the leaves in the distance, they could see a beautiful blue bird, sitting in a nest made from Midas twigs.

"Hello, pretty blue bird," chirped Joshua almost as cheerfully as the bird had been doing.

"Hello, young man. Hello, Devany. How are you?"

"Hello, Mrs. Bluebird, I am very well."

"Please call me Belle; I'm past holding on ceremony here. Besides, it's almost time for my chicks to be born, and I could do with some help and encouragement from a master."

"Oh, you are too kind, my beautiful blue friend, but in any case I would be delighted to help you in any way I can. By the way, my companion is Joshua. He is a new teacher in the Midas Tree, still working on what he will specialize in, but probably he will be helping new arrivals I should think. Isn't that right, Joshua?"

"Yes," said Joshua, although he wasn't at all sure how things were going to develop. "I am pleased to meet you, Belle, and might I add that you sing so very beautifully."

"Why thank you, Joshua. Of course, I have a lot to be thankful for, what with my new chicks about to come. You know I never stop being grateful to Morfar and the Midas Tree for the bounteous gifts that we are blessed with."

"Would it be okay if we could see your eggs?" asked Joshua.

"Why, of course." Belle stood up and stepped aside onto the rim of her nest, so that Joshua and Devany could peer inside.

She had laid four eggs in all. Three were tiny blue ovals, but the fourth was a great enormous whitish-grey egg.

"Aren't they all beautiful?" chirped Belle. "All my lovely chicks, just waiting to be born."

"Oh yes," said Joshua, not wishing to sound shocked, or to draw alarm to what they were seeing. He threw a glance at Devany, who reached her hand out and held his forearm, as if to calm him down and stop him from saying anything.

"Well Belle, you truly have done yourself proud. They're going to be lovely chicks I can tell. Now you sit back down there and relax, and Joshua and I will just go and get a few things, and then we will be right back here to help you with the lovely moment when the chicks hatch."

"Right you are, and thank you Devany. I knew you would come. I was just asking Morfar to send me some help, not a moment before you arrived.

Joshua and Devany walked away quietly, until they were far enough that Belle could not hear them.

"Why is one of her eggs bigger than the others?" asked Joshua. "All the little blue eggs seem to fit in just right, but that big white one looks really out of place."

Devany laughed. "Yes, well, it's true that the little blue eggs were laid by Belle, but not the great big white one, that's for sure. She's so petite, and that thing is almost as big as she is."

"How can you laugh at such a terrible thing?"

"Joshua. Why are you judging this to be a bad thing?"

"Clearly that egg is an imposter. It's not her real chick, and what will she think when it hatches and it doesn't look like all the others? And how will she feed it? It looks like it will need ten times as much food as the others."

"Even though it may not be her chick, I can tell you for sure that it is her creation, and that she has manifested this situation to learn about something."

"By the way, I laugh because I am running my vibration of amusement. It helps me to stay neutral and in the center of my head, so that I don't make judgments or get carried away by my emotions. I have faith that everything is as it should be."

"Can I learn to run my amusement?" asked Joshua.

"Absolutely, it's very simple. I can teach you in jiffy," laughed Devany. "All you need to do is create a ball of your unique vibration of amusement above the top of your head, and then let it trickle down through your whole body until it tickles you."

"Oh, like the cosmic energy?" Joshua asked.

"Yes, except this energy travels everywhere, not just through your energy channels."

Joshua did what Devany suggested. He created a ball of amusement above the top of his head, which he noticed was pink, and he let it flow down all through him. Soon he was chuckling away alongside Devany.

The two only stopped giggling when they heard a rustling above them, and his old friend Mr. Woodpecker descended to a nearby branch.

"Hello, Joshua. Hello, Devany. What are you two doing up here so high in the tree?"

"Hi, Mr. Woodpecker. Devany was bringing me to see Deval, and on the way we bumped into Belle, the bluebird who is about to have chicks. She showed us her eggs, and one of them is much bigger than the others."

"Well the very nerve of it!" fumed Mr. Woodpecker.

"Do you know something we don't?" asked Joshua.

"Bob is going to think all sorts."

"What do you mean?" asked Joshua.

"Bob is Belle's mate," explained Devany.

"The cad, the imposter!" said Mr. Woodpecker.

"What is it?" pressed Joshua.

"It's that old cuckoo again, isn't it? She can't be bothered looking after her own chicks, so she lumbers them on other birds to look after. It happened to the sparrows last year, and the robins the year before. Oh, it really is a terrible state of affairs."

"Why? What will happen when the chicks are born?" asked Joshua.

"What will happen when the chicks are born? Well, I'll tell you what will happen. That great lumbering cuckoo chick will take over the nest, and it will oust those other poor innocent chicks. Belle and Bob will be so exhausted feeding it, they won't notice what is going on."

"What can we do about this?" asked Joshua.

"Nothing, really," said Devany. "We can help Belle hatch her chicks, but we can't intervene. There is nothing stronger than a mother's love, and she will love those chicks as soon as she sees them – each and every one of them.

"That's true," said Mr. Woodpecker. "Same thing happened to Sarah and Rose, and what stories I could tell you about that. Those cuckoo chicks pushed their brothers and sisters out of the nest, so that the sparrows and the robins only had one child. As soon as those cuckoos were ready to fly the nest, they did, and they never come back and visit. Good job they were able to have other chicks after that."

"We'd best go back to Belle," said Devany. "Joshua, grab some leaves and petals, and we'll try and make her and the chicks as comfortable as possible.

Devany and Joshua hurried back over to Belle, who by now was perched on the side of her nest, again looking down at the eggs. They were moving from side to side, and where the shells were visible, little cracks could now be seen.

"Oh my chicks, they're being born," cried Belle. "Praise Morfar, praise the Midas Tree! I'm going to be a Mother."

As she continued chirruping, the cracks got larger, and soon little beaks started poking out. Devany whistled a high-pitched, barely audible whistle, and a stream of her little black Devas arrived. They started working with the chicks to help them emerge from the shells with as little struggle as possible. Then as they emerged, Belle moved the eggshells aside, while Joshua laid the petals and leaves down for the little chicks to rest on.

"Oh??" said Belle once she got over the euphoria, and had a good look at her chicks.

"Let me see, here are Betty, Barney, and Bertie and..."

"Let me see... this last one here, this big boy here, he's called Boomer, yes that's right, Boomer. I'd better call their father in, as they'll want feeding soon. Oh Bob, Bob! Come and meet the brood."

Then she turned to Devany and Joshua. "Thank you both so much for your help. They are all lovely and so perfect, two legs, two wings and one beak each. My beautiful blue chicks, well three blue ones and a... grayish-white chick. Coo, coo are you hungry Boomer? Bob? Bob? Where are you?"

"Yes, they truly are beautiful chicks," said Devany. "It was our pleasure to help you, but we'd best leave you now to settle in and get acquainted with your new chicks."

"Yes, Belle, good luck, all the best," said Joshua.

Once again Devany and Joshua waited until they were out of earshot, before they discussed Belle's brood some more.

"How can we just walk away without saying anything?" asked Joshua. "It seems so cruel to know what is in store, and not say anything."

"First of all, we don't necessarily know what is in store. We just believe what is most likely, based on our experiences. However, Joshua, the past only exists as a thought. It is the here and now that matters. Belle and her chicks all have free will to create what they want out of this. Second of all, each of those creatures is in full agreement with the situation and what will happen."

"How can a chick be in full agreement with being kicked out of the nest before it can fly?"

"I know it sounds terrible, but hear me out, Joshua. I deal with a lot of souls who are coming from Morfar and the garden of color and light, into the Midas Tree. Sometimes, some of the souls only want to be here for a short time."

"Really? Kind of like me when I first arrived here?"

"Yes in a way, but then again not in another way. You see these souls may only have one little lesson they want to finish off from last time..."

"Hold on. What do you mean 'last time'?"

"What? You don't know?"

"What do you mean, I don't know?"

"All the physical creatures that live in the Midas Tree are eternal spiritual beings. They come to the Midas Tree from Morfar and the garden of color and light in order to expand themselves. They focus on learning certain spiritual lessons and truths along the way, but they don't just come here once. They come over and over again. Each time they choose certain areas to focus on."

"So you are saying that Belle's chicks may just be popping in for a quick experience, and then they will get born again at another time for a different lesson?"

"That is precisely what I am saying."

"What about me, have I been here before? Because I don't remember. Plus I get lots of lessons all the time, without going back to Morfar."

"Yes, Joshua, you have been here before. You would not have reached this stage of development unless you had been here many times before. You came here this time because you wanted to teach, and you needed to stay long enough to learn enough that you could remember that choice."

"But I wanted to go back in the beginning, and like I said, I don't remember any of this."

"Yes, that's part of the agreement."

"What agreement?"

"The agreement we all make with Morfar not to remember the past. Anyway, we're here now, so you will have to save any further questions you might have about this for later."

Chapter 18

Painting New Fruit

They entered a beautiful open space, surrounded by paper-thin leaves and pink and white blossoms. Bees were buzzing around and hopping from flower to flower. Over in the distance was a tall thin-boned, white-bearded Deva in a long flowing sky-blue robe.

He had a paintbrush, and was delicately sprinkling a yellow powder onto the blossoms.

He appeared to be swathed in purple mist, but as they got closer, Joshua could see that this was a busy cloud of purple elongation Devas, who were following his every move by sprinkling a dust of silver sparkles everywhere Deval's brush had touched.

"My dear Devany, I am so delighted to see you. And this must be our new young guide, Joshua?" Deval nodded his head towards Joshua as he spoke.

"Yes, I'm Joshua, and I am very pleased to meet you. I am also very curious about what you are doing."

Deval twisted his white moustache so that it turned upwards, and with a smile answered, "I'm working with the bees to pollinate the flowers. As we've been short of pollen lately, I'm just going around with my personal supply, and ensuring that all the flowers are ready. Of course once the flowers have been pollinated, the purple elongation Devas come and sprinkle their magic dust, and so the process of bringing new fruits and seeds into being begins."

"Oh, I see."

"Would you like to come and help?" Deval pulled a second paintbrush out of his pocket and handed it to Joshua. "Devany, would you be a dear and go and find Devina, and tell her we're just about ready for her to come and start the incubation process? I think she's with Devalicious and Devora over to the south side of the canopy." Then he added with a wink, "Joshua will be quite safe with me."

"Absolutely, your Royal Highness," quipped Devany with a smile and a curtsey, and off she went stepping across the branches.

"Right, young man, let us put together a palette of pollens for you." They wandered over to an area where there were about twenty large baskets full of pollen. Each basket had a large magnifying glass and a small shovel tied to it with string. On the side of each basket was a symbol, which presumably gave a clue as to what species of pollen was in the basket.

"Now then, you take a hold of this." Deval handed Joshua a plate with six indentations in a circle. "Ah yes, put your brush in your pocket for now, that's right." He handed Joshua one of the magnifying glasses. "Now take a look at these ones."

Joshua held the magnifying glass to his eye, and pointed it at the basket of pollen. What had looked like a pile of yellow dust was instantly transformed into a pile of little round balls with spikes all over them.

"Alright, now put that one down, and what about these?" Deval handed him another magnifying glass from the adjacent basket.

"Wow!" exclaimed Joshua. These ones transformed into little ovals that almost looked like peanuts.

"What about these ones?"

These were tiny pyramids. They continued until Joshua had looked at the pollen in all twenty baskets. He saw a myriad of shapes from little balls, to doughnuts, acorns and fur balls.

"Now choose half a dozen of your favorites, and we'll get started shall we?"

"OK," said Joshua, "but how shall I choose them? Which are the best ones to pick?"

"Well there's no rhyme or reason really, just choose the ones you like the best."

Joshua looked at the baskets, wandered over to the fur balls, and took a scoop of them. Then the little sea urchin look-alikes, tiny brains, oranges, almonds and pyramids.

"Got them!" he called to Deval, who had wandered back to talk to the purple elongation Devas, as Joshua seemed to be taking quite some time to make his decision.

"Great, come on back over here then. Now hold onto that palette carefully."

Deval put his arm around Joshua's waist, and they levitated above the canopy of the tree. They were just high enough that they could see all the different types of blossoms, stretched out into the distance.

"Now Joshua, I want you to take your palette of pollens, and go forth and pollinate all the flowers of your choosing. Take a good look from this vantage point, because when we get back down there, you'll have to be crossing through the branches to get to them."

Joshua couldn't believe what he was seeing. There seemed to be every type of flower in creation spread before him. How on earth would he remember where they all were, let alone decide which pollen was the right pollen for them.

Deval moved his other arm forwards, and they shot forward. He used his arm to steer them in the direction that he wanted them to go, until they had done a couple of circuits of the entire area, after which he brought them to a stop right back where they started.

"Deval, what am I doing, actually?"

"Why, you are creating, Joshua. You will be helping to create the new fruits of the Midas Tree."

"How will I know what to do?"

"Use your brush, choose some pollen, choose a flower, and sprinkle it in. Simple really! You just have to remember to clean the brush between dips, that's all."

"Yes, but how will I know I matched the right pollen with the right flower?"

"That's the whole fun of it really. You won't, and that's not a bad thing at all, as this is how we manage to create new combinations. I made a pomenana last week, and a tangango the week before, and both of them were delicious."

Joshua really wasn't sure at all about any of this. He didn't like this seemingly haphazard approach to creation.

"Go on, off with you now. Everything will be all right. You wouldn't be here if you weren't a capable creator."

Joshua smiled and timidly wandered off in the direction of some fuchsias and a patch of orange blossom. He smelled the orange blossom. It really was a lovely smell and he liked oranges, but he actually always had an inkling that orange and mango would go particularly well together. "A mangage," he said out loud.

The only problem was, could he make a mangage? Did he have everything required to make his desired creation? He doubted it. He didn't think any of his pollen grains were particularly mango-like, although he did have one that looked like an orange. Maybe he could find a mango blossom, whatever that looked like. He wandered off in search of a mango tree.

He felt like an intrepid jungle explorer, wandering off into uncharted territory with only his wits and his intuition to guide him.

"Chirrup, chirrup, chirp a cheep, cheep"

Joshua looked up into the branch above him, and there sat another bluebird.

"Bob?" he asked.

"Yes, hello, do I know you?"

"I'm Joshua. I helped Devany deliver your chicks."

"Oh yes, well thank you, I think. Although by Morfar, I never knew being a father would be so much work. I should be out there now looking for grubs, but I'm so tired I just had to have some respite here among the mango blossoms."

"Is this a mango branch?" Joshua looked at the tiny sprays of fine flowers.

"Yes, that's right."

"Great!" He got out his palette, and dipped the brush into the pollen that he hoped belonged to the oranges, and started tapping the little yellow grains into the mango flowers.

"Oh it's wonderful, isn't it, the art of co-creation? Although it seems you can never be quite sure what you will get. Take Belle and me for example, two beautiful bluebirds. You would think we would make more beautiful bluebirds, wouldn't you?"

Joshua made himself busier with his job of sprinkling the pollen.

"And that is what we got. We got three lovely bluebird chicks, Betty and Barney and Bertie. They're lovely they are, apples of my eye, so to speak. Yet that Boomer, if I didn't know my Belle better, I'd swear he came from another type of bird."

Joshua made himself even busier making his mangages.

"Oh well, I expect it will all turn out for the best," said Bob.

"Oh yes," agreed Joshua, standing back and looking at his handiwork. "I expect it will all work out for the best."

"By the way, have you met the chimera yet?"

"Sorry, met the what?"

"The chimera. He's a funny looking chap, according to the rumors anyway. He lives up here in the highest part of the canopy. Never met him myself, but I've heard the stories about him."

"What kind of stories, exactly?"

"Just that he's constantly changing, and you never know that you've met him until after you've met him. If you meet him again, he never looks the same, but he can tell you a thing or two about creating things, being an expert in it himself and all."

"Is he dangerous?"

"Not that I know of, but then I've never met anyone who's actually met him face to face. I've just heard the stories. Anyway I'd best be off, or the Missus will be mad at me. It was very nice to have met you." With that, he took off towards the lower parts of the tree, no doubt in search of the biggest juiciest bugs he could find for Boomer.

Joshua wandered through the canopy of the Midas Tree, deeper into the jungle of blossoms. He went past blackberry and raspberry blossoms and the grape fronds, into a grove of yellow papaya and red pineapple blossoms. He wondered if he should marry the fur ball pollen with the pineapple or the papaya. On the other hand, perhaps the almond-shaped pollen grains? Maybe they would make almaya or pineond. He was just pondering this further, when he heard a rustling sound off to his left-hand side.

He turned to see what had made the noise, but there was nobody there. He moved closer and pried the branches apart to look. No sign of anyone, although on a level hidden under the branches were some very unusual and striking-looking flowers indeed. They looked like beautiful silk wedding dresses, with long salmon pink and pale pink ribbons in the center.

There was another rustling sound, this time off to the right. Joshua stayed where he was, and turned his head ever so slightly. He still couldn't see anything, but he could hear a faint mumbling and muttering.

"Them's durians... them's durians... them's durians... mix 'em with the fur ball... Mix 'em with the fur ball, then you'll get a furian. That'll be nice, that'll be nice."

"Hello, there. No need to be shy, my name is Joshua and I would love to hear what you have to say about these blossoms and my pollens."

"Mix 'em with the fur balls, then you'll get a furian, or maybe even a durball if you're lucky."

"Actually though, don't the fur balls belong to a type of fruit, rather than being an actual fur ball?"

"Well aren't you clever." There was some more rustling, and a tiny man wearing animal furs, with a thick brown head of hair, a beard and quite a hairy body emerged from the branches. He was wearing furry boots and carrying a little club.

"The fur balls are rambutans. So if you mix them with the durian, you'll most likely get a durbutan."

"Huh!" said Joshua. "Well, that sounds good, have you any idea what that will taste like?"

"Rather like a sweet almond custard is my guess," said the creature, "but without the nasty smell of a durian. So all in all, it's worth it.

"Good. Then I'll do it," said Joshua.

"Joshua, you say your name is?"

"Yes that's right."

"I've heard the legends about you."

"Oh? That can't be me! Although I hear there is a legendary creature somewhere in here, called the chimera."

"Really? That may well be true, but I have heard the legends of Joshua the golden boy, who will teach us all how to live."

"That cannot be me. I mean I did turn the Midas Tree to gold, and myself for that matter, but I'm just learning to be a teacher. So far, all I've done is help deliver three bluebirds and a cuckoo, and help a white sticky grub to live a better life. That is hardly the stuff of legends."

"Maybe you need to change your perspective on that? Perhaps you should believe in yourself more? Maybe if you believe in yourself more, you would be more confident about your ability to create new fruit for the tree, and for all its creatures to enjoy?"

"Joshua. Oh, Joshua." Devany's light voice came drifting through the air, and Joshua turned in its direction. When he turned back, the curious man was gone. In a few moments, Devany appeared in his place.

"How are you getting on?"

"Alright I suppose. Look at this lovely blossom here. It's a Durian."

Devany peered over his shoulder. "Yes Joshua, I do believe you are right. You know how I can tell? It's because of the color and structure of the blossom. This long salmon pink protuberance here is called a stigma, and these pale pink protuberances around it are the anthers. The anthers hold the pollen, and the stigma has a tube called a style, which reaches into the ovary. So when you sprinkle your pollen, make sure it dusts onto the tip of the stigma, this bit in the center."

"Ahh!" exclaimed Joshua, who hadn't quite got that part from Deval's explanation. Luckily, he still had lots of all the pollens left. He refined his technique so that he was doing what Devany had explained.

"These are going to make durbutans," he said.

Devany laughed. "Is that what you want to create, Joshua?"

"I don't know really, I'm just experimenting."

"Experimenting is great. Although I always find it helpful to know what I wish to create first, that way I can consciously put my energy behind it. I put my request out there to the universe, and the power of my visualization is sufficient to put the universe in motion to bring that creation into being. Would you like to learn how I do it?"

"Absolutely," said Joshua.

"Let's find a comfortable branch to sit on. You can put down your brush and palette for now. Great! Joshua, let's start by grounding and centering." Devany paused for Joshua to prepare.

"Then get your earth and cosmic energies flowing. That's right, first the earth energy in through the arches of your feet, and then the cosmic energy in through your head and down your back, up the front of your body, out the top of your head. Don't forget to branch some off at the cleft of your throat, and let it flow down your arms and out the palms of your hands... wonderful..."

"Now take a nice deep breath in and out, and think about something you would like to create..." Again, she allowed time for him to come up with something. "Now visualize your desired creation as clearly as you can, and in as much detail as you can."

Joshua imagined the reddest juiciest berry he could. It was as big as a plum, and as red as a pomegranate, but it smelled like strawberries and peaches, and it looked like a giant raspberry. The juice was red as wine and the flavor as sweet as honey. His mouth was watering just thinking about it.

"Now place your creation into an imaginary pink balloon, fill the balloon full of helium, and let the pink balloon float off into the universe. Let it go; don't hold onto it. Simply let it drift away, so that the universe can do its work and bring it back to you when it is ready. Take another deep breath and open your eyes. Now how was that?"

"Great," said Joshua, "just great. I saw the exact fruit that I want to create."

"That's wonderful," said Devany, "but you know that's only part of my recipe for successful manifestation. You also have to really desire your creation."

"Oh yes, I definitely do want this delicious fruit."

"And you have to believe that you can have it."

Joshua's brain went on pause. He had momentarily forgotten about his doubts while he was meditating. Now that Devany said this, they all came flooding back in.

"Not to worry, Joshua. Close your eyes again, and we'll do some work around this too."

Joshua closed his eyes, and Devany continued. "Let all your doubts and disbeliefs flow away down your grounding. In fact, create a rose and place anything that says you cannot have your creation into this rose, and then explode it. Keep creating and exploding roses, until all your doubts have disappeared."

Joshua kept working on this for quite some time, until eventually he opened his eyes again. "I just have one question. How is this going to come into being?"

"Great question, and a great lead into another ingredient for successful manifestation. You have to follow up with some actions in the physical world too. So go ahead and dust your raspberry blossoms, and I'll leave you alone for the next little while, for you to finish using up the rest of the pollen in your palette."

Joshua excitedly ran back to the raspberry blossoms and sprinkled the flowers with the pyramid pollen. He felt so happy doing this work that he started to whistle, so he barely registered the rustling noise coming from the branches behind him. Then he noticed his whistling seemed to be getting louder, even though he wasn't purposefully making it louder.

He scratched his head, and blew more quietly. The whistling continued loudly for a couple of seconds, and then adjusted itself to match Joshua's pitch. Joshua whistled loudly again, and the accompaniment increased in volume. Joshua abruptly stopped, but the whistling continued.

"Ahh, you caught me," said a funny voice, and a little man dressed in flower petals that resembled red velvet emerged from the canopy. He had a pixie hat and a clean-shaven and cheeky grin. He looked at Joshua with a twinkle in his eye, and then let out a shrill whistle and disappeared back into the undergrowth.

Instantly Joshua found himself surrounded by clouds of purple elongation Devas. They were sprinkling their magic silver dust wherever he placed his brush, exactly as they had been when they were helping Deval. Joshua started whistling again, and soon he noticed that the whistling was influencing the work of the purple Devas. A shrill whistle drew them to attention, a quiet whistle slowed them down, and a loud one speeded them up. If he stopped altogether, then they retreated into the canopy. All he needed to do to get them to come back was let out another shrill whistle, just like the man in red velvet petals had done.

Joshua sat down on a tree branch to contemplate what he would like to create next from his palette of pollens. He really liked figs, and so he wondered what would be a good combination. Once at supper, he'd had a delicious salad of figs and mint. "I could make a figment," he thought out loud.

"That's a just a figment of your imagination, I'm afraid. You need to stick with the fruit combinations. The mint is an herb, so it's a much more difficult combination to achieve."

Joshua turned his neck to see a short and wizened old man approaching from the canopy behind him. "What do you suggest I make then?"

"Hmm. Let's take a look at that palette of yours again."

Joshua turned around on his branch, and showed it to the old man.

"Again? Sorry, I don't think we've met. I would have remembered you."

"Not necessarily. We have met before. We are meeting now, and yet we have never met."

"I'm not sure I follow."

"Well, I'm not the same as when we first met. I'm in a constant state of flux. I almost don't recognize myself from one moment to the next. There's only one thing I'm sure of besides constant change, and that is there is one sure part of me and that's my spark."

"What's your spark?"

"You know, I'm very glad you asked that question. My spark is me, my divinity, that eternal piece of Morfar that I am."

As Joshua was looking at the old man, he noticed that his form was shimmering and shifting before his eyes. Before he could mention anything the man said, "Must dash," and he dipped back into the canopy.

Joshua sat back on his branch and tried to relax. "I wonder what I should make next?" he asked out loud.

"How about creating something with an interesting shape and texture like a coconana? I always like those. Or if you want something for a more refined palette, how about a lycheonut, or cocochee?"

A short young woman was approaching from the same direction that the old man had gone to.

"Oh, hello, this sure is a busy and crowded part of the tree," commented Joshua.

"Oh, no. It's mainly just me and a few birds that live here."

"No, not at all. Since I've been here I've seen a short hairy man, a clean shaven man in red velvet, a wizened old man, and now you."

"That's right, just what I said, mainly just me and a few birds."

"Sorry, I don't understand. I haven't met you before."

"Joshua, don't you recognize me? It's the same old spark that was here before in the three little men."

Joshua recoiled in shock, and then he remembered what Bob the bluebird had told him about the Chimera.

"Ohhh. Are you the Chimera?"

"I'm not sure what you mean by that."

"I was told that there is creature that lives here that is always changing its form. It's known as the Chimera."

"I am always changing, so they could be referring to me, although I prefer to be called by my first name – Daphne."

"Daphne, I never heard of a little old man called Daphne, or a hairy little man for that matter."

"Well no, you met Ug, Simeon, and Alfred."

"But I thought you said they were all you?"

"I did, and they are. Oh, no. I feel a change coming on, got to dash."

Joshua let out a big sigh, sat, and pondered his new friend. Surely, this was the Chimera. The same creature that kept changing into different forms, and calling itself by a different name for every form it creates. Like the creature said, the same eternal spiritual spark, present in different forms.

He looked down at his palette. He was almost out of pollen, so he wandered over to a nearby gooseberry patch and tipped the entire contents over it. He let out a shrill whistle, and the Devas came and swirled around the branches, sprinkling their silver powder.

He wandered off in a direction that he hoped would lead him back to Deval.

Chapter 19

Seeds of Inspiration

Joshua had been wandering around the canopy for what seemed like hours without seeing anyone. No bluebirds, no chimera, and no Devas at all. He felt like he was going in circles. One set of branches looked pretty much like the next set of branches, until he came to an area where there were no blossoms anymore. Instead, there were tiny fruit, just beginning to form.

He leaned in closer, until he was almost swallowed by the canopy, and he reached in and pulled one of the fruit laden branches toward him. As he peered at the fruit, he noticed some tiny green bugs were stuck to the stalks. As he looked closer, he could see that they had little tubes coming from their mouths that they were using to pierce the stem under the fruit and suck out the juices.

"This can't be good for the fruit," said Joshua out loud. "They're siphoning off nutrients before they reach the fruit."

He started to wipe at the bugs with his fingers to get them off, but they were so sticky his fingers just ended up all goopy.

"Out the way, stand back!"

A ladybug flew past Joshua's ear, and landed on a fruit on the branch he was holding.

"I am Wing Commander Laddy Lady Ladd at your service."

A second ladybug carrying a bugle landed next to him, and blew a loud trumpet call.

A swarm of very fat ladybugs carrying dust cloths instantly descended on the bushes and started dusting and polishing the fruits and their stems.

"Hello, I'm Joshua," offered Joshua.

Wing Commander Laddy Lady Ladd and his lieutenant both saluted him.

"We are happy to be of assistance in polishing off these greenfly for you, Sir."

"Thank you, Commander," said Joshua, "but I thought ladybugs usually eat greenfly?"

"Yes, that's right Sir," interjected the bugle-carrying lieutenant, "but our army is only so big, and there's so many of them. We're full, we just can't eat anymore."

"Yes, so we are polishing them off using dust cloths," said the Commander.

"Oh, I see," said Joshua. "That's very funny, polishing them off, ha, ha."

The two bugs glanced sideways at each other, shifted, and shuffled their feet a little bit, and then there was an awkward silence.

"Well, good on you!" said Joshua. "You get top marks for ingenuity."

"Quite," said Laddy Lady Ladd.

"Quite," said his sidekick.

"Have you ever thought about expanding your army?"

"Ahem," said Laddy Lady Ladd.

"Ahem," said the lieutenant.

They shuffled and looked sideways at each other again.

"Shall we tell him?" the lieutenant asked.

The Commander looked at his feet and said, "You go ahead, lieutenant. I'll be over here checking on the troops." He flew a few feet away, to oversee the ladybugs that were polishing aphids from the branches over there.

"Ahem," said the lieutenant again.

"Tell me what?" enquired Joshua.

"Ah, you see it's like this," stumbled the lieutenant awkwardly. "How can I put this? You see, it's rather a delicate matter."

"I'm a good listener," encouraged Joshua. "What's your name by the way?"

"Lieutenant Ladybug."

"No, I meant your first name."

"Oh it's Toby, Lieutenant Toby Ladybug."

"Toby, it can't do any harm and it just might help."

"Yes, I see your point, quite." He shuffled and looked awkward some more. Then he took a couple of deep breaths and began. "You see it's the ladies, they're on strike. They won't do anything and they have us doing everything, including all the housework, as well as keeping in check these aphid populations."

"Do you have any idea why they went on strike?"

"Yes and no. It started with Jessica Lady Ladd, who said she was watching her figure, and so she wasn't going to eat any more aphids. Then as she started to shrink, all the other ladies wanted to shrink too. They stopped eating, and as they stopped eating, they stopped laying eggs. Then they lost interest in pretty much everything else too. All they do is sit around all day comparing the size of their thorax, the redness of their wings, and the number of black beauty spots they have."

"That doesn't sound good," said Joshua.

"So then we found ourselves eating twice as much, and putting on weight, even though we are also doing twice the work. We just can't keep up with it. The aphids are expanding faster than we can eat them or dust them."

"Can I meet with the ladybug ladies?" asked Joshua?

"I don't know what good that will do. The Commander and I have already ordered them back to work, and threatened them with a court martial if they don't do as we ask."

"But did you talk to them, to find out why they are behaving this way?"

"There's no talking to them, they just say we are being unfair, but all we are attempting to do is get them off their fat lazy behinds and doing what ladybugs do best – eat bugs!"

"Toby, did you hear what you just said?"

"What?"

"You just referred to them as fat and lazy, and yet you also said that they are not eating and are trying to get thinner?"

"Ah quite, I see your point."

"Perhaps if you were kinder and more sensitive to them, they would feel better about themselves, and not think they need to be thinner? Please let me talk to them, they might feel better talking to a neutral party."

"Righty ho. Just let me check with the Commander." Toby

flew to where the Commander was and had a conversation with him. Then they both stood to attention and saluted Joshua. "Good Luck!" they said and waved him off.

Joshua turned and started to walk away. Then he turned back toward them. "Just a moment. I don't know where they are. Could you point me in the right direction?"

"Befuddled if we know. They said they didn't want anything else to do with us. We haven't seen them in three days."

Joshua sighed and walked off into the canopy, still hoping to find Deval and perhaps the lady ladybugs as well. At least he seemed to be walking into areas of riper and riper fruit. He walked past some banana leaves replete with clumps of fruit with long hairy fingers. "Coconana," he thought as he reached out and picked one. This wasn't going to be as easy to peel as a banana, that was for sure. He found a rock embedded in the bark, and bashed the hard shell against it until it eventually broke open. The flesh inside was much softer and whiter than a banana, but it still looked and tasted like one. As he ate, Joshua realized he was actually quite hungry, and before he knew it, he was ravenously digging in to his second and then his third fruit.

"How are the banonuts?"

Joshua turned to see an ethereal, tall, thin-boned female Deva with white hair knotted in a straggly bun on the top of her head. She had beautiful, piercing blue eyes, was wearing a sky-blue robe the same color as Deval's. She was wearing silver spectacles perched on the end of her nose and held in place by a silver chain.

"Devina?" asked Joshua.

"Yes, indeed, how are the banonuts?"

"Delicious," said Joshua swallowing down what was left in this mouth.

"Well, keep some more room, as there's plenty of other

crops to try out. Come over here and tell me what you think of this rasbutan." She popped a round red fruit from the center of a little fur ball, and handed it to Joshua.

"Mmmm, that's delicious!" he said.

"Wonderful. That means we've been doing a good job ripening them, not too much sun, and not too little sun; not too much rain and not too little rain," she said.

"Yes, and not too many aphids, and too little ladybugs," said Joshua.

"What was that, dear?" said Devina, who was leaning into another vine, laden with apricot-colored bunches of grapes. "Grapicot?" she said handing one to Joshua.

"We need to make sure that the aphids don't get out of control, and ruin the next set of fruit crops," said Joshua in a little more detail this time.

"Oh, not to worry the ladybugs, will take care of all that."

"Not this time," said Joshua. "The lady ladybugs are on strike, because they want to lose weight so they can look like Jessica Lady Ladd."

"Stuff and nonsense," said Devina. "Where did they get an idea like that from?"

"I think it's partly because the male ladybugs have been calling them fat and lazy," said Joshua. "So they told them they can do it all themselves. The males are over there, dusting the aphids from the bushes." He pointed back to where he had left them earlier.

"Dusting? ...and where have they left the female bugs?"

"That's just it. They don't know where they are."

"Oh. Let's see. Come over here with me, and we'll scry them."

"We'll what them?"

"We shall scry them. Scrying is a way of seeing what is, through a physical medium. It's a form of remote viewing, where you can use your inner vision to see where they are, and what they are up to, in real time. I have a little bowl of water over here, and we'll take a look and see if we can locate them."

Devina beckoned Joshua to an indentation in one of the branches of the Midas Tree. It was full of water. She sat down by the side of it and beckoned Joshua to join her.

"Now ground and center yourself. Get into a meditative state using all the tools and techniques that you know, and then peer into this still dark pool of water, and let your mind run free."

Joshua did as she asked. He made his grounding cord and placed his consciousness in the center of his head. Then he ran his earth and cosmic energies and started creating and exploding roses. When he was ready, he stared into the pool. At first, all he could see was the sky, the leaves, and the branches reflected back at him. Then the leaves began to form patterns, which looked like people and places and things.

"Now ask that you might see the lady ladybugs," said Devina.

Joshua asked to see them, and a new image unfolded in the rustling of the leaves reflected on the water. The female ladybugs appeared to be lying on the leaves at the very top of the tree, sunbathing. One of them, presumably Jessica, as she was the most emaciated of the group, was standing before them displaying her wings. She was surrounded by lemons hanging from the branches around her. She had poked a hole in one of the lemons so the juice trickled out, and was now rubbing the juice over her wings to bleach them. They had also been bleached by the sun, and appeared orange with grey spots. The other ladybugs watched her, and then eagerly lunged and poked at the lemons until they were all standing in a shower of juice. They frantically started rubbing their own wings and spreading them under the sun.

"Can you tell where they are?" Joshua asked, assuming that Devina had seen what he had.

"Oh, we have other things to do at the moment, but we can start right here, right now, by communicating with them as spirit. Joshua, be grounded and centered, and contact the guiding light of each and every one of those lady ladybugs." She gave Joshua a moment to do this. Then she said. "Tell me what you see, Joshua?"

"I see a cluster of bright lights."

"Just so, you have contacted their spirits. Now speak to them in your mind, while you maintain your psychic awareness of these lights."

"OK, what shall I say?"

"Tune into your guiding light at the same time, and you will know what to say.

"Hello, lady ladybugs. I want to talk to you about your physical appearance. You are beautiful exactly as you are. You do not need external validation from your male ladybugs, or from any of the other lady ladybugs to know this. It comes from inside you. Tune in to your everlasting light, and know your eternal beauty. Feel the love of Morfar in that light. You are ladybugs. You are red and black, and you eat aphids. Know who you are, and be who you were meant to be. The Midas Tree and all its creatures need you to fulfill your purpose, which is to control the population of aphids so the fruits can ripen and grow."

"That was great, Joshua. Now create a rose and let it represent the lady ladybugs."

Joshua did as he was asked.

"Give the rose its own grounding cord, so the ladies are connected to and in harmony with the Midas Tree. Then connect them via a line of light with Morfar, so they are in alignment with their source and their purpose. Bring a waterfall of golden light through the rose, and help them release their feelings of not being enough, and let go of what is misguiding them. Then create a rose for Jessica Lady Ladd, and give her an extra healing. Help her pull her energy off the other ladybugs, by running a gold net through the them to gather her energy, and then bring it back to her."

Devina watched Joshua as he worked, and then said, "That's great. Now let's go taste more fruit and we can check in with them again later."

Joshua followed Devina.

"So I was talking to the spirit of the ladybugs?"

"You were talking to the ladybugs, who are spirit!"

"But I was not in the same place that they are, talking to them?"

"No, you were not talking to them in their physical bodies, but you were talking to them. The physical body is like a house that the spirit lives inside. The body exists in time and space and is finite, whereas the spirit, as you quite rightly said, is eternal and exists outside of time and space. We can communicate as spirit always, and for all time. You do not need to be in the physical presence of someone to communicate with them, but you know that, Joshua!"

"Yes, I know it, but I don't know it. Or I need to know it on a deeper level than I know it."

Devina laughed. "As spirit we know everything we need to know. However, sometimes it takes time to get our knowing completely into our bodies, and into our conscious awareness. You did a great job, Joshua, and I'm sure we will see a change in the behavior of the ladybugs as a result."

"Should we not also speak to the Commander and his army, so they no longer feel the need to criticize the lady ladybugs?"

"That's a great idea Joshua. Why don't you do that now? You can do it while we walk to the place where we dry the seeds, readying them for planting."

As they walked in silence, Joshua summoned the lights of the male ladybugs, and told them exactly what he told the females. That they are great the way they are, and they don't need to make themselves feel better by making someone else lesser than they are. He gave them a healing, and he helped the two groups get some space from one another, so they could see themselves and each other more clearly.

When he had finished, he turned to Devina. "That's the first time I did something like that while walking around. I usually do it when I meditate."

"Devina laughed again. Why, your whole life is a meditation, Joshua, surely you know this? Everything that happens in your life is a symbol that has great meaning for you. Everyone you meet is there to reflect an aspect of you, so that you can see yourself more clearly. You are here to grow yourself and know yourself. Talking of things that are here to grow themselves..."

Joshua and Devina turned a corner and climbed a ladder to the top of the canopy. Almost as far as the eye could see, seeds of all shapes and descriptions were laying on the leaves to dry. There were hundreds of tiny crystal light Devas flying overhead, so that beams of light from the sun were reflecting through them and hitting the seeds. Off in the distance, a swarm of lady ladybugs was taking flight from the top of the canopy, and heading off in the direction of the male ladybugs and the ripening fruit.

"Now Joshua, once the fruit has ripened, we share it amongst all the creatures of the Midas Tree for food, taking care to save the seeds for planting later. See here we have papaya seeds, avocado and peach pits, as well as some of our more exotic combinations. My little crystal clear light Devas gather them up when everyone has finished eating, and bring them here so we can dry them and store them."

"What are they doing with the light beams?"

"They are reflecting the light of Morfar into the seeds, and ensuring that they are charged with their full potential."

"What does that mean, their full potential?"

"In each seed is contained the full potential of what that seed can become. Morfar gives enough energy so that the seed has everything it needs to become the best version of itself that it can possibly be."

"Does the Midas Tree make its own seeds?" Joshua asked.

Devina smiled. "What a wonderful question. In a way, you are the seed of the Midas Tree."

"What do you mean?" asked Joshua.

"Come with me. I have some special seeds to show you."

Joshua followed Devina into an inner chamber, away from the sun. There were bags of dried seeds stacked up everywhere. The walls were full of shelves, laden with jars of seeds of different shapes and sizes.

Devina picked up a piece of sackcloth and laid it on the floor. Then she leaned her long slender arm up to the topmost shelf, and pulled down a large golden jar. She opened it up, and tipped the contents onto the sackcloth.

They looked like little golden acorns, each a golden egg inside its own little golden cup.

"What are these?" asked Joshua.

"They are the seeds of your future selves. One day when you are ready to leave the Midas Tree, you must come here to the seed room and put all of your remaining dreams and desires into these seeds."

They were radiating golden light, and Joshua peered at them in awe. While he was lost in wonderment, Devina reached for a second clear glass jar with a silver lid. She opened this one up, and spread its contents on a second piece of sackcloth.

She tapped Joshua on the shoulder to stir him from his trance, and then she pointed to the second set of seeds. These looked like little silver helicopter blades.

"These are your seeds of inspiration for those who are yet to come to the Midas Tree, and who are yet to walk the path that you have walked. As you learn new things, you may come here and place your knowledge into these seeds. Now I am going to go and find Deval. I'll leave you alone here with your seeds, and what you need to do is charge them with everything you have learned so far, just like the crystal clear Devas are charging the seeds out there in the sun."

Joshua was so busy staring at the silver and gold seeds that he didn't have the presence to ask Devina exactly how he was meant to do that. When he finally came out of his reverie, she was nowhere to be seen. He went outside again, but all he could see were the crystal clear Devas, still hard at work charging the seeds from the fruits of the Midas Tree.

He watched them for a while, to see if he could learn from what they were doing. They were receiving the sunlight, and then directing it as beams of light into each of the seeds. Joshua whistled to see if he could attract their attention, but they just kept on working, so he addressed them. "Crystal light Devas, can you please explain to me how to charge the seeds?" Once again, they kept on with what they were doing. Joshua sat silently and watched some more.

They moved so fast it was difficult to see. Joshua grounded and centered, and brought his energy into the present moment. Then, by narrowing his eyelids and relaxing his eyes, he could almost slow down time. That allowed him to pick up a little more on what was happening.

The sun entered the Devas at their crown, and flowed down to the energy center near the base of their spine. Then it flowed up the front of their bodies and fountained out of the top of their heads. However some of it branched off near the cleft of the throat and flowed down their arms and out through the palms of their hands. They were pointing their little hands at each seed, directing the energy into the seed they were focused on. Once they finished one seed, there was a small pause, and then they repeated the action to do another seed.

Huh, thought Joshua. In a way, this is just like flowing cosmic energy, except they are focused on using it to create potential in the seeds, instead of melting energy blocks and healing themselves. "I wonder why they pause in between seeds?" he said out loud.

"It's so they can bring through the unique piece of Morfar that belongs to that individual seed." He heard Devany's voice from behind him.

"Oh Devany, am I glad to see you. Come in here please." He led her into the room where his seeds had been laid out, and pointed to the golden acorns. "These are the seeds of my future selves." Then, pointing to the blades, "These are the seeds of inspiration for those who are yet to come and walk my path through the Midas Tree."

"They are truly beautiful," said Devany.

"Yes they are, but Devina said I need to charge them with energy, and I don't know how to do it. Can you help me?"

"I can help you with advice. I can suggest a technique that you can use to do this, but only you can charge these seeds. They are your unique gifts of wisdom to those who will follow you, and they are your unique intentions for your own future lives."

"Great, I'll take whatever I can get. Where do we start?"

"Let's start by meditating. Ground and center, and then get your earth and cosmic energies flowing. Now pay particular attention to the energy flowing down your arms. Feel the energy flowing out through the palms of your hands. Do you feel that, Joshua?"

"Yes, I think so."

"It might help you to get this, if we play with the energy a little. Cup your hands and make a concentrated ball of energy. Then pass this ball between your hands... Great. Then make it grow bigger, and then smaller and denser."

Joshua did as she asked. He felt the energy in his hands.

"Now pass the energy in a beam, from your right hand to your left hand."

Joshua obliged, and he could feel the energy tingling in his left hand as it hit his palm.

"Now open your eyes, Joshua, and shoot the beam of energy over to me. Aim here for the palm of my hand... that's great. Now sit back and receive energy from me.

Suddenly Joshua felt a strong current hitting his left hand. "Wow, Devany, you are so powerful!"

"So are you, Joshua, so are you. Now what you need to do is take what I have just taught you, and one by one focus this beam of energy to the seeds. Start with the ones that are for those who will come after you. Place everything that you have learned and would like to teach them into the seeds. Allow your learning and wisdom to be available to all who come after you. Try with this one now."

Joshua focused the beam of energy in his hands at the seed. He felt like it was glowing as he did this. "Right, but how do I transfer the wisdom?"

"You need to focus your mind on what you have learned, and then direct this information down your arms and into the seeds."

Joshua did as Devany suggested. He thought about his first lesson in the Midas Tree, which was to talk to and be kind to his physical body. He focused on the meditations where he sent happiness and love into his body, and sent the energy from these thoughts down his arms, out the palms of his hands and into the seed.

He asked, "How will I know when the transfer of information is complete?"

"Place your consciousness in your crown, at the top of your head, instead of in the center of your head as you do this. You will simply know."

Joshua moved his attention from the center of his head into his crown, and focused on the seed. After a few seconds, he knew he had completed his task and the seed was ready.

"Great, Joshua, and now do the others," Devany turned to leave. "Place all your knowledge that you have learned so far in these seeds. Remember, you can always come back later to add additional lessons as you learn them to more seeds."

"Wait, Devany. How can I charge the seeds for my future selves?"

"What new experiences would you like to have, that have not yet happened? What do you need to learn that you do not yet know? Who would you like to meet whom you have not yet met? Think on all these matters and place them into the seeds when you are ready." Devany turned her back and left the room.

Joshua set to work on all the other silver helicopter seeds. He selected the next seed to be charged with his wisdom. The next lesson I learned was how to ground with Devadne and the bronze Devas. He grounded as much as he possibly could, and then he held the thought of everything he knew about grounding in his mind and channeled this energy into the seed, until he knew it was done.

Then he put this seed together with the first seed, and chose a third silver helicopter blade. Another important lesson I learned, from Mr. Woodpecker, was how to center. From the center of his head, he visualized himself being in the center of his head, neutral and free from judgment, above the denser levels of his physical body such as his emotions and intellect. Then he channeled these thoughts into the third seed until he knew that it was done.

Next, he remembered his adventures with Deverall and the ice blue Devas. He ran his earth energy through the energy centers in the arches of his feet, and up the energy channels in his legs, until the flow reached near the base of his spine, where he allowed some of it to flow down his grounding cord. He allowed the flow of earth energy to gently bring him into balance with the Midas Tree by melting away energy blocks, just as Ariadne had shown him. Then he captured all that he knew about earth energy, and placed it into a fourth seed.

The fifth seed was for cosmic energy, taught by Devandra and his forest green Devas. Joshua envisioned a ball of gold cosmic energy above the top of his head and brought it in through his crown. He allowed the energy to travel down energy channels in his back, all the way down until it met the earth energy. Then he blended the earth and cosmic energy together and brought it up his front channels. After allowing it to branch from the base of his throat and flow down his arms and out the palms of his hands, he switched his focus to charging the fifth seed with this information.

Joshua continued until all the silver helicopter seeds were charged with the wisdom he had gained from his time spent in the tree. He was amazed with how far he had come since he first entered the Midas Tree.

He now knew that we each create our own reality through our thoughts and beliefs. He learned this first with the manna of the Midas Tree and then with the lessons in the spider's lair with Ariadne. She had also taught him that creativity lies in being in the present moment, and if we struggle or try too hard, we only get stuck.

He had also learned about clear seeing, the interpretation of symbols, and the power of inner vision from Ariadne, Mr. Woodpecker, Devon, Devora, and Devalicious. He'd studied how to create and destroy energy, and visualize a symbol, like a rose, to learn more about a situation.

Joshua learned how to communicate as spirit, with Devalicious and Devina, and from the time he spent with almost everyone in the Midas Tree. In particular, Araneus, Mr. Woodpecker, and Bertie Bat helped him know that help and guidance is always available. Joshua also now knew that he was an eternal spiritual being. Devalicious and Devina had made sure of that.

He knew that he could heal himself, and help others to heal themselves. He knew that part of healing the self was to let go of the ego, which is a false created self. He knew all this from his time with the Antimony's and the ladybugs, where he learned how important it is to be yourself.

Araneus, his deceased spidery friend, taught him unconditional love, and he knew to truly be free you have to know yourself and love yourself exactly as you are. He also learned compassion through his experience with the chipmunks.

Mr. Woodpecker also taught Joshua to have patience, because you are always exactly where you are meant to be. He wanted those coming after him to know that they should walk their journey at a pace comfortable for them. That they should keep their giving and receiving in balance, because they would not be able to help others unless they were taking care of themselves. He laughed when he thought of those crazy chipmunks. He even learned from the little white grub how important it was to live in balance and harmony with those around you.

Deval had taught him that he was a truly creative soul. Now here he was using his creative energy as Devany had just taught him, creating seeds of wisdom to help teach those who would walk his path. He thought about how our creativity sometimes involves creating difficult lessons, as part of our reality, as the bluebirds had done.

Most fascinating of all, he learned from the chimera that souls can choose to return to the Midas Tree for further development and exciting adventures. Plus, according to Devina, he could plan these adventures ahead of time using the golden acorns.

By the time Joshua had reviewed all of his experiences in the Midas Tree and committed each one to its own seed, he was exhausted. He wandered out into the sunshine and sat down on a branch, leaned back and dozed off to sleep. He was too exhausted to think about programming the acorns for his future selves. Anyway, he had plenty of time for that later, he thought.

When he awoke, it was dark. The faint glow of candle light was coming from the seed storage room. Joshua rubbed his eyes, stretched and yawned and then stood up and wandered back inside. Deval and Devina along with their Devas were packaging up Joshua's seeds into little silver packages, and setting them into a trolley ready to take them somewhere.

"We see you have been busy, my son," said Deval.

"Yes," said Joshua. "I have learned so much since I have been here in the Midas Tree. I had not realized how far I had come until I reviewed all my new knowledge."

"You truly are a child of Morfar," said Deval.

"Now though," said Devina, "you should sleep some more." She waved her arm and a cot appeared in the corner of the room. "Lay down here, Joshua and rest your weary body. Tomorrow is another day."

Joshua was very tired it was true, but he also wanted to know what they were doing with his seeds. He went over to the corner of the room and sat down.

"Deval and Devina?"

"Yes, Joshua?" they responded in unison.

"I see you are packing up my seeds. Where will you take them, and what will you do with them?"

"Why my child, we will place them all around the Midas Tree, so that our new students can find them when they most need your help."

"It will be so wonderful to share my knowledge with others," said Joshua, leaning back on the cot and yawning again."

"Sleep my child, and know that your work has not been in vain. Not only have you benefited from your adventures, but so too will all souls who now enter the Midas Tree, should they choose to learn your story and ask for your help." Devina stroked his head, and blew a kiss from her lips in Joshua's direction.

In no time at all, Joshua was fast asleep again. His dreams were a kaleidoscope of his past adventures in the Midas Tree, his wanderings in the garden of color and light, as well as scenes that he did not recognize from past and future existences. All the times and places and ideas folded into one until he could not separate them apart.

*"Now that you have almost finished your journey through The Midas Tree, what have YOU learned? To post your knowledge for others to benefit from go to **www.themidastree.com/readers***

Chapter 20

Return to Morfar

After a long and full life as a teacher in the Midas Tree, Joshua's yearning for Morfar became almost overwhelming, and he returned to the seed room. It looked the same, except Deval and Devina were no longer there. The little Devas and the cart with his silver seeds was also gone, but the golden acorns were still where he had left them. There were even candles still burning, although they were almost finished.

He got up, walked over to the doorway, and glanced outside. It was pitch dark, and so he reached out a hand to touch one of the branches. It felt cold and damp, and there did not appear to be any leaves anymore. Plus he could smell a wet earthy smell that reminded him of the time he had spent in the root chambers.

He went back inside and lit a few extra candles that he found lying around on the shelves. Then with one in hand, he ventured back outside. He reeled back in shock, because he was no longer at the top of the canopy, but instead he appeared to be at the base of the root system. There was a single tunnel stretched out before him, with a bright pinpoint of light at the end. Unlike other times, there was no choice between alternate routes, just one long tunnel.

Joshua knew he was meant to go towards this light, but he also knew that it was not time just yet. He went back into the chamber where the golden acorns lay. He sat and pondered what to do with them.

Devina had told him they were the seeds of his future selves, and Devany had told him to charge them with all the things he wanted to experience in the future. He imagined he should use the same visualization and energy transference technique that he had used before, except this time he should visualize his future desires. Where to start though?

I have really enjoyed healing myself and helping others to heal. I feel I only scratched the surface of what is possible in the realm of healing. Therefore, I would like to explore being a healer in much more depth in one of my future journeys in the Midas Tree.

Joshua willed this intention to learn as much as he possibly could about being a healer, into the first acorn. He thought about what he had been told when he first entered the Midas Tree: that there were others just like him, who came there not knowing how to survive and thrive. He intended that he would help them learn about the physical reality of the Midas Tree, and empower them to heal themselves.

As he was intending this outcome, he caught a glimpse, through the seed, of something he did not understand. There was a wooden train. It ran on some tracks down in the roots of the Midas Tree. It was laden with sacks that were full of fertilizer. Joshua was pouring them onto the roots of the tree. A dark hand grabbed his shoulder, and Joshua was pulled backwards into a dark chamber.

He looked intently at the first acorn after he was finished. It seemed to be glowing and emanating light. That's curious; maybe that is how I know I have done a good job of programming the acorn? The glow was comforting and he felt good about it, in spite of what he had seen. He felt strong and confident, as though he could handle anything he could ever encounter.

He did not allow himself to reflect on his handiwork for too long. There were another six acorns left for him to program, and he soon switched his attention to them.

Hmm, he thought. I really enjoyed creating those fruit combinations, but I wonder what other amazing creations I could make if only I had more time. I would like to come back as a skillful co-creator in the Midas Tree. First, though, I would like to meet some masters of manifestation, so I can learn much more about how to create my reality consciously. Then I'd like to put what I learn into practice.

He imagined a time when teachers such as these were present within the tree. As he focused on his intention, a future time vignette opened up before him, and he caught a peek at some of the struggles he would go through to achieve this level of mastery. There was a very powerful Deva. One he had never seen before, and this Deva was focusing a powerful beam of energy from his hand onto various objects. When the light hit the objects they shattered - disintegrated into a million particles. Then they dissipated into the air around them until all that was left in their place was empty space. Joshua saw that some of the creatures of the tree were crying, and others were cowering in the corner at such a great display of power. Others were angry. They were fighting with each other about how to deal with the situation.

This truly was a troubling vision. Joshua visualized that all the creatures in the Midas Tree would learn to work in harmony, including the Deva with the powerful beam of destructive light. They would work through this turmoil and create a joyful adventurous life together. He transferred this intention into a second golden acorn.

Joshua moved on to the third acorn. I had fun with Devon and his rhymes, and I never did quite spend as much time as I would have liked learning about symbols. I didn't fully understand what happened when I entered the dream world to learn about the symbols. So I wish to explore the interface between dream reality and waking reality a lot more. What better way could there be to do that, than to put my energy into becoming a mystical artist, just like Devon? I will write poetry of profound mysticism and my works will touch all the creatures of the tree in a deep way.

Just as he finished programming the third acorn, a flash of a future time scenario popped into his mind. He saw his body laid on the floor with a crowd of panicking Devas around him, trying to wake him up. Try as they might, Joshua's body remained limp and unresponsive. The only movement was in his eyelids, which were rapidly flickering. On the walls around this scene, Joshua could see beautiful artwork, full of symbols and bright colors.

Joshua stirred uncomfortably in his seat. His intentions were good and yet each time he programmed an acorn, he saw something unexpected. What if he was creating situations, through his intentions, which were beyond his ability to handle?

He shrugged off his discomfort. He grounded and centered. Then he called to Morfar for help in understanding the three scenarios he had witnessed so far. A blanket of comfort and encouragement surrounded him. "My Child, you know by now that the path to wholeness is honed by challenges of the will and the ego here within the Midas Tree. Make it through the barriers of your mind and the fires of opposition and you will see. The prize is worth it all. Your light will join with mine, and then there will be only love."

Joshua felt calmed and he continued with his task. Now, I love my body, and I have made it gold all over, but I would like to radiate this light further and further out. I would like to come back and focus on radiating love and light to all creatures that live in the Midas Tree, so that they may be transformed by it. Joshua focused his spiritual vision on this desire, and this time he was so amazed by what he saw, he gasped out loud...

Instead of seeing radiant light, the Midas Tree was in darkness. It seemed to be dying, and was covered with a black fungus that was blocking the light and draining its energy. Joshua again heard the voice of Morfar "My child, if you wish to learn to radiate light to all within the tree, you will attract challenges to overcome. This is not a bad thing, it is how we learn. Trust yourself to meet the experience that comes, and overcome it. You will not create anything that you do not have the power and strength to work through."

Then, as Morfar spoke, Joshua saw himself as a point of light, with radiance so bright that it lit up the whole tree. His light shined on the tree and everything in it, until they all merged into oneness. "But where is my body?" he exclaimed, and then he heard Morfar's voice. "You are not your body, Joshua, you are the light." As he heard Morfar's voice, he remembered the brightness of the garden, and yearned for its comfort. He would bring as much light as he could from the garden into the tree. He focused this intention into the fourth acorn until he knew it was done.

Joshua knew that he was a teacher, so that whenever he entered the tree he would always learn and teach. He so loved the Midas Tree and all its crazy creatures and spirits. He wanted to come back with a strong focus as a teacher. He visualized a time when there were students just as he had been, journeying through the Midas Tree.

As he grounded, centered, and focused on this vision, more vignettes of future events played out before him. He saw that the new students were just as green as he was when he first arrived. They had no idea how to navigate the world of the Midas Tree. They were all over the place, up in the branches and down in the roots, getting themselves into all sorts of sticky situations. Joshua saw one student who was hanging by his fingertips from one of the branches, looking as though he was about to fall. Another was trapped in Ariadne's lair, and yet another was being sick from something he had eaten in Devi's chamber.

Surely, Joshua could come back and help them. He would teach them the techniques that had helped him so much. He visualized how he would use all his communication skills to help these students. He would use his ability to communicate as spirit, as well as his telepathy and other abilities to guide these youngsters. Thus, he programmed the fifth acorn.

I also enjoyed using my spiritual sight to see. I will come back to the Midas Tree as a seer, who has amazing gifts of spiritual vision. I will come back at a time when the tree and its inhabitants need my help to see more clearly. Joshua watched as another vignette unfolded. He saw that all the creatures of the tree were wandering around with a cloud of thoughts around their heads.

He also saw the ants, except they had now taken over the whole tree, and they were forcing their way of life on everyone else in the tree. "They are so wrapped up in their thoughts that they are not using their spiritual sight," he said out loud, "I can surely help them with that." This was Joshua's intention for the sixth acorn.

Now he was left with the final acorn, but he could not think of anything else that he wanted. He connected with the spirit of Morfar and said. "Oh great Morfar, who knows all things, I love and trust in you to will what is best for me and the Midas Tree into this final seed. Please work through me and let this seventh sojourn into the tree be a surprise."

He felt the love and light of Morfar travel through his being and into the last acorn. Then he stood up, took a deep breath, and walked out of the room with his hand in his pocket clutching the seven golden acorns.

As he walked down the tunnel, he felt a stronger and stronger pull towards the light. Sweet music filled his ears, and it became louder and more intoxicating the further he walked. The light was getting brighter and more intense, and Joshua's heart swelled with love. The further he went the less clear his adventures in the tree became. They seemed to merge into a great ocean of oneness that contained everything that ever was, is, and ever will be.

Soon there were no thoughts, only being, light, and love. Joshua's body seemed to dissolve into the light, until he no longer needed his legs because he was floating. He wafted on through the tunnel in a state of bliss towards the exit. A warm breeze urged him onwards, until he both emerged from the tunnel and merged with the light.

He was in a beautiful field of golden grasses and colorful flowers. Behind him stood a magical tree, with all the seasons and all the fruits and leaves and flowers and seeds of any plant that was ever known. He would have seen it, had he cared to look back. But he was entranced by flowery trellises he could see in the distance, and the sound of running water coming from afar.

Joshua floated over to the passageway, and through the middle of the wisteria-festooned trellises. He admired the purple flowers and their pretty companions, some pink climbing roses. On the other side was a patch of golden yellow sunflowers, with bright faces peering up to the sun. Next to them, clump upon clump of ethereal red poppies wafted in the breeze. Joshua stayed and absorbed the beauty of these flowers. It was not certain how long he did this for, as time did not exist.

Then in his reverie of golden suns and red buttons, he once again awakened to the sound of a babbling brook. He floated to the edge of the flower patch, where there was a bridge over a stream.

Joyously he wafted into the middle of the bridge, and watched the waters flowing beneath him. He became aware that he was holding something in his hand. How bizarre, he was holding seven golden acorns. He did not know what they were, only that they were beautiful. He absentmindedly dropped them one by one into the water and watched them drift away, wishing them well on their journey, wherever they were headed.

He continued watching for eternity, until the still sweet voice of Morfar floated into his awareness, and he floated off in search of its source.

The voice appeared to be coming from the top of the stream, so Joshua followed the water. He glided effortlessly above the stream, admiring the glints of sunlight on the ripples of the water. He liked the way the water frothed and foamed as it ran past the rocks, so every now and then he paused to enjoy this sight.

There were fish in the stream, beautiful golden carp. They were swimming in the opposite direction to Joshua. There was a ball of light dancing amongst them, darting in and out of the water, in front of and behind the fish. Joshua watched in fascination as the fish jumped out of the water towards this light, mouths open as if it were a tasty morsel.

Joshua became entranced by this scene and switched directions for a while. They were almost back at the bridge, when one of the fish succeeded in swallowing the light. As soon as it swallowed the light, it took on an inner glow and swam faster downstream.

Joshua was standing on the bridge again, being mesmerized by the water and the light, when once again the sweet voice of Morfar beckoned from upstream. So he wafted along, this time hovering over the riverbank. Occasionally he dipped in amongst the reed beds to watch the dragonflies. They were so beautiful, with all the colors of the rainbow reflected on their wings.

Joshua lost himself in the light beams coming from their backs. While he was joyfully playing, a cluster of light particles came from upstream and joined in his games. They buzzed around in and out of the reeds, and in between the dragonflies. They played what felt like an endless game of tag, until all at once the light particles entered the swarm of dragonflies. As soon as this happened, the insects took on an internal glow. They stopped their play and bounded away swiftly, following the flow of the stream.

Joshua watched them go, and then turned back upstream towards the sweet voice of Morfar, who he knew was at the source. In fact, Morfar **was** the source.

The further Joshua went, the narrower the stream became, and the brighter the light in the garden. Eventually, and yet in no time at all, Joshua found himself standing amongst the smooth round pebbles that surrounded the source. He was amongst the spray, watching the water spring forth in powerful spurts.

He could not see Morfar, but he could feel the radiance and love of Morfar's presence all about him. He radiated love and light back in response to this. The more love he radiated, the more love he found he could radiate. The love and light kept expanding, as Joshua realized there were higher levels of radiance that he could reach. His being was vibrating at ever higher and higher frequencies, until he felt that he might explode into oneness with Morfar.

As soon as he reached that edge between his individuality and the oneness of Morfar, he once again heard that still sweet voice.

"Joshua, you have grown in soul development. You have learned many lessons and have expanded yourself greatly. However, you are not yet prepared to enter my light completely. Follow your golden acorns as they float along the stream. Watch over them as they take root, and nurture their growth. Enter them as they grow and help them become all that they can be. Live out your dreams, and return to me when you have completed your plan. You always have my support, and I am always with you."

Joshua felt a gentle pull backwards, and as the radiance of light lessened, he became aware once again of the stream. He ambled his way back down into the garden, following the voice of Morfar all the way, and watching the stream to see if he could catch the golden beams of light that might lead him to an acorn.

About the Author

DR. LESLEY PHILLIPS

Dr. Lesley Phillips is a speaker, author, spiritual teacher, healer and clairvoyant reader. She is passionate about the benefits of meditation and intuition and believes everyone can use them to live a happy and purposeful life.

She has helped 1000's individuals receive guidance through her readings, healings, classes, workshops and mentoring program. Dr. Lesley is known as a caring, gifted teacher and speaker who brings out the best In people.

Dr. Lesley is also a Ph.D. microbiologist who used to search tropical regions of the planet for natural product medicines. Later she was a business negotiator in the life science industry, who travelled the world brokering multi-million dollar deals. Nowadays she focuses on using her spiritual gifts to help others.

She has extensive training in metaphysics. Rev. Dr. Lesley is a certified spiritual counselor, having graduated from the CDM Spiritual Teaching Centers' two year Clairvoyant Training Program as a minister in 2003. Two years, in 2005, she also qualified as a spiritual teacher. Prior to this Dr. Lesley also trained at several mystery schools in the U.K.

Dr. Lesley regularly appears on radio and TV and is the Psychic Advisor to the Earth Needs Rebels Show. She is also the creator of the Portico Card Deck.

 You can learn much more about Dr. Lesley, Phillips, The Midas Tree and her intuitive card deck "Portico" on her websites:
http://www.drlesleyphillips.com
http://www.themidastree.com
http://www.afreecardreading.com

About the Illustrator

Cody Chancellor

Local/international artist Cody Chancellor has been dedicated to the arts his whole life. He was raised by two creative parents deep in the woods of Northern California, sculpting clay, drawing crazy inventions, climbing trees. He went on to graduate from San Francisco State University refining his professional craft. Since then he has expanded up and down the coast expressing his ideas in a myriad of mediums, from metal to wood, theater to books, and fine art to commercial art.

Cody aims at spreading hope, inspiration, and a reconnection to nature through his art. His current illustration style is a fusion of rich traditional mediums and contemporary digital technology. The surface of Cody's work is happy and light, yet there are many layers of meaning underneath— sometimes a metaphor, sometimes a lesson. The story might be a moral message, a reworked fairy tale, mythology, personal insight, social commentary, or the beginning of a novel. This made Cody the ideal artist to illustrate The Midas Tree.

Currently, Cody lives on the Sunshine Coast keeping in pace with the seasons, with roots nourished by the spirit of nature, as an environmentalist, and a gardener. His wife Jennifer, also a dedicated artist, and Fern their new baby girl fill his days with purpose. He is always looking forward to share fresh inspiration, the next dream to create.

To view many of his fantastical creations, visit his web site http://www.chancellor.net